To Marguerite
So glad you are enjoying on Topsail
Carol Ann Ross

The Trill of the Red-Wing Blackbird

A novel and continuing
Topsail Island Saga

Carol Ann Ross

D1416067

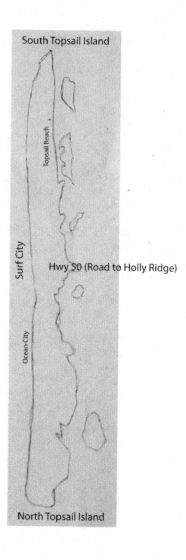

South Topsail Island

Topsail Beach

Surf City

Ocean City

Hwy 50 (Road to Holly Ridge)

North Topsail Island

IRONHEAD PRESS

COPYRIGHT 2014 by IRONHEAD PRESS

DEDICATION

This book is dedicated to the pioneering families who came to Topsail Island in the 1940s, 1950s and 1960s. Thank you for enriching my life.

ACKNOWLEDGMENTS

I love writing about Topsail Island. So it adds to my joy when those individuals who love her too are eager to help me with historical information. I want to thank Doug Medlin, Doug Thomas, David Justice, Rudy and Rosa Lea Batts, P.H. Padgett, Sonny Atkinson, and most importantly Diane Batts Geary. Diane, you have been a great source of not just knowledge, but encouragement.

Thanks to Patti Blacknight, Kellie LaFar, Juliet Madison and Debra McKnight. You have been so very helpful with information, ideas and technical support.

INTRODUCTION

After Paul's death Pearl was as she had always been, an attentive and loving mother. No one could argue with that.

She spent hours on the docks at either her home or her parent's home fishing and even attended local pig pickings and seine pulls. But each time someone would mention Paul, she would politely smile and nod her head, often rubbing her growing belly and reassuring them that she was doing just fine. Then she would change the subject.

She really did appear to be getting on with her life as she did all the usual things expected of a mother. She tended to her children; sewing their clothes, cooking, cleaning and taking them over to the island to play on the beach. She did all that would be expected of her except talk to her children about their father.

She helped Josie and Frank with homework and readied them for school. However, once they rode off in the big yellow school bus, Pearl, within minutes, would hop into the truck and make her way onto the hard road, Highway 50, and across the pontoon bridge to the Sea Gull Restaurant. There, she and Lottie prepared for the day's customers.

Even though business was slow during winter months, Pearl kept everything spotless. She made new curtains, mended the tablecloths, and she and her father, Jess, stripped the bar and put on a new coat of varnish.

Lottie had given up arguing with her daughter about staying off her feet. She was, after all, expecting her third child in the spring. Often Lottie mentioned that Pearl needed to rest more, but she ignored the requests and went about keeping herself as busy as possible.

"At least sit," Lottie pleaded.

Pearl usually responded by rolling her eyes and shrugging.

"She's trying to keep herself so busy that she doesn't have time to think. I wonder what she does at night when the kids go to bed."

Jess reached for his wife's hand and squeezed it gently. "You've seen those dark circles under her eyes. That's what she's doing—covering up the hurt."

"Whenever I mention Paul she changes the subject. It's as if he never existed." Lottie shook her head as she released an exasperated sigh.

"She's just not the same girl anymore," Jess shook his head. "Paul's death changed her in a way that I don't think you or I understand. I don't know how or what to do to help her move on with her life." Jess scuffed his shoe against the floor. "She's always told me what is in her heart. Now she acts as if she's just going through the motions."

"She's like the cabinet we keep the radio on, all veneer—she won't let anyone see what's beneath it."

"Maybe when she has the baby, things will change."

It was difficult for Jess and Lottie to see their daughter pull away from them, from everyone. There had never been a time when Pearl had not opened up her heart to them, and it left them feeling confused and worried about the thing Pearl had always been about—joy.

****

The birth of Emma Jewel in May of 1953 found Pearl to be accepting of her new child. She had not talked much about this new baby as she had the others. She never even mentioned which she preferred, a boy or a girl.

Her friend Ellie found this very curious. She chided Pearl about gaining weight, getting older, anything—simply trying to provoke Pearl into opening up. Nothing worked. In fact, Pearl's retort of 'it's none of your business' shocked and pained Ellie to the bone.

"This is not our girl," she explained to Lottie.

Ellie had moved to the island in January, into a little cinderblock house that she immediately had painted pink. The place was within walking distance of the Sea

Gull Restaurant, about three quarters of a mile, just beyond the old officers' club.

A large screened-in porch skirted the home and she decorated it with fishing nets, seashells and glass balls. Monroe was living with her now, much to everyone's surprise. They attended seine fishing events together and went to pig pickings; Monroe fit right in with her polished nails and current fashions. Physically she seemed a replica of her mother; however, her personality was nothing like Ellie's. Monroe was not condescending; she seemed more concerned with other's feelings.

Pearl was annoyed by the attempts of her friends and family to involve themselves in her life. She refused to admit that there was anything wrong, that she was still clinging to Paul or that she was melancholy.

"I can take care of myself," she retorted defensively when anyone expressed concern for her. She continued to keeping herself busy and within a few days after Emma Jewel's birth, Pearl began taking the baby to the Sea Gull Restaurant, laying her in a crate box.

She sat close by and peeled potatoes, washed carrots, made cole slaw—whatever needed to be prepped for breakfast or lunch. And when it was time for Frank and Jo to come home from school, Pearl gathered her baby and drove home.

She explained to her family that she was the owner of the Gull and that she would do as she pleased. It was spring, after all, and she was not going to miss out on the fishing season.

****

Fishermen came to the beach in droves, lining the shore of the island from the north end to the south end, wading out into the cool water to cast their lines.

For the Sea Gull, it was a busy time of the year. There was no lull in business; it was nearly as busy as it had been in the summer, just with a different kind of clientele.

"A little more smelly," Jess liked to joke.

The seine fishing continued too, but now the men brought the dories across on the pontoon bridge, pulled by farming trucks and an occasional tractor.

Rawl West was still a spotter, he'd always done a good job at it, and Leo Weldon brought his magnificent seine. He never did give up making them.

During the 40s when no civilians were allowed on the island, he traveled to some of the farther south barrier islands along the east coast and with other locals, made a fine living from his work.

Carl Burns started seine fishing with the old group as he had before the war. Strong as ever, he helped propel the dory through the water. His wife, Sarah, still had the prettiest yard around for miles and miles.

Enid Abbott and his wife, Bella, had a baby girl and another one. Arlo, the youngest of the Abbott children had been born a month before Emma Jewel.

10

They were still part of the old group of people doing things as they had done before the war, but perhaps a little differently; after all, the banks had changed quite drastically. Buildings had been left there by the military and other houses were being built by landowners.

No longer referred to as the banks, the twenty-six mile stretch of sand dunes, beach grasses and abandoned military buildings, became Topsail Island. The central part, where the Scaggins, Rosells, Burns, Butlers and others had always frequented, was now known as Surf City. The rest was referred to as the south end and the north end, although homes and businesses were being built there as well.

The main intersection in Surf City was abuzz with workers as construction began on a shopping center where there would soon be a grocery store, barber shop, laundromat, soda fountain, hardware store and realty office. Everyone was anxious for the new shops that would make everything a little more convenient.

Diagonally across from the shopping center site was the reservoir, a large cement building that stood about twelve feet tall. On the side was painted a girl in a bathing suit, welcoming visitors with a wave of her hand: *SURF CITY, THE FISHERMAN'S PARADISE*, the painting boasted.

Things seemed different; after all, the island had opened up for development. There were businesses everywhere. There was even a post office that Ron and Janie Butler were operating along with a small general store and restaurant.

11

Their daughter Sarah Elizabeth had been the first child to have a residence on the island, and for a long time found her best friend to be her dog since there were no other children to play with.

Military families would come for a few months, then leave, they might have children, but they never stayed for very long, and soon Sarah would be back to playing with her dog.

Not many wanted to live where the closest hospital, movie theatre, or clothing store was thirty miles away. And it took a special kind of person to adjust to the tourist season way of life, where seven months out of the year you struggled to make ends meet if you had not made a good living in the vacation and fishing seasons.

Changes were happening fast in Surf City, and on the south end of Topsail Island as well. The south end of the island, New Topsail Beach, had a growing population itself, and businesses were being built there, too, along with homes. Most of the homes were second homes for the business owners, however several families chose to stay year round.

The Cracker Box and Godwin's Grocery Store were two of the most frequented places, along with Warren's Soda Shop that sold food and beach paraphernalia. The Breezeway Inn and Restaurant was a seasonal business, as was the Jolly Roger Fishing Pier.

The drive north from Surf City was lonely, since hardly any construction there had taken place by 1954.

Dunes and scrub oaks populated the landscape until reaching the Onslow County line where stood the Mermaid Bar.

Pender County, the most densely populated part of the island, was a dry county, Onslow, the northern part of the island—barren and unpopulated most of the year, was wet. This is where locals and tourists went for a drink.

Miss Williams ran the establishment. She wore bright red muumuu dresses and wore her brilliant red hair piled high on her head. She had decorated the Mermaid with fishing nets, buoys, sea shells and neon beer signs.

Traveling farther north, there was the occasional fishing shack until reaching Ocean City, a small black community made up mostly of summer homes. The area was usually only populated in the summer months or during fishing season.

Still farther north there may have been a few homes, but mostly the land was barren. Fishermen, both surf and seine, fished there where the fishing was said to be the best.

By 1954 bait shops selling rods and reels, tackle and assorted baits were abundant on the island; at least four shops lined the road leading up to the little pontoon bridge at Sear's Landing.

Plans for a fishing pier were underway. It would be Topsail Island's first pier, located in the heart of Surf City, close to Pop's Pavilion.

Already construction had begun at Sear's Landing for a swing bridge that would open and close to allow boats to pass. Dump truck after dump truck had deposited dirt on either side of the landing for the graded ramp to the bridge. No more would people worry about losing their mufflers, and access to the island would be simple and easy. Everyone was excited about the new bridge and all the new development happening on Topsail Island.

At the intersection, where the shopping center was being built, stood a new Gulf gas station. It had two bays for working on cars and a downstairs where a winch was installed for lifting motors.

Down the road a few blocks, Bart Ralston opened up a mechanics shop. He quickly established a reputation for being able to fix just about anything.

In Surf City military barracks from World War II were being bought up by families eager to take part in the development of the island. Before his death, Paul had spoken to Pearl about buying one of them and renovating it as an apartment house. Rather than live on the farm, he and Pearl would move to the island and lease out the farm. That was something he wished for, something he looked forward to doing in his future. But by the fall of 1953 nothing had come to fruition.

A few weeks after his death Pearl received a deed to the building they had been looking at, the one a couple of blocks adjacent to the old officers' club.

When she received the deed, she wasn't happy about it or unhappy. It was just another reminder of what could have been. Now she was content to live on the farm, it was familiar.

Paul's brother Phil was now working with her father and helping to run the farming business that Paul and her father had built.

From her kitchen window Pearl could view the men in the distance working or talking, and she could not help but watch Phil; he moved so much like her late husband. She did her best to get out of the house as quickly as she could once the children left for school.

Clarence, Paul's father, helped out now and then to the best of his ability. He had become unfocused and rarely could finish a task. He had become withdrawn, too, after Paul's death and often mumbled to himself. He wandered around a lot, often walking down by the sound where he tossed his cast net, bringing home fish and shrimp.

Clarence didn't talk very much to anyone, but when he did, it would undoubtedly be about either Josie or Paul. He recalled events that no one else seemed to remember, but none the less, they brought him joy. All the events he related were about the family and the closeness they shared. Phil, exasperated with his father's condition, grew even angrier when the older

man, confused and baffled, insisted on calling Phil by
the younger son's name.

It was perplexing to all how Phil reacted to his
father's senility—that is what his behavior was
considered among most. One day Clarence would know
who Jess was and the next day he would not. One day
he would be very accommodating, performing small
tasks like taking out the trash, and other days he would
be argumentative, childlike in resisting any request to
do chores.

Phil's display of anger worried some as he cussed or
yelled at Clarence for forgetting to perform a task or
when the elder Rosell made a mistake. It was apparent
that Phil had little patience for his father.

"Odd...something's brewing," Rawl West
commented on more than one occasion. "One day Phil
is gonna take care of past business and that old coot is
gonna wake up dead."

That was pretty much the feeling around the
community. No one understood how Phil could forgive
Clarence for beating Josie and for humiliating his sons
time after time. He had done so much to hurt his family
that no one blamed Phil for his actions toward his
father.

Whether fishing or working the tobacco at the farm,
as the months went by it was obvious that Clarence
could do less and less.

Enid came to help out more and more often, taking
over the tasks that once Clarence had been able to

perform. Mostly Phil's father spent his time sitting by the tobacco barn staring off into space.

Concerned that Clarence would hurt himself or even worse, burn the place down, Jess and Lottie often tried to convince Phil to leave his father at home. But Phil reassured them that he would keep a keen eye out for the old man.

He avoided Pearl like the plague. He could not abide her staring at him. He assumed it was because he favored his brother so greatly. She made him feel uneasy. But he did so enjoy spending time with his nephew and nieces. They were the one thing that brought joy to his life.

Adding fuel to the awkwardness of this was Clarence.

"What's a matter with you two? You been married how many years? You ain't even sitting together? What's wrong?"

The embarrassment was too much and Phil gave up going in public at all with Clarence. He kept mostly to himself, rarely going to pig pickings, the Gull or even Pop's Pavilion.

Pearl felt the awkwardness too, but she found herself staring at Phil, nonetheless. He did look so much like Paul. She was glad when he no longer attended the social events. She busied herself with her children and her business and tried to forget that the love of her life was gone.

CHAPTER ONE

1954

Pearl stooped, twisting her body low to the ground to hammer a nail into the plywood, slamming the hammer once again into her thumb. "Dag blasted, son of a biscuit eatin'..."

"Pearl Lorraine Rosell! If I hear you cussin' one more word, I'm gonna..."

"I ain't said the first cussword, Momma," Pearl hollered back. "Now, I can, if you want me to...*damn* it all, rotten ol' hurricane, I can't wait..."

"You listen to me little gal, I ain't so old that I can't bend you over my knee." Lottie walked out onto the patio of the Sea Gull Restaurant where Pearl sat cross-legged, holding onto a piece of plywood with one hand, a hammer in the other and nails held in her pursed lips. She looked up at her mother and spat out the nails.

"Momma, this is nearly impossible. I can't hold all of this and nail too." Throwing her hands in the air, Pearl sighed. "I guess I shouldn't have had that argument with Roger. Maybe I'll just call him back and have him come help us before this hurricane hits."

"Why in the world you want to even mess with that Yankee is beyond me. I haven't trusted him since the day I met him."

"At least he could help me with this." Pearl looked defiantly at her mother.

"Humph. I'll hold the plywood. If *that's* all you need that bag of worms for." Lottie gazed at her daughter accusingly. "I ain't no fool."

As Lottie held the plywood, she sighed and shook her head. "Gal, I ain't trying to be mean, I just for the life of me don't understand why you ever started seeing that man."

Pearl's jaw tightened. "You wouldn't understand." She continued hammering, rising up to reach the sides and top of the plywood that covered the side window to the Sea Gull Restaurant. "I finished this one, now there's two more oceanfront."

Lottie followed her daughter to the other side of the patio, considering what she could say to make Pearl open up about what she was feeling. Since Emma Jewel's birth Pearl had been acting more like her old self, somewhat. But there was still something that Lottie could not put her finger on.

She watched as her daughter bent down. *Yes she laughs more and is more eager to participate in going places and doing things. But...*

Lottie watched while Pearl maneuvered her body to hold the plywood against the window.

"You helping or not?" Arching an eyebrow, Pearl pointed her hand toward where she wanted her mother to place her own.

The corners of Lottie's lips turned up as she thought of how Pearl had regained her figure within two months of having her baby. Ellie and she had donned bathing suits and played on the beach with their children. Lottie had felt a little odd about Pearl leaving the baby with Bella Abbott. But she minded her own business and said nothing to Pearl about it. She considered that this was a way for her to move on with her life and get past the death of Paul.

Lottie could see bits and pieces of the old Pearl, in the laughter, but there was still something missing. Something had changed about her daughter. She didn't understand it—didn't question it, but for sure, her daughter was not talking to her about it.

"Are you gonna stand there staring out into the ocean or are you gonna hand me that hammer? It's the third time I've asked for it." Pearl's voice rang sharp as she slapped her mother's shin.

"Oh, sorry dear." Lottie bent down, handing the hammer and nails to her daughter. "I was just daydreaming." Flipping her hand through the air as if whisking away a pesky fly, Lottie continued, "I wish we wouldn't have made these windows so low to the ground."

"If you remember, we had all agreed that the larger the windows, the better the view." Slamming the hammer against the nails, Pearl rose, nailing along the sides and top of the plywood. "*We* didn't know *shit*."

Immediately Lottie's open hand fell against Pearl's cheek. Her chest rose and fell as her opened mouth gasped for air. "I'm tired of this, tired of it, you hear me! What is the matter with you? You've never spoken to me like this before." Lottie turned her back and stomped across the patio.

Pearl heard the screen door slam, and then heard it slam again. A few seconds later she heard the rev of the Scaggins' truck. As she rolled her eyes, a loud sigh escaped her lips. She shook her head and turned to resume covering the remaining window with plywood. Grabbing the last sheet by the edges she tripped over the box of nails and slid her hand along the edge of the wood.

"Damn! Fire and hell! God, why are you doing this to me?" She looked at her raw hand and the splinters imbedded in the thick meat of it. Catching her breath, she calmed herself. "No. It ain't God's fault. I'm sorry God." She closed her eyes and felt the tears welling. "Momma, I'm sorry," she whispered. Gazing upward she shook her head, "It's my damn fault. It's all my fault."

****

The new bridge would be in place soon. Already mounds of dirt were piled high on either side of the waterway to build support for the swing bridge that Lottie hoped would be there by spring.

She recalled Janie Butler telling her how her oldest son, Raymond, jumped into the waterway from the dirt mounds. *Oh my Lord that must have scared the heck out of poor Janie,* Lottie thought as she grinned about the adventurous young boy.

Now her heart was breaking as she thought of her own child, and how Pearl must be so confused.

Someone called out her name loudly and waved her on in the line at the pontoon bridge, still operating next to the mounds of dirt.

Within the year no one would have to worry about losing their muffler on the pontoon bridge. Yes, Lottie, along with all the inhabitants of the island were ready for that. Oh, how she would be happy when it was up and running; she had lost three mufflers in the past year.

This afternoon it seemed that the new bridge could not be in place soon enough as she waited in line with others who were making their way off the island before Hurricane Hazel hit. Surely before long, Pearl would be along in her car. Pearl had only one window left to secure when Lottie had so angrily stormed out of the restaurant and left. *It was a smaller window,* Lottie paused, lowering her head in shame and fighting tears, regretting that she had left the restaurant without

22

waiting for her daughter. *Surely* Pearl would be along soon.

Traffic was creeping along—stop, start, stop, start—inches at a time, all waiting to cross the only access to the island. Lottie's mind wandered.

Before she had left, Lottie had noticed how the incoming tide was lapping at the picnic tables. Paul had built four directly in front of the Sea Gull for tourists to enjoy. He'd also put up a volleyball net. Lottie could not count the times it had been replaced, due to strong winds. Still, Paul had insisted that it be one of the amenities the Gull offered its patrons. Out of love and respect for her deceased son-in-law, she and Jess had made sure it was a fixture at the business.

During the past summer there hadn't been a day when a group of young people couldn't be seen laughing and enjoying themselves at the net. But there seemed to be good and bad about everything.

In late August of this year, when she had been watching the young folks playing, she noticed a familiar face that kept turning, scouring the patio area of the restaurant while he played—Roger.

Why in the hell had he come back? She fussed over the thought all day and by eight o'clock that night, when nearly all the customers had gone, she watched as he came slinking through the front door.

"You guys aren't looking for any help in the kitchen are you?"

Ellie nearly knocked over the sugar bowl she was filling as she turned toward Roger's voice. "Well, well,

well. Look what the cat dragged in." She gently strolled over to his side.

His arm circled her waist and he drew her close for a kiss on the cheek. "Hey Babe." Roger pulled away from Ellie and walked toward the bar, his eyes scanning the restaurant as he spoke to Lottie, his tone respectful. "Hello, Miss Lottie, you're looking well. I'm glad to see you again." His eyes never met hers, but she had expected that.

From the swinging kitchen door, Pearl emerged. She was wiping her hands on the white cleaning cloth she used to wipe down the counter. "You serious about a job?"

Ellie and Lottie shot each other a questioning look. Both were amazed at what they just heard as they stared at the other in disbelief.

*"We're expecting a good fishing season this fall, so if you're serious about working—and I mean **working**—I could use you." She turned and walked back through the kitchen door.*

A car horn honked loudly, waking Lottie from her daydream. She moved ahead a little in the line, stopping once again after only a few feet.

Gazing off toward the little islands in the waterway, she picked up her thoughts of Pearl and Roger.

She had known from the evening he walked through the restaurant door that Pearl would take him as her lover. She had felt it in her bones.

24

Lottie knew that he often came to Pearl's farmhouse after she closed the Sea Gull in the evenings and she had seen him leave early in the twilight of the morning to go to work. But he stayed mostly in the barracks building that Paul had bought before his death.

"He's a gold digger. Doesn't give a hoot about you and he's using you for everything you have." These words or ones to the same effect had been spoken to Pearl by Lottie on numerous occasions. In response, Pearl had simply agreed, then either walked away or changed the subject. Eventually Lottie quit mentioning it at all.

"Everything was moving along in the right direction until that...that..." She searched for a word to describe the man manipulating her daughter. "...That no good, worm infested, cow paddy." Blinking back her anger, Lottie shook her head remembering words she had always lived by: you can always find something good even in bad situations.

Ellie and she had become closer since Roger had come into Pearl's life. Who would have ever thought that she and Ellie could find common ground?

"They're over there right now, speculating, as Roger puts it, on what renovations need to be taken care of." Ellie's neatly manicured fingernails pressed her cigarette butt against the glass ashtray.

From the window of the Gull, Lottie and Ellie could see the barracks building—a long, brown, building with a broad wooden porch running its length. Halfway

25

along the length of the roof, a tall brick chimney rose skyward. In the back of the barracks were three two-story sand dunes.

Lottie smiled to think of how much fun her grandchildren would have playing on them.

"What are you smiling about?" A puzzled look crossed Ellie's face as the smile vanished.

"The kids will have a ball playing on those dunes behind the barracks." Suddenly her smile faded as she recalled the man, at this moment, enjoying the company of her daughter. "I can't believe Pearl is carrying on like she is. She needs to be taking care of her children."

Ellie nodded in agreement, "Yeah, this is so unlike our Pearly White."

"Jo and Frank are okay with their grandpa and Uncle Phil, but Emma Jewel needs to be at home with her momma, not toddling around this restaurant or having a babysitter."

Pearl had asked Lottie to stay home with the kids but she had refused. There was no way she was going to encourage her daughter's affair with Roger, though she would have been glad to watch them for any other reason.

"You'd think that with E.J. being Paul's, that Pearl would want to spend all the time she could with her."

"Now, don't you start calling that darling baby E.J. That just doesn't sound right."

"Well, none of y'all will settle on either Emma or Jewel and saying it all together is a mouthful. E.J. is just easier."

"Humph, I guess a name doesn't matter so much if the poor child's mother doesn't even want to be around her."

"Don't say that, Miss Lottie. She takes her out on the beach some."

Lifting her head to meet Ellie's eyes, Lottie nodded. "I know."

"And Bella comes over with her kids; she says she likes watching the boys and E.J. After all, her Sally is the same age as our baby. Monroe likes it too when Sally brings her kids. They have fun."

"I guess you're right. Kids like to be around other kids, and as Miss Bella says, 'the more the merrier.'"

****

Lottie woke once again from her daydreaming as another car honked its horn. She shook her head. "I guess everything will be okay. Jess says that I worry too much, but...well, things would have been okay if it hadn't of been for Roger. Where in the heck is he anyway?"

That's what had prompted the anger between she and Pearl in the first place. Why wasn't he helping Pearl? After all, putting up plywood was man's work. What kind of argument would keep him away from the woman he loved—if he loved her at all? Lottie doubted

27

that. She had always known what he was after. Still...he should have been there helping her.

Putting the truck into park as she waited in line, Lottie wondered if she should turn back.

"No, don't be silly." she told herself. "Pearl will be along; the kids are waiting for her." Beating her thumb against the steering wheel she looked out across the sound and waterway. It was one of the highest tides she had ever seen. Fidgeting in her seat, worry building, Lottie pulled her truck out of park and into reverse and looked for a way to turn the truck around. There was none. She would get stuck in the sand if she would have left the pavement. And that would have really caused a commotion. "No, better to just go on home, the kids are waiting there with Jess and their Uncle Phil."

Her hand reached to turn on the radio. The dial clicked and she turned it to move along the numbers and stations she was familiar with. Mostly crackling sounds emanated from the speakers along with garbled and static filled sentences.

"This is useless." She twisted the knob to off and leaned back in her seat, recalling that the weather reports on the radio earlier had said that the coming storm was a big one, and that all should vacate any waterfront homes or businesses and seek shelter at least five miles inland.

That didn't make a lot of sense to Lottie. She knew enough to not be in a boat during a storm, and she sure as hell knew not to be on the banks during one. But where she lived, by the sound, she pictured a rising tide and maybe lots of water, lots of wind that might blow down a tree or tear up the barn. But five miles inland? That was a bunch of baloney. After all, Lottie had been living through hurricanes her whole life; they were something she knew about. Some were nothing more than a hardy gale. Others uprooted trees, destroyed porch fronts and changed inlets. And if your house was not up on pilings you might get some flooding. That would be true for anyone who lived soundfront. It was the banks that took the brunt of the storms, that's why they were there, to protect the inland areas. So she never worried too much, putting her faith in God and believing that a little Hell comes with paradise; no place was perfect.

A mighty storm had not been through the area since 1940, right before the Army had come. And then back in '33 another storm came through, too. Those were the only ones that had worried her and Jess. They boarded up their windows and brought the boats in from the dock and sheltered them by the barn. But it wasn't too bad. Some shingles came off the roof, and the lean-to shed fell on the flats boat, and part of the dock was destroyed. But there was nothing damaged that could not be fixed.

After the 1940 storm they had gone over to the banks with Pearl and the West family, and walked north for a couple miles to find that the storm had made a new inlet, albeit a shallow one. Before long it filled in.

One of the little shacks where a dory was kept had been destroyed; the dory nowhere to be found. A few small boats had washed ashore along with someone's stairs. They found lots of chairs, a screen door, lots of shoes and several pieces of pipe—she had no idea where that could have come from.

Rawl West found a radio full of shells and sand, and Francis found someone's winter coat. A few other miscellaneous items of that nature were strewn hither and yon, buried halfway in the sand.

Pearl had been such a young girl then, and as she walked along the beach front, well ahead of her parents, she ignored the debris as she filled her dress with sand dollars and whelks and starfish. To Lottie and Jess's amazement, Pearl had even found some of her precious purple heather.

It was astonishing that, despite all the destruction, the plant was hale and hearty and blowing in the breeze as if nothing had happened.

Back then, before the development of the island had begun, there was not very much to damage. Now, there was a fishing pier, restaurants, grocery stores, cottages and homes.

Lottie was worried about the Sea Gull Restaurant. She and Jess and everyone else in the family had worked night and day to make the place a success. And it had been a booming success. The business had changed all of their lives.

The thought of living without the extra income, and the new way of life they had begun, scared her.

Lottie worried for the island and she worried again as she studied the white caps in the sound and waterway. The merkle bushes and little oaks alongside the road were swaying wildly; already a few limbs lay about on the ground. Hazel was on her way.

"Hazel," Lottie spoke aloud. "Who in the world came up with the name Hazel—and why in the world are they giving names to hurricanes?"

It started last year—the naming, that is. Before, they had simply been numbered. 1953 held hardly any damaging weather for the coastal area of her home. However, in August, just two months ago, Hurricane Carol had hit the coast of Connecticut and had done devastating damage, tearing down power lines, destroying businesses and homes. The flooding lasted for days and days, causing even more ruin. *Surely Hazel couldn't be that bad,* Lottie thought.

Finally reaching the bridge, she slowly drove across, the rear of her truck fell hard on the pavement as her truck bumped against the decline. Glancing back, she expected to see her muffler lying on the road. Perhaps luck was with her today, it had not been torn from the truck.

But as she had glanced back she had not seen Pearl's brown Packard either.

Disappointed, she pulled the truck to the side of the road, into the driveway of a small bait and tackle shop. She rolled her window all the way down and stuck her head outside surveying the slow stream of cars slowly moving.

The pontoon bridge looked as if it would sink beneath the weight of the vehicles on it. And even though the population of Topsail Island was small, the bridge was its only access. Progress was at a snail's pace.

"Sorry, Miss Lottie, you're going to have to move along. Traffic's pretty backed up now with everybody trying to get off the island before that hurricane hits." Billy Burns' lanky frame leaned down to speak apologetically. "Miss Lottie, is there something I could help you with?"

She gazed up and smiled at the young teenager. "Well, I was hoping I could turn around. Pearl's still at the Gull and I want to make sure she comes on home."

The older Burns strode slowly to the truck. "Lottie, is there a problem?"

"Hi, Carl. I was just hoping I could get back on the island, shouldn't have gone off anyway. Just want to make sure Pearl is coming along."

"Sorry Lottie, we got strict orders to not let anyone on the island, and I'm sure Pearl has enough sense to leave." His neck stretched skyward as he studied the clouds. "It's mighty bad out here now, gonna get worse. That Sergeant right up the road," Carl pointed and nodded his head, "will have my 'you know what' if I let you back on there."

"You sure?" Lottie's eyes pleaded.

"Pearl would never stay. She's got the car, doesn't she?"

Lottie nodded.

"Well, I'm sure Pearl will be right along. She was putting up plywood, right?"

Lottie nodded again.

"You go on home now, and I'm sure she'll be along soon."

There was no way to avoid the worry depicted in Lottie's face, Carl sighed. "Ya know what, you rest assured, if I don't see her come off this island, I'll go check on her myself. I'll keep a sharp eye out for her and so will my boy. How's that?"

"Oh, I'm just worrying too much." Lottie smiled; a faint blush crossed her checks as she realized she may have appeared too overwrought. "But I just got this feeling, you know. And it ain't a good one."

Carl held her eyes for a moment. "I'm sure you are worried, Lottie, but after hearing about that storm that hit up north, well, I guess lots of people are worried. We all are, but you go on home now. She'll be along soon." He smiled and waved her on as she pulled out onto the road.

CHAPTER TWO

The last of the boards was finally nailed into place. Pearl hoped it would be enough, but she had doubts. Hurricane Carol had really devastated the northeast in August. She'd seen pictures in the newspaper of buildings destroyed and had read how families had lost their businesses and homes. The thought of losing her precious Sea Gull was unthinkable. She shook her head and walked in through the side door; it would be the last to be secured.

A final check around the restaurant to make sure that everything was unplugged and that all the doors and windows were sealed tightly would be all she needed before heading home.

She breathed a quivering sigh and felt her entire body chill as she thought of all the work she and her family had done. She treasured each hour they had all spent building the restaurant and deciding the colors and tablecloths and even the menu. Why now did she feel as if she had taken so much for granted?

My happiest days have been here. And Momma and Daddy. I can see the sparkle in Daddy's eyes when he got out of the hospital and started helping here. It really made him get better faster. God knows, I believe that.

Pearl could feel the pit of her stomach ache—the ache moved up to her chest and shoulders. "And Paul," she whispered. Pushing tears and despair away as she had learned to do over and over again, Pearl raised her chin. "No."

The Sea Gull Restaurant was she and Paul's baby nearly as much as were their own children. The thought of loss once again angered her and as she felt the dark cloud of hopelessness filling her body she shook her head. "Hell no, this is not going to happen to me again! I am not going to leave here."

As she spoke, she heard the wind pick up, it howled loudly and she heard the *flut, flut, flut* of something perhaps caught in the corner of the building. She could only guess as the gust of wind continued pushing against the outside of the building.

The wind whistled louder still and she heard the thud and grate of something hit the side of the restaurant. She found herself looking toward the windows, boarded up so tightly that they prevented any view at all.

I guess I did a good job, Pearl smiled to herself. Unlocking the side door, she stepped out and rounded the corner of the building to the patio. The impact of the wind as it burst against her skin was amazing. It pushed her back hard against the side of the building. Like sandpaper it blasted against her, stinging as it nearly blew her sideways, and then seemed to push her back toward the door.

Holding her head down and her arms tightly against her body, Pearl hugged the wall as she moved toward the loud fluttering sound.

A dead seagull, half wrapped in a cloth awning, lay pushed up against the south wall of the patio. The awning fabric popped and fluttered, the wind beating hard against it.

That's it, Pearl thought. The sight of the twisted body of the bird would have normally repulsed her. Rather, in this case, it calmed her.

The whole sky, everything, was filled with thick mist and sand; shielding her eyes she gazed out toward the ocean.

"Wow! Oh my God." Her hands went to her face as she stood before the Atlantic. As the wind had tossed her from one side to the other, waves were being tossed—one on top of the other, crashing southward, northward, straight to the shore and some even seemed to go backwards.

Swirling around the picnic tables, the water tugged at their pilings. A smile and shake of her head belied the realization of their eminent destruction. How toy-like they looked as she watched the rising water lap at the benches.

Licking her lips, she tasted the salt; it was even heavier than usual and had amassed in the corners of her lips. The thick mist coated her face with droplets of water.

Southward, Surf City Pier was being pummeled by waves as they crashed over the end of the structure. The huge crane at the end of the pier, where construction was still underway, sort of shivered a bit. Spray lifted high into the air over the crane as waves curled repeatedly, one after the other over the end of the structure; each wave reached higher than the one before. In awe, Pearl stood amazed, consumed with the sights around her.

She watched as wave after wave crashed against the sand, the picnic tables, each other. In the distance she could see telephone poles sway, their lines now seemed loose as they flapped in the wind.

A swirl of varying shades of grey encompassed the sky and ocean; it seemed to reach all the way to the ground where little jetties of sand fingered out, daring to stand against the rising, pounding water that changed from one second to the other.

Overcome with the sights and sounds around her, Pearl was hypnotized by the cacophony—the ear-splitting hiss of Mother Nature and the pull of emotion that surpassed any physical love she had ever experienced.

All this beckoned her as she carefully stepped down the stairway leading to the beach. It was all so beautiful, so angry. "Miss June was wrong, this *is* where

God lives—this is life, this is death, this is everything," Pearl whispered the words, closed her eyes, and felt the spray against her body and the wind whipping about her, pulling and pushing.

Holding on to the railing she rested on the last step, leaned back against the stairs and slid off her shoes, letting her feet sink into the wet, gritty, sand.

A half smile crossed her lips as she felt her body lift a bit on one side and then the other. The thought of not being in control, letting go, was enticing. It reminded her of her life with Paul, whom she had always been able to rely on.

Her life with him had been one of trust. Whenever she was troubled she let go, and Paul found the way for them both. He had lifted her from loss and despair and saved her.

Paul's image appeared in her mind, the clearest it had been in months. This time she did not push it away, rather, she relaxed into a trance-like state of conjuring his breath and being.

"Let me go," she whispered.

She felt the wind pulling her hair away from her scalp and the sand as it stung against that tender skin. The wind reached beneath her blouse and blew, flapping and tugging against the buttons, one popped briskly off. The wind was filling her shorts, she could feel it across her back where it stung her buttocks and thighs. She felt again the thick wind lift her body.

"Let me go," she called. "Please."

Pearl listened to everything, the wind, the waves, the roar...it was consuming her, and she became less and less aware of her being.

A loud crash disrupted her state and she nodded; awareness clouding her consciousness. Another disruptive sound echoed, and she thought she heard the calling of her name. Fully aware now of her surroundings, she listened intently. Was that her name she heard? Was Paul calling her? It seemed she heard his voice. At first it startled her, but that is what she wanted, wasn't it? Why wouldn't he call to her? He must long for her as she longed for him.

Again she heard her name, it blurred with the pounding of the wind. It called again, louder, differently.

That was not Paul's voice. Shielding her eyes from the blowing sand, again she heard the voice call out; it came from the top of the stairs. She slumped down and pulled herself beneath the stairway, against the spinning sand. *Was that Carl Burns? What was he doing there?*

The pounding waves muffled Carl's pounding fists as he beat on the front door and boarded windows of the Sea Gull. "Pearl, your momma and daddy are waiting for you and your kids too." Carl's voice came closer. "Ya hear me? Are you here?"

Part of her wanted to rise and make her way up the stairs. Her family, her children needed her, this was true. But she could not move. Instead she closed her eyes even tighter and pulled her knees up to meet her chest.

Again Carl called out, "Pearl! Pearl!"

His voice seemed farther and farther away as he called out her name again and again.

Finally she heard the calls no more.

Holding herself as still as possible, Pearl listened to the sounds around her. They were thunderous, but at the same time soothingly deafening. She watched an angry wave tear at the last step, groaning came from somewhere and she turned her head toward the fishing pier and watched as the end of it, where the huge crane stood, buckled and fell into the ocean—swallowed by waves curling higher than she had ever seen before.

A loud noise, though muffled, seemed to rip by her and she jerked to notice that one of the awnings of the picnic tables had been blow away. Turning her head left then right, she gasped, realizing that it was gone, completely—as if it had vanished into space.

"Carl!" Pearl scrambled from beneath the stairs, her vision blurred by sand. Her eyes burned and she did what she knew she shouldn't do, she rubbed them hard. "Carl! I'm here!"

Her searching feet found her shoes and she hurriedly slipped them on as she pulled herself up to the first step, her left leg becoming engulfed in the rising water; it ebbed back only slightly. Pearl stood mesmerized as she watched the ocean consume the picnic tables. In a second they were gone.

The sand-filled wind stung sharply against her skin; her eyes burned and ached. *I must flush them out with water;* she panicked and raised her arms to shield her face as she pushed against the wind to the front of the restaurant. Carl was gone.

"Oh God, what have I done?" She hugged the outside of the building until she reached the unlocked side door. Pearl couldn't help but look out toward the ocean. Fear swept over her, overwhelming her thoughts.

"Calm down, calm down," she told herself as she took a deep breath before reaching for the screen door. She pulled it open; a gust of wind swept wrenched it out of her hand and into oblivion.

She pushed against the thick wooden door, holding onto the knob as tightly as she could and slid inside. It slammed hard behind her as she moved toward the front of the restaurant and the counter where she had set her car keys. Her eyes scanned the counter and rested on the cash register where her eyes sat. Yes, they were where she remembered putting them. Hurriedly she ran to grab them, and then made her way back through the door, around to the front stairs and down to her car.

By then the rain had turned into a stream, a torrent of water pouring, it seemed, from all directions. Sheets of water fell and as the wind picked up, what she thought could not become any more forceful, did become so.

The wind, sand and rain against her body was excruciatingly painful as she inched her way to her car that seemed a mile away.

Reaching for the handle, Pearl pushed herself inside and slid the key into the ignition. Nothing. She tried again. Nothing. The car swayed as the wind pushed against it. The rain poured so heavily, she could not see out the windows. *Entombed*, the word flitted through her thoughts; immediately she brushed the thought away.

What to do, what to do; looking about the car, Pearl felt her breaths quicken; her body shook uncontrollably. Pearl could feel the fear welling—"the Lord is my refuge and my fortress," Pearls lips quivered as she spoke nervously, bowing her head she gripped the seats of the Packard tightly. "My God in whom I trust." Pearl repeated the lines she had learned long ago over and over. Slowly she calmed herself and looked about the car for something, anything, that would help her or shield her in some way against the storm.

Surely she could not stay there in the car. It would only be a matter of time, she thought, before it was blown away or the windows became broken. "I am going to have to get back to the Gull to even have a chance of survival."

In the back seat of the Packard were her jacket and an umbrella. She grabbed the jacket and jerked it on her damp, gritty body.

"Oh God, please let me make it back," Pearl prayed, opened the car door, pushing hard against the wind. A gust caught the door, slinging it back; she did not bother to try to shut it.

Pearl fell to her knees, and began inching her way toward the front of the restaurant. At times, nearly flat on her belly, she pulled her body.

Finally reaching the steps she made her way to the front porch. With her jacket pulled to protect her face, she looked toward Surf City Fishing Pier, even more of it was gone, nearly half. It was too hard to make out if the tackle shop was there or not.

The oyster house that had once been the officers' club was still intact, or at least it seemed to be as she fought to see. Everything was blurred by the wind and rain.

Telephone poles stood tilted with lines drooping from them. She heard a loud pop and sizzle and turned, hugging the walls until she made it to the side door. Immediately Pearl pushed two tables in front of it, and then stood back with her hands on her hips listening to the incessantly beating wind and rain. She moaned aloud, "Oh my God, what am I going to do now? They're all going to be so worried about me."

My babies, her hands went to cover her face as she shook her head. "What in the world have I been thinking? Stupid, stupid." Pearl rolled her eyes.

"Shut up! Think! What are you going to do NOW?" Pearl looked around the kitchen listening to the howl of

Hazel. *The kitchen is the only room with no windows. It's probably the safest.* She nodded, reassuring herself.

The side door that led outside to sand dunes and merkle bushes was the only source of ventilation for that room. And during the summer months it stayed open with a large fan whirling away in front of it.

She and Paul realized too late that at least one window should have been built into the room. Now she was happy they had overlooked installing one. It made her wonder if perhaps *this* had been the reason they had forgotten to make a window for the room.

Pearl walked toward the swinging door that led to the dining area, pushed against the door and scanned the restaurant. "There's not much between me and Hazel, is there?" She asked herself.

Turning, she re-entered the kitchen and settled herself on the floor next to the freezer. She could feel her heart beating against her chest. Taking deep breaths she listened as the fluttering, banging and knocking about; of what, she did not know, as it went on and on and on. The rain sounded more like white noise, a background for all other loud sounds.

She pictured the rain tearing through the walls of the building and her heart raced more, drowning out the thoughts in her head. She felt numb. "What is going on with me?" Her voice trembled as she gasped for breath.

Afraid, the loud beating of her heart joined the ear-splitting, rhythm-less cacophony booming on and on just on the other side of the wall where she sat. It was unlike anything Pearl had experienced before. Fear was welling and coming at her from all directions.

What was that! It sounded as if the roof was being torn apart. She gasped, then gasped again. It seemed to her that her breath was uncontrollable. The rhythm to her breathing seemed gone and she found herself forcing each breath.

Pearl felt herself rocking as she pulled her knees close to her chest. "Oh God," she whispered, her eyes closed tightly as she tried to pull her knees in even closer into herself. "The Lord is my refuge and fortress."

Another loud crash exploded outside and she heard something slide across the patio. She knew that any minute something would come crashing through the walls.

The entire building was shaking; the crashing and sound of things slamming against the little Sea Gull were constant. The floor seemed to move beneath her and she scrambled atop the long freezer. She thought of climbing into it, *but how could I breathe? Am I going to die today?*

Closing her eyes, Pearl took a slow, deep breath and forced her body to release the tension. "The Lord is my refuge and fortress," she whispered.

Stretching the length of the freezer, now damp with condensation, Pearl prayed again, asking God to be with her, to be with her children and family. "I'm so sorry. I have hurt so many people. Please forgive me Lord."

Repeating over and over her regret and pleas for her family, lulling herself into calmness, Pearl concentrated on long, slow breaths. Breathing became easier. Tears welled in her eyes, *I am going to die today.* She felt an overwhelming sense of regret fill her.

Who was there now to reach out to for a helping hand, a shoulder to lean on? Who was the someone she could trust to bring her through?

"Who have I loved?" Pearl called out angrily. Tears rolled down her burning cheeks as she pulled her lips tight. Roger's image came to mind.

He held the door as she entered the large knotty pine-paneled room. Moving close behind her, he rested his hand on her shoulder.

"I like the paneling. Whoever put that up did a good job. But the flooring...what you need here is some tile."

"No, I don't like tile."

Pearl remembered moving away from his touch. Even then she had ambivalent feelings about him.

"A nice linoleum, maybe light brown or something like that. Something that isn't going to show too much dirt, you know, we're going to have lots of sand."

"Come on baby, I know about flooring and..."

Pearl watched his mouth moving but like so very often, she turned off his words. He knows about flooring, he knows about this, he knows about that. She didn't even bother to roll her eyes; she simply grinned and let him continue.

The sink, do you want to move it in front of the window so you can watch the kids playing while you do dishes?"

Now that was a suggestion worth considering. She turned and walked toward the dining room, remembering walking there with Paul.

Then it was so sweet, making plans and designing their future. It seemed as if he moved through her body even now as she closed her eyes to feel him.

He stood there by the window, sunlight kissing his blond hair and lighting up his blue eyes.

"Come on over here," Roger's words startled her.

She felt numb as he slipped his hand to her shoulder and as they entered the long hallway of the barracks building. Moving closer, he grazed her body. At first it annoyed her, and then, as it had been since he returned to Surf City, she allowed it. Why?

"Why did I allow that jerk to do that to me? Why did I do that to myself?" Shaking her head, she closed her eyes again.

"The first thing I'll do is tear down some walls and do something with this hall." Roger touched his hand to the small of Pearl's back and moved her gently in the direction of the back door. He leaned in slightly.

Pushing the past away she leaned into Roger. She bit her lip, too hard, and tasting the blood, she thought of how she didn't even like him.

He pulled her closer still. "I think we're going to make this into a mighty fine place—a home."

Pearl's eyes settled firmly on Roger's. They held and she watched the muscles in his arm flex as his fingers stroked her skin. He had a new tattoo, one she had not noticed before, a wolf with its head stretched back to howl.

"When did you get this?" She asked.

"Lone wolf," Roger moved his fingers from her shoulder and ran them across the ink work. "Last year. That's how I feel sometimes and I thought that you must feel like that too."

Her eyes met his gaze again. Not for one minute did she believe he cared or even had a heart. If he did, she didn't care anyway. She did not like him, didn't trust him. But he was the only one to come to her; the only man to offer something resembling love. She pushed him aside.

"The kids are going to love playing in those sand dunes," Pearl said as she walked to the little porch facing the backyard; she leaned against the side rails. It was dusk and the muted shades of the beach were everywhere—the dunes were covered with beach grass, the yucca had lost most of its bells, though a few browning ones held on. Around the base of the dunes was the hairawn muhly, Pearl's beloved purple heather.

As she squatted down to sit on the step, Pearl scanned the landscape of dunes, scrub oaks and merkles and listened to the song of a red-wing blackbird. It called soothingly, mystically, reminding her of the good *times, good things, smiling friends and family. Sighing, she furrowed her brow, trying to push the images away. But the bird did not stop, it trilled louder. Another joined in and within seconds, it seemed the trees were filled with the trill of the red-wing blackbirds.*

Awash in the feel of the past, Pearl relaxed against the sweaty box freezer. Warmness flowed over her body as she pictured Paul and his ever-forgiving smile. Lottie and Jess came from the periphery to bend and kiss their daughter. Even Jay came holding her hand and asking for her trust.

The corners of her lips lifted as she felt her loved ones course through her. She had been loved so much in her life. And what had she given back?

"Roger. I gave myself to Roger because I couldn't have the others anymore. I deserved him, I guess."

Stretching her legs and lifting herself from the freezer, she stood, shaking her head. "Yucky!"

Hammering winds beat and beat, but there seemed to be at least a second or two between the beats, now.

"Jeez, I'm going to die today and I just figured out how stupid I've been." Pearl moved to her original spot on the floor beside the freezer.

"Is this the way it's going to be? My poor babies, I have so neglected them since Paul died." Tears poured down her cheeks, "He died. He died." She had known this all along. Why had it taken so long to comprehend it? "Paul is gone...shit."

The floor seemed to move again, Pearl watched in silence. She turned her head toward a ripping sound; "Something got torn apart," Pearl spoke calmly and heaved an exhausted sigh. She listened. Outside the beating continued as the wind whistled louder, and then less loud, and then even less still, until Pearl's eyes closed to a rhythm that had begun.

CHAPTER THREE

Local home and business owners assembled at Sear's Landing awaiting their turn to board the DUKW, an amphibious military vehicle. Unless owners and families had their own boat, it was the only way to the island. The pontoon bridge had been damaged. It lay cockeyed against the marshy shore of Goat Island, one of the tiny islands dotting the sound and Intracoastal Waterway between the mainland and Topsail.

People launched their watercraft from landings in Hampstead, Sloop Point, Holly Ridge, and Snead's Ferry and motored over to Topsail to check out their homes and businesses. Surf City had the largest influx of people since it was the most densely populated.

Silently Lottie and Jess watched from their flats boat as a group of around twenty people boarded the Duck, as the DUKW came to be called.

Gently pushing the throttle of the outboard on his flats boat, Jess motored slowly to the island where Bart Ralston stood waving.

Holding hands, Lottie and Jess stepped from the boat and walked over to Bart. Nodding to one another, they immediately began walking toward him.

"Too much of a mess to drive the Jeep up here; everyone's in a fuss and in a bad mood," Bart shook his head in disgust. "Got the Jeep parked up by the reservoir."

"Lots of damage," Jess muttered as he looked at the devastation surrounding him. "Lots of damage, but you made it out okay, right?"

"Yeah, she was a bitch." Bart quickly turned to Lottie. "Excuse me ma'am, my language."

"Well, that's one way of putting it," Lottie snickered.

"You rode the whole thing out, didn't you Bart?" Jess queried.

"Humph, if that's what you want to call it. I was hugging the toilet most of the time. Thought I was gonna die."

"Bad, huh?"

"Yeah, near about as bad as Guadal or Bogansville. At least then I could aim at something and shoot back. This, this thing, storm, hurricane, whatever you want to call it—you better believe I was scared."

Looking for a little levity, Bart added, "But I'd do it again."

There was no response from either Lottie or Jess and they continued walking toward the reservoir, picking up their step a bit.

"I guess you're wanting to drive on down to your restaurant—find out how it fared."

Jess and Lottie nodded in unison. Tight lipped they avoided Bart's gaze.

"Don't worry too much, now. I'll help you build her back if she's blown away."

Walking in silence, Lottie heaved a loud sigh, and swallowed hard. Jess pulled his wife against him and wrapped his arm around her shoulder. He kissed the side of her head.

"Okay, you two..." Bart studied the couple.

"Pearl never made it home yesterday. We..."

"Hell, why didn't you say so. If I'd of known that, I'd of gone and checked on the place. You could have called me...oh, that's right, the power lines are down."

Picking up his pace, he walked quickly, making it to the reservoir ahead of Lottie and Jess. "Come on," Bart waved his arms. "Let's get going." He hopped into the jeep and turned the key, sliding into reverse he stopped, allowing Jess and Lottie to get seated.

"The going is gonna be slow. We're gonna have to pull any debris out of the road." Bart clucked his tongue anxiously then added, "That is if we can find the road.

"I was pretty lucky, my place didn't blow away. Not much of it, maybe some shingles and part of the back porch. But at least I've got a vehicle." He turned to Jess and Lottie, clucking his tongue again—one of his many nervous habits.

"I told them that the best place to leave their vehicle was on the other side of that reservoir." Shaking his head, Bart snickered. "Glad they didn't listen to me, there wouldn't have been room for everybody. I'm one of the only people that has a working vehicle and can travel around."

Flipping his thumb against the steering wheel, Bart surveyed closely the surrounding devastation. "Every few feet or so we're going to have to stop and move debris out of the way, you hear? I know this Jeep will make it through sand, but not if it's waist high, and it ain't gonna go if the tires got nails in 'em."

Jess nodded and quietly squeezed Lottie's hand.

"Look, I'll get you there as soon as this old Jeep will let me." Bart licked his dry lips, "Don't worry too much. If I can make it through this damn hurricane, I know that gal of yours can, too."

It was expected that in a couple of months the new shopping center, the Superette, would be up and ready for business, but it was obvious that was not going to happen. Hazel had blown out all the windows in the building under construction, and sand stood more than a foot deep over the floor. Pilings and two-by-fours jutted out of the walls. The category four storm had indeed wreaked havoc on the new complex.

As Bart drove past, he shook his head. Glancing at Lottie and Jess, he realized that all the devastation didn't offer a great deal of hope for them about their daughter. The road to the left was covered densely with debris; part of a house sat squarely in the middle of it. Bart shifted into first, then reverse and back to first, and instead of trying to maneuver his way around it, he drove straight to where Pop's Pavilion stood. It had indeed sustained heavy damage with nearly being blown off its foundation. In fact, part of the building was gone. The remainder sat a bit tilted where part of the sand dunes had been washed away. Pop Jones stood out front, surveying the damage. He waved as they slowly drove north.

From the Jeep they could all see the main building of Surf City Fishing Pier, the tackle shop. It had been damaged, but not destroyed. A few of the railings had disappeared and sand covered much of the stairway and ramp that led to the tackle shop. But the fishing pier itself had been nearly destroyed—fully half of it was missing. The crane that was used for putting the pilings in place was gone. Pilings jutted out of the now calm and slow rolling water, askew and seemingly naked without the boardwalk above them.

As Bart drove along, stopping intermittently, so that one thing or another could be moved out of the way, he chatted a bit trying to lighten the slow journey toward the Sea Gull Restaurant, where they all hoped Pearl had ridden out the hurricane safely. Occasionally the three would wave or call out to others scouring through the debris and wrecked or damaged buildings. It was odd to drive past the Finley home and see the swingset frame still standing upright, though the swings and teeter-totter were missing. An oceanfront barracks, now serving as apartments, was missing half of its porch, but a rocking chair stood on one side as if nothing at all had happened.

One of the old towers from the missile launching days after World War II stood staunchly in the dunes. It had defied Hazel and won. Hope welled among the passengers of Bart's Jeep.

"Those things will be here for centuries." Jess nodded his head assuredly. "Ain't nothing gonna tear them down—built strong. We built the Sea Gull strong too. My little gal's holed up in that restaurant and I know she's fine."

"Hell, if I can go through it, I know your Pearl can. That's one tough gal you got."

Lottie grasped Jess's hand tightly and nodded, her eyes begging for reassurance. "I shouldn't have left her."

"No matter. She's fine." Jess squeezed Lottie's hand in return.

Driving up to the old officers' club they gasped in disbelief; much of the structure was gone. The front outdoor patio had been swept away, leaving the oyster bar looking naked and desolate. The long concrete walkway along the dunes still stood, though at least a half of it was missing. The remaining walkway was tilted a bit toward the ocean.

All three stepped from the Jeep to pull boards and other debris from the sand covered road.

"This looks familiar," yelled Bart as he picked up the edge of what looked to be an awning. "Isn't this one of yours?"

Lottie's hand flew to her lips. "My baby."

"No, no, now Miss Lottie, that was right on the beach. It was bound to be destroyed. I helped you guys build that place. I know it's strong. Just hold on."

"I think we're going to have to drive around this one," called Jess, as he nodded toward a large slab of concrete that blocked the road ahead. "Isn't this the rest of the walkway that led toward the stables?"

"Looks like part it," Bart answered.

"I think we'll be able to get around," Bart called as he beckoned for Lottie and Jess to get back in the vehicle. "We need to get on down to the Gull."

They could all see it a short distance north of where they stood. There seemed more urgency now, and Bart, though going slow, swerved in and around chunks of debris blocking the road.

"Roof's still on," Jess beamed, as they reached the Gull. "Told you, told you. My little gal is fine in there."

As she nodded in agreement, Lottie held back tears of doubt, praying that Pearl would be okay despite the odds.

Bart stopped short as they reached the building. The jerking motion nearly threw Jess out of his seat as his feet touched the ground. His eyes couldn't examine fast enough the damage to the building. Yes, the stairs were gone, except for a lopsided banister. But he pulled himself up by it anyway, and then reached out a hand to help Lottie.

The front door was intact and boarded. All the windows were still boarded; an awning from one of the picnic tables lay propped sideways against a window and the porch. In front of it, mysteriously, were a pile of about six dead seagulls. A mattress lay flat on the porch with a stop sign atop it. Seaweed gathered in clumps along the edges.

The door facing the ocean was intact, but sand was packed nearly halfway to the top. There was no way they were going in that door. Jess beat loudly with his fist, "Hey gal, gal. You okay?"

"Daddy?"

"Pearl!" Lottie and Jess hollered in unison as they ran to the side of the building where nearly a foot of sand covered the porch. A pathway had been carved out and footsteps were visible, obviously Pearl had already ventured out. He pushed on the side door, and to his amazement, it opened.

"It took you long enough." Pearl pulled a long swallow of Dr. Pepper through her lips. "I've been waiting and waiting. Even took a stroll down the beach. Look what I found." Holding up a Florida license plate, she smiled, "Think Ellie could use this?"

Silence followed as all seemed awe struck by Pearl's cheerful attitude.

"I'm so…" Lottie began.

"No Momma…and Daddy too, I'm so sorry."

Pearl reached out her hand and pulled her mother close. "I'm so sorry, I'm such a brat. I've been so stupid."

Jess nodded. "Rawl West came here looking for you and couldn't find you. He thought for sure you had gotten a ride with someone."

"But then you didn't come home and..."

Her head lowered, Pearl started, "I..."

"No, it doesn't matter, now. Our gal's okay." Lottie pulled her close for a hug. "We both are so bullheaded." Her eyes meet Pearl's and she smiled, "So, what's the damage here?"

"It's amazing. I don't think there is a single thing inside that is damaged, though maybe a window or two is cracked. But everything looks okay inside. Outside is another story."

****

Jess stepped out onto the patio alone, as Lottie, Bart and Pearl examined the inside of the Gull.

He looked northward, next to the restaurant, to where a new cottage had been built last winter. The site was completely vacant; the structure had been totally blown away. His heart beat rapidly and fluttered. *Thank God, thank God.* He closed his eyes for a moment and sighed. He walked slowly past the debris on the porch and walked toward the stairs to the ocean. Yes, just as he expected, all the picnic tables were gone. Pilings lay askew on the shore along with broken boards, twisted pieces of metal and tree limbs. The banisters around the patio were askew or gone, as well. Beach grasses were strewn everywhere, except where they were supposed to be. But the sea was calm, rolling, as if nothing had happened at all. He hated it when someone didn't own up to their actions.

"Look what you did," He called lowly, shaking his head and sighing. Halfway expecting some kind of response from the entity he'd known all his life. "I've seen you do some really bad stuff." He glanced down at the half-gone stairway to the beach. "Well, you did leave us more than you did others."

The stairway to the beach was hanging in mid-air; standing there he noticed an indention in the sand-covered bottom step. Pearl had been sitting there, no doubt, looking out to the ocean. Maybe talking with it too, as he often did.

"It must have been a hard journey through the storm for my Pearl," he said to himself. "I hope she learned a lot."

He wondered and hoped that it had opened her eyes to some things; her children, that man...Roger, and their order of importance. Jess had never approached her on the matter, felt awkward about discussing it and had left all of that to Lottie. But there had been some discussion between the two of them regarding their daughter's indiscretions. Mostly they talked about the children, always trying to figure out a way to have them with them at work or at home on the farm. Jess didn't mind keeping an eye on the kids at the farm. That was much easier than trying to watch them at the beach. And at the farm Phil was around, or Bella would be there with her brood while Enid worked.

Emma Jewel was simply too young to bring to the beach. She needed lots of attention. The least of which was potty training.

Jess winced at the latter. He had never been keen on changing diapers.

****

"So, you're out here staring out into space again, huh?" Wrapping her arms around her father, Pearl kissed him quickly on the cheek.

He turned slightly and gathered his daughter to his side. Silently they stood before the ocean and the damage so visible on the beach.

"Was it a fun ride?" Jess asked. There was no sarcasm in his voice.

Quietly turning her face toward her father's, Pearl gazed deeply into his eyes. They held their gaze for a long time.

"Yes, Daddy."

CHAPTER FOUR

"The Mermaid Bar was destroyed, flattened. There were yellow boards strewn everywhere, I'd say, for at least two miles up and down the beach. Ol' Hazel had a heyday with that place." Jess leaned his chair upright from the side of the tobacco barn.

"They'll build it back. A man's gotta have some place to play cards and have a beer."

"Now Phil, are you going to tell me that you're really going to miss that place?"

Shrugging, Phil curled his upper lip, "Paw always said hootch provided the fuel for entertainment."

"You aren't going to start quoting your father now, are you?"

Phil's face reddened as his eyes slid to his hands where he held a twig. Twisting it between his fingertips he spat, "I hate that bastard."

"I can understand that." Jess crossed his arms across his chest. "He's done a lot of bad."

Phil looked over to where Clarence sat stupor-like, with his legs sprawled wide, his chair leaning against the side of the tobacco barn. Phil eyed his father coolly as he nudged Jess.

"He ain't really here, you know."

"Wonder what he's thinking about now?"

"Beats me Jess, but as long as it keeps him occupied, I don't care. I'm just trying to figure out what to do with him."

The silence between the two men was palpable and Jess wondered just what Phil meant.

"You know," breaking the silence, Phil continued, "as much as he drank, I don't think I ever saw him go into a bar."

"Me neither...maybe he didn't want to give the competition anything." Jess guffawed.

"Yeah." Sliding a glance back toward his father, Phil shrugged. "I don't have too much use for bars, but then it's all in the reason you're going there. Don't ya think? I go now and again to have a beer and play a little poker. But like my brother, I never did have any desire to swill the stuff. Anyway, my old man never needed a bar to get sloppy drunk or beat his wife and kids."

"Yeah, he was mean to y'all, that's for sure." Pausing, Jess considered whether or not to ask the question he'd had on his mind for quite a while. Taking a breath, he spoke. "We all been wondering about something, Phil. Why are you taking care of him now that you're back?"

Phil did not answer, rather he turned his gaze to the old man he called Paw. He sat his chair upright and sucked on his lower lip. "Taking care of him? I'd like to *take care of him.*"

Again silence rested between the two men for a number of seconds.

"You have any idea where I went for all those years, Mr. Jess?"

"I heard you'd gone up to Detroit and was working in one of those car plants. But that was just hearsay."

"Good boy, Enid," Chuckling, Phil ran his hand across the back of his neck, turned it as he heard the pop-pop of the vertebrae.

"I was in Chinquapin. Enid's the only one that knew that. I was working on a farm and went by another name—Delbert James. Now, how's that for making up a name, pretty good huh?"

Jess chuckled. "I never knew." Squinting he asked, "Did Paul know?"

"Nope, no one knew. Enid promised me, no matter what, that he wouldn't tell a soul. Yes sir, you can trust ol' Enid."

"You didn't come around when your maw died. Why?"

"The war was just winding down and Enid wasn't home yet. Otherwise, he'd have told me. As it was, I didn't hear about Maw's passing until a couple months later."

"It was a nice funeral, lots of folks came." Jess's sorrowful eyes met Phil's. "Why didn't you just come on home when you finally did hear?"

As he rose to stretch, Phil yawned. "And come home to a lovin' Paw? Yeah, just what I needed. Never could see how Paul put up with all that, but then he had Pearl and y'all as a family."

"You should have come back, son. Things would have worked themselves out."

"Yeah." Phil nodded his head. "Well, you never know do ya?"

"Paul had his problems with Clarence, don't think he didn't. Why do you think he joined the Navy when he did, or that Pearl moved in with us?"

Phil shrugged and bowed his head as he fidgeted with the twig he held in his hands.

"They went round and round, you know, fighting and hating; the old man trying to tell Paul what to do all the time. Then one day, it was as if a switch was turned off, and Clarence just started going downhill. He was easy as pie to get along with—didn't argue or try to tell anyone what to do. He was pretty good help when we were building the Gull." Jess gestured a thumbs up toward Phil. "Your old man could hammer a nail.

"Now, he didn't or wouldn't recall all the bad things he did to your brother, you and your maw—and that made Paul mad, just like it's making you mad. Then after Paul's death, it's been a landslide. You can attest to that."

Phil stared deeply into Jess's eyes. "I won't ever forgive him for what he did." Turning, he walked slowly toward Clarence. "Hey old man." He tapped a leg of the chair with his foot. "Hey old man."

Clarence looked up to his son and smiled a toothless grin. "Paul, hey boy. Don't ya think we oughta be heading on back to the house? Yer maw's sure to have supper ready?"

As he chuckled loudly, Phil kicked at the dirt. "What do you think I oughta do with him, Mr. Jess? What would you do?"

Jess watched Phil and Clarence as they walked to their truck; Clarence slow and plodding, his arms barely swinging by his side and his bottom lip hanging as if it were detached from the rest of his mouth. He shuffled along, Phil walking far ahead of him.

"Y'all welcome to stay for Sunday dinner if you want. Lottie's frying up some chicken and making some collard greens. I know she's got some of those biscuits your paw likes so much."

"No thanks, Mr. Jess. I think we better just head on to the house." Phil opened the passenger door of the truck for his father, looked defiantly back at Jess and waved.

Jess waved back and nodded his head. "Keep it 'tween the lines, son."

He watched as the truck drove down the cart path and on to the hard road. His brow furrowed, confused about the relationship, concerned about the whole situation.

"I guess I oughta get on home too," he said aloud, "Lottie's got her famous fried chicken tonight—don't want to miss out on that."

As he pulled the truck up to his home, things were just as he expected. Lottie stood leaning against the breezeway screen door. *She still has a figure*, Jess thought. His eyes followed the outline of her waist and hips: her hands propped against their sides. A yellow dishcloth lay draped across her shoulder.

"What took you so long? Your chicken is getting cold, husband."

Upon reaching the steps to the breezeway, Jess leaned forward and wrapped an arm around his wife's waist.

"Phil sure has a lot on his plate, sweetie." He pushed his lips to Lottie's cheek, "I don't know if he's gonna make it."

"You invite him for dinner?"

"Yep."

"You talk to him about things?"

"Yep."

On the table sat a plate of fried chicken, a bowl of collard greens, new potatoes with butter sauce and parsley. Steam still rose from the cornbread set neatly in the center of the table in an iron frying pan.

"I don't know whether the old drunk's condition is due to all the moonshine he's drank in his life, or if he is really just plain senile." Settling himself in his usual chair, Jess placed his napkin in his lap.

"Dear, we've known Clarence his whole life. He's always been causing trouble in some way or another. I think he's been hell on wheels his whole life. And I think it's time somebody quit letting that old bag of worms control theirs. It's time to quit caring."

"What? You think we oughta just let Phil go ahead and kill him?" Jess stared at his wife, holding his fork in midair.

"Is that what you think he's gonna do?" Lottie grinned.

"I guess it's something he's considered along the way, don't you think? But I sure do hope that boy doesn't do something foolish like that."

"It would be a shame to have to go to jail for the likes of Clarence. I'm thinking that we ought to just cart him up to Dix Hill."

"Maybe," Jess muttered through a mouthful of potatoes.

"In the past year he's gone from gentle conversation with nearly everyone, complying with simple requests to pull the suckers off the tobacco leaves or to wipe down the tables at the Gull, to losing his train of thought in mid-sentence. He doesn't know if he's coming or going, and it might be the kindest thing to go ahead and put him away before he hurts himself."

"Or somebody does it for him."

****

68

Clarence sat on the porch staring, at what, Phil did not know. But his gaze seemed to point to where an old barn had stood with a rusted-out truck, car and parts to a tractor lying about it.

That was one of the first things Phil had cleaned up when he returned to his homesite.

His eyes followed the old man's gaze, and he watched as Clarence raised his hands, making motions as if to reconstruct the items that had been there before.

Phil watched as his father's lips mouthed unintelligible words.

"Hey Paw, you gone crazy?" Shaking his head, Phil turned and entered the house.

****

"You'd think it would have been just the opposite with old Clarence," Lottie commented. "As fierce and loud as he always was, he has turned into a bumbling lamb. I think if I said 'boo' to him he'd pee in his pants. But I sure do not feel sorry for him, no, not one bit."

"Blub, blub, blub." Ellie pursed her lips. "Pfft...his brain is cooked." Ellie stood on the top step of the breezeway. "I sure as hell do not feel sorry for that old cow turd either."

Lottie grinned, "How long have you been standing there, Ellie?"

"Just a few minutes, but I know who you're talking about."

"You're getting sneaky; I didn't even hear you drive up."

I didn't drive up, I took the skiff. I've been fishing and I'm tied up at your dock right now." Ellie laughed and pulled the brightly colored scarf from her head.

"I don't believe I ever saw you behind the tiller of any boat," Jess gently chided.

"Yessiree. I'm learning new things all the time." Holding out a stringer of fish, Ellie stepped into the open doorway to the kitchen.

"Have a bite with us, gal." Jess pulled a chair out from beneath the table.

"Yes, we have plenty of fried chicken." Lottie squinted a questioning look toward her daughter's friend. Since she had been working at the Sea Gull, their relationship had improved. But she still was a little wary of Ellie.

"Oh no. I'm so sorry for interrupting y'all's super.

Wiping her hands on her apron, Lottie reached for the plates in the cabinet. "Come on now, we got plenty."

"No ma'am, I just wanted to give you these fish me and Monroe caught after church today. There's more than she and I can eat, so I thought you and Mr. Jess might like them. There might even be enough for you to use at the restaurant tomorrow. You know, tomorrow's special—fish sandwiches, twenty-five cents."

Jess stood, wild excitement filled his eyes as he ran to the window and threw back the curtains.

"What! What's going on? What are you looking at?" Lottie asked.

"Looking to see if pigs are flying around."

"Huh?"

"Looking to see if pigs are flying around."

Jess bent down to touch the ground. "And if hell's frozen over. Except for when you're working at the restaurant and *have* to be polite to one another, I've never seen you two agree on one single thing."

Ellie's head tilted back as she laughed loudly. "Me and Miss Lottie agree on lots of things. Right Miss Lottie?" She gently jabbed Lottie on the shoulder.

"More than we used to. I guess you're growing up some, Ellie."

"I know one thing we agree on, and that's what your daughter has been doing here with Roger."

Lottie's face reddened and her lips pursed. With her hands sitting squarely on her hips, she spat, "That's over. It's been over since the hurricane. I thought you knew that."

"But...just the other day we were talking about that."

"That's done with. My little girl wouldn't continue on with something *she* knew was wrong..."

"Ha, ha, ha." Ellie folded her arms across her chest and tapped her foot. "This coming from the queen herself of judgment...you've spent most of your life judging—putting me in my place, until your own little goody..." Stopping herself, Ellie watched sadness fill Lottie's eyes as her shoulders fell. "I'm sorry."

"It's over, I tell you." Lottie looked from Jess to Ellie, "This is something that belongs to Pearl. We all got our demons. I never should have talked about it, I was just—well. I never thought my daughter would do things like that..."

"And that I did do things like that, right? You didn't think your little Pearly White could stoop so low as to be like me."

"No, I'm sorry Ellie. I guess I always have judged you, not that you didn't do some things you shouldn't have, but you're right."

"Ladies, ladies, let's make nice now," Jess interrupted. "We've all done some things we shouldn't have." He looked sternly at the women. "Ellie, you've been too loose and flirtatious...I think 'cause your Momma and Daddy gave all their time to your older brother and sister, and when you came along they were just simply too tired to do much.

"Lottie, you're too bossy sometimes...I've spoiled you...partly because I know you blamed me for little Billy dying...

"Clarence was always a mean old bag of worms and yes, he was responsible for Josie dying so young.

"Paul was the kindest man in the world, the hardest working man in the world, but he had no confidence in himself. Probably never would—too much like his momma, and—"

"And you!" Lottie called sarcastically.

Shifting in his seat, Jess slid his eyes to the floor. "I'm perfect."

"Get outta here, you're full of blue sky." Ellie giggled. "You, who've always kept your own mind about things, never passing judgment on anyone. Now, listen to you."

"Making out like the wise old owl."

Jess nodded, "Well, if the shoe fits."

Lottie gazed at her husband questioningly, *He is a new person; my strong silent man is telling other people what he thinks. He always let me know, in some way or another—a touch, a look—but now he's actually speaking out.*

"Well, I'll be." Lottie walked over to Jess, put her arms around his neck and kissed him softly on the lips.

"You two beat all. I think you're the luckiest people in the whole world to have each other." Ellie cooed. "Sometimes I wish my daddy was still alive and that we could all get together like we used to."

"Umm," Jess nodded.

"But Mother wanted to move up to Raleigh after he passed." Uncharacteristically, Ellie's eyes filled with sorrow. Quickly she changed the subject.

"Well, I just wanted to drop these by for you." She placed the fish on a small table situated in the breezeway and waved a goodbye. "See you at work, Lottie."

It surprised Ellie, as she walked toward the Scaggins' dock, to feel the ache in her chest. She was not used to feeling regret, and this feeling seemed to overwhelm her.

Time stared her in the face as she had looked at the couple. Why had she not noticed their aging? She worked with Lottie every day and saw Jess at least once a week. But here at their farm they had seemed so old, so unlike what she remembered in her youth. The feeling made her feel uncomfortable and she slipped into the skiff, untied the line around the piling and started the motor to the outboard.

CHAPTER FIVE

1955

Jay rested his arm around Feona's shoulder as they drove along Highway 17. Her breath was slow and easy and smelled faintly sour. He brushed his cheek gently against her brown hair as he studied the road ahead.

Familiarity swept through him, as he crossed the Cape Fear River Bridge in Wilmington.

He recalled driving this way from the island with Pearl, Ellie, and one of her many beaus to go to the drive-in theatre. A couple of times he had driven with Jess to downtown Wilmington for parts and supplies. Yes, it was familiar, though changes had occurred; there were a few more houses, a few more businesses. Still, the recollection of the times he had come to the port town brought a sanguine smile to his lips.

He peered into the rearview mirror, his young son, Lafayette. "Fate," as he was called, lay sound asleep, stretched across the back seat of the Chrysler station wagon, his wavy brown hair mussed and lying gently against his brow.

Jay pulled Feona closer to him and kissed the side of her head. Still sleeping, she turned her head away and moaned softly.

They had married not long after his return from the banks back in 1949. Yes, he *had* put the past behind him, believing and knowing that his son Frank was in the best of all possible worlds with people who loved him and would take care of him.

Paul, he knew was a good father. Jay had always thought highly of him; he was a good man whose integrity was beyond question.

Pearl, he still loved. She was, after all, part of his youth—one of the sweetest parts. Who would want to forget that? He respected that love they had once shared, though it was much different than the love he had for Feona. Perhaps the love he had then was not as mature as he now felt for his wife.

After his return from the island, Jay had felt relief knowing that things were as they were, as they should be. He trusted in Pearl and Paul; there was no need for worry in that situation. What had been between he and Pearl was the past, and he had pushed the past where it belonged.

For several years he had felt at peace with the decisions he had made, and had moved on to make his own life, his own family. But when the letter came from Ellie telling him of Paul's accidental death, it brought doubts and questions that he needed answers to. Who was going to help Pearl with Frank? How was Frank dealing with his father's death?

He began thinking of ways to get into Frank's life without disturbing the status quo. The thoughts plagued him as it did not seem right to stay away from a son who no doubt needed a father or father figure in his life.

Jay asked himself over and over about the role he could possibly play in his son's life. Would he be injecting himself into a situation where he wasn't wanted? Would Pearl hate him for trying to be a father? There were so many questions.

Jess, what about Jess? He's old now and can't do a lot of things with the boy. Who is going to teach my son?

What man is going to come into Pearl's life and be a part of my son's childhood?

The answer to Jay's questions was always, *me.*

Feona had never known about Frank or Pearl. Thank God, his mother had the good sense not to bring it up. Oh, how he regretted confiding in her when he returned from North Carolina in '49. She had been so judgmental, so accusatory, insisting that the bastard child could not possibly be his—that the "little whore" didn't even care enough to write back after she had sent a letter telling Pearl about his internment in a prisoner camp.

"If she cared, she would have written, Jay. Don't you see that? She didn't even respond."

How could he argue with what his mother said?

Madge was enraged the first time one of the letters arrived from Ellie. To avoid any further explosions from her, Jay changed his address to a post office box in Brownsville, Texas, nearly twenty miles away from Donna, where he lived.

At least once a year Ellie sent a manila envelope. It always included a short note asking about Jay's family and perhaps a line or two about what was happening at the beach. She kept him current with pictures of the area and the new developments taking place on and around the island.

Always a boy would be included in the photos. Once she had sent a picture of the Sea Gull Restaurant with hordes of bathing suit-clad customers crowding the patio. In the corner were Pearl, Paul, Frankie and Josie. Another picture, taken about a year later during seine fishing season, showed scores of people gathered at the beach, some pulling on the seine and others simply enjoying themselves. Paul was easy to pick out; a young growing curly-haired boy stood by his side.

Since the news of Paul's death, Jay had been ready to drive to North Carolina, but Madge would have nothing to do with it. She forbade it, threatening to tell Feona about Pearl and her bastard son.

Pictures came, and Jay studied the sullen expression of his son standing next to his sister and mother.

More pictures came of Frank sitting next to Lottie and Pearl at the damaged Sea Gull Restaurant. Pearl held the hand of her youngest daughter, Emma Jewel. She had now survived her husband's death and a devastating hurricane.

Jay wrestled with the thought of his son being fatherless, and periodically he mentioned a desire to move to Surf City, North Carolina.

"Your wife is a very shy girl, it would be hard for her to be somewhere where she doesn't know anyone," Madge chastised her son, "and you know she is a fragile thing, Jay. You can't go moving her across the country."

"What do you mean?"

"Jay, Feona is a simple—no, not simple, but a naïve girl. She doesn't know a lot about the world."

"You don't like her. You don't like anyone I fall in love with."

"That's not true. I like Feona, but you have to be gentle with her. She's been sheltered her whole life."

"She's shy," Jay retorted sharply. "And she doesn't know how to be around other people very well."

"She's not very good at socializing."

Jay rolled his eyes. His lips tightened as he clenched his fists. "You didn't even like Pearl when I told you about her before the war."

"Oh my goodness, son, that was so long ago—and I turned out to be right, didn't I?"

Shrugging, Jay knew he dare not tell his mother the whole story, and how Pearl was such a good mother, and how he knew in his heart that Frank was his. As he turned away he listened to his mother's sigh.

"Dear, I'm not against Feona. I *want* you to be happy. Truly I do. Feona may be the one for you, and you and she may have a happy life together, but I just worry. You've been through so much and she needs so much."

He wrapped his arms around his mother as she wiped a tear from her cheeks. She had never been one to cry openly or to sob. Always a strong woman, the simple tear on her face left Jay thinking that his mother did truly care. She just had a funny way of showing it.

Oh, if we had just not moved in with Mom. Jay thought often. But at the time, it seemed the most practical thing to do.

His mother had meant well, attempting to run the farm during her husband's illness and subsequent death. She relied on the advice of neighbors and other business owners in the town who had misled her. It was not long before most of what his father had worked for all his life, was gone. All that was left were the groves. They had always been small and yielded only little profit each year. It was not nearly enough to support the family.

Jay began taking on day labor jobs to help supplement the income of the family and when Madge suggested that he and Feona move in, it did just seem like the most beneficial thing for everyone.

Initially everything moved along smoothly. His mother and Feona got along well. He was happy about that, and his mother did try—she was not too intrusive, but there were times when he wished she had not included herself in their problems. He felt inadequate, unable to provide for his family and unable to live up to the type of lifestyle his mother had been used to during most of her marriage to his father.

He knew she was unhappy, so he was not surprised when one evening, after his return from working for his friend Larry Cale, Madge gathered him and Feona at the kitchen table and told them of her plans to move in with his sister, Marsha, now living in Corpus Christi.

"You can stay in the house as long as you like. I'll charge you a minimal rent and you can send it to me." She looked apologetically to her son. "I wouldn't do that son, if I didn't need the money."

Jay did not argue with his mother. He stayed in the home for the period it took her to gather her belongings and move in with Marsha. He knew his mother would be happier living with his sister and her children. Madge loved the grandchildren and was always nagging him and Feona about having children of their own.

Within a few months of his mother's departure, he sold the groves, and rented the home he had grown up in. Madge was happy to see the money and agreed to split the incoming rent. She seemed comfortable now, living with Marsha.

Now, there was nothing to stop Jay from moving. And he made preparations to move his family to North Carolina. Feona was excited. She loved the idea of living on a barrier island and listened to her husband as he described what it had looked like when he lived there more than a decade ago.

On their way out of Texas, Jay and Feona stopped in Corpus Christi to see his mother and Marsha. She apologized to him for being so hard on him about the boy. He watched as Marsha winked at him, understanding that perhaps she had had something to do with his mother's change of heart.

"Send me pictures, Jay. And visit me often," she called as he, Feona and Fate drove away.

******

Traveling down Highway 17, Jay slowed as he entered the town of Holly Ridge.

Where are all the buildings? He felt his hand go to his mouth to muffle a gasp. *The barracks, movie house, Laundromat, fire station—endless rows of buildings? It was all gone, as if it had never been. No, there were the pillars where the main gate to the camp had been. There was the old fire station, deserted.*

His eyes scanned the landscape in disbelief. Someone had wiped the past away, or had made a great effort to do so.

All the roads were still there, but the majority of the buildings were gone. A few still stood, and some looked as if they were now homes and businesses for the people of Holly Ridge.

He turned right off of 17 and drove a couple of blocks. Yes, a few of the buildings from the war were still there and yes, Boom Town was still there. A smiled beamed across his face, his cheeks hurt from it. He remembered the many times he would go there to buy steaks for a barbeque and the times he went there to buy a saw, hammer, a pair of sneakers, a scarf for Pearl; Boom Town had everything.

He made another right and drove behind the restaurant that used to be one of the lounges where celebrities performed—a café was there now. From the opened back door the smell of frying beef tickled his nostrils. He could hear loud music as it escaped into the afternoon air.

Making a right, he returned to Highway 50, the beach road.

This was the road where he had first seen Pearl so many years ago, centuries it seemed. He felt a laugh rise inside him and his chest heaved a bit as the laugh escaped his lips. He saw her again leaning into the roadside trees, her silhouette visible through her thin dress; she was barefoot.

He thought of the young couple pretending that they were not looking for one another, and the Jeep ride to the sound to go crabbing.

"What's that?"A startled Feona shifted her shoulders away from Jay and sat upright.

"Hey Sweetie, sorry to wake you. I was just driving around the old town where Camp Davis used to be."

"Oh, let me see." Pressing her lips against her husband's cheek, she squeezed his arm. "Come on honey, I want to see the place you always talk about. It must have been a really wonderful place to be."

Jay turned the car around and then stopped at the intersection of Highways 50 and 17. He turned right and pointed out again the tall brick pillars that had once led to the camp. He calmly explained that at one time there had been well over one hundred and ten thousand troops stationed there.

A perplexed look crossed Feona's face. "Where in the world did they all stay?"

"Well, you have to picture it. There were barracks all along there." He pointed to where they would have been, and then explained to her where all the buildings and facilities had once stood. He got lost in the explanations, recalling his work at the stables and how he spent hours marching, cleaning, and preparing for what would be the turning point in his life.

"But early on, I had to move the horses over to the banks." Jay turned to Feona, her face focused on a shop across the highway.

"Did you hear me?" He asked.

"What? Oh...that's strange."

"What's strange," Jay brushed his hand to ruffle his wife's short hair.

"I could have sworn that your momma was standing over by that building looking at us."

"Huh?"

"Your momma...looking at us...she didn't even wave."

"My momma is in Texas, my dear." He laughed and ruffled her hair again. "You must have been dreaming."

"Hmmm."

Quietly Jay turned the car until he was back on the road to the island.

"I'm hungry," cooed Feona.

"We'll get something in a bit," he reassured her with a kiss.

Jay drove silently while his wife seemed lost in thought. He worried that perhaps she might feel left out of his life here as she had in Texas.

Had he not spent enough time with her since the baby had been born? Had his mother been too intrusive in their lives? Feona always seemed so insecure, so doubting about herself. Why she worried that he didn't love her, didn't spend enough time with her, was beyond his understanding. He lived to please her as he strove for a perfect love, a perfect relationship.

Feona's quietness was something he always liked about her, though it was evidence that she had led a sheltered life. Yet, she seemed so eager to see and do and learn. It was one of the things that excited him, her willingness for change. And she was so in love with him. She relied on him for everything.

Jay had not realized how insecure a person Feona was when he married her. He chalked it up to the shyness—she had, after all, no siblings and had been raised solely by her grandmother. Why wouldn't she be shy? He fully believed that once they moved away from his farm and his mother that Feona would break out of her shell.

He loved her very much—her giving manner, her caring and thoughtful ways; she was the most gentle person he thought he had ever met.

Feona had worked behind the cosmetics counter at the corner drugstore in his hometown of Donna. It perplexed Jay, since Feona didn't wear a stitch of make-up, except for a light smear of lipstick. She explained later that the job was an effort on her part to meet people and learn how to socialize.

She wore her short brown hair in a pixie cut, and she always wore small hooped earrings in her pierced ears. That, he thought was a daring thing for a girl to do. His mother scoffed at it, saying that nice girls didn't pierce their ears.

"That's the Coca-Cola girl," Jay's friend Larry had commented when he'd told him about wanting to go out with the girl at the drug store.

"Yeah, she does have a great figure," Jay responded defensively. "But I can't even get her to look at me, she sure is shy."

Jay spent nearly twenty dollars at the cosmetics counter on lipsticks and polish that he eventually gave to his sister, Marsha, before Feona would consider talking to him about anything other than make-up. He liked her, especially her hazel eyes that sparkled when she smiled. She made him feel happy, and he found himself thinking less and less about what he had lost in life. Being in her company relaxed him and brought about a feeling that there could be a future for him.

After all that had happened in North Carolina and in Germany, Feona was just what he needed. She soothed away all the pain from both experiences. There weren't any questions, any feelings of inadequacy, none of guilt when he was with her. She didn't question his past but accepted him as he was. That was very welcoming to Jay who had come back from the war physically scarred. What could not be seen were the scars from the banks, the rejection, and the lost love.

He never mentioned Pearl or any of the Scaggins family to Feona. He did not want to worry her; he didn't want to lose her. She seemed such a fragile young woman. Besides, all that was in the past. Sometimes it seemed as if it had all happened to another person.

Frank was a distant reality secured by the knowledge that he was surrounded by the love of a perfect family. Jay felt that his son was safe—that he would have a good life, that is, until he heard of Paul's death.

CHAPTER SIX

"Sarah Elizabeth!" Janie Butler hollered for her daughter. "You need to come on in now; it'll be dark pretty soon."

Sarah nuzzled her face into the German Shepherd's dense coat. "Come on, Skipper, we better get home." Rising from the floor of the dune valley where she and the dog had been playing, Sarah Butler, grasping the sand with her toes, made her way up a dune and down another. She loved playing in the dune valleys, rolling down them, her dog chasing her as her body turned over and over. And she really liked making sand castles for her doll babies.

Not many children lived on the island, and so she spent much of her time with Skipper. He was not a bad playmate. Sometimes even, he let her put hats on his head.

Sarah was very glad when Miss Pearl moved to the island with her children. Josie was so much fun to play with. They played with their baby dolls and had tea parties; it was lots of fun.

Sometimes Josie's brother Frank would walk with his sister to Sarah's house, leaving her there while he ventured across the road to play basketball in the big abandoned military warehouse.

The building served as a sort of clubhouse or gathering spot for the youth of the island, though girls rarely ventured into the building. Only the bravest would venture into the cavernous building and play among the abandoned military vehicles. But since one of the Butler men had erected basketball goals at either end of the building, the boys had claimed ownership; usually during the off season they could be found there.

Sarah thought Frank was a nice enough boy, but he did tease her sometimes and so she was glad when he left to play with the other boys at the warehouse. But her cousins, who had moved to Surf City recently, teased her too. Maybe it was just something all boys did. Anyway, she was glad Josie had moved to Surf City and she hoped that as her mother called her, Josie would be visiting with her mother, Miss Pearl. Sometimes they stopped by in the afternoons.

Today, as she dusted the sand from her clothing, she wondered if anyone would find the castle she had built in the dune valley. She hoped no one would destroy it before she came back from school tomorrow.

She looked back at it as she and Skipper trudged down the dune.

Sarah held the screen door and eased it shut; her mother did not like to hear the door bang when it closed. As she entered the living room of her home, soft voices met her ears. *Is that Miss Pearl? Is Josie here?* Her face beamed a broad smile.

"Momma?" Sarah stood at the doorway.

Janie Butler smiled proudly as her daughter entered the room. "Come say hello to Miss Pearl, Sarah."

"Hello." Walking slowly toward Pearl, Sarah blushed, *I'm so sandy, I've been playing in the dunes with Skipper. Is Josie with you? Where's Josie?*"

"She didn't come with me this time, Sarah. She's helping Grandpa take care of Emma Jewel and she has a few chores to catch up on this afternoon." Pearl gently took the child's hand. "But I promise you one day this week I'll make sure she comes for a visit. Okay?"

"Yes ma'am." Sarah smiled. "I'll see her on the school bus tomorrow." Returning the knowing nod from her mother, Janie excused herself from the living room and padded down the hall to her own bedroom; Skipper was fast on her heels.

Pearl watched as the child left the room and then turned her attention back to Janie; she reached for her cup of coffee. "I think a lady's club at the church would be wonderful. It would give some of the new people a chance to get to know one another. Especially Mrs. Bishop, Feona is her name, isn't it?"

"Yes, she seems so shy, and I'd really like to make her feel more welcome." Pearl sipped from her cup. "Thank you so much Janie. You've been so helpful. I'll make sure I ask Feona if she wants to come."

"Tell her that she is more than welcome, and that we all can't wait to taste some of her Texas food."

Pearl stood and extended her hand. "I sure will, and you be sure to say hello to Mr. Ron for me. Okay?"

All her life Pearl had trudged up and down sand dunes, but today they seemed especially high. Topping one, she sunk her bare feet into the sand as she skirted the trough of the dunes to avoid the spurs and cactus there. Imprints in the sand from Sarah playing reminded her of her own childhood. She sighed as she wished to herself that she had driven to Miss Janie's house rather than having walked.

Jay's move to Topsail had not bothered her at all. In fact, it felt that it was as it should be—another person there from her youth to rely on. She saw him often as she stopped at the corner gas station for a fill up or to have her oil checked. They talked as old friends, with trust and respect.

"Feona likes it here. She really likes the ocean and going there in the summer with Fate. But she's feeling very lonely lately now that the tourist season is over. It gets real quiet around here after Labor Day." Jay grinned and settled his hands on his hips. "I guess she needs to make some friends."

Had she made a mistake when she had offered to hire Feona for a couple of days a week at the Sea Gull? She had thought that it might help her get out of her shell. Maybe she just needed to feel welcome and to make new friends.

She can bring little Fate; he and EJ are real close in age and I bet they would have a lot of fun. She remembered saying those words to him. Had it been a mistake?

"Nah," she said aloud as she walked along the shore. Her sneakers, tied around her waist bounced gently against her hips.

Smiling to herself, she felt reassured that Jay was in love with Feona. That made her happy. It made her feel good that he had what he had always wanted, a family. What in the world would she have ever done without hers?

Nearly a year ago, she had been in such turmoil. Of course, she had been in a different frame of mind at the time. But things were better now; she'd passed a milestone and felt good about it.

Turning, she skipped as she walked backwards; it was fun. The cool autumn waves licked at her bare feet. Walking on the beach was always a good time—a productive time. "Clears out the cobwebs," Pearl spun around, "and it feels so good to be freeee..." She felt wonderful as she walked along the beach.

The old officers' club was fairly close now; it had made a wonderful oyster bar and had been a little competition for the Sea Gull during oyster season. But Hurricane Hazel had taken care of that. The storm had done quite a bit of damage. Now there was talk of building a fishing pier there.

She pondered the possibility for a moment—how would it affect business at her own restaurant. She wasn't sure if she liked the idea or not.

In the distance she could see the Gull. *Was that Feona standing on the patio?* It seemed that the young girl was always wandering out to the patio to look at the ocean.

I can understand that. It is calming. She sighed and touched her tongue to her teeth; she could feel the salt on them too.

But Feona does seem forlorn quite often. What does she have to be sad about?

Toying with the idea that perhaps Feona knew of she and Jay's past, Pearl considered that to be a possible reason for the shy behavior.

"But I have no romantic feelings for Jay, not anymore." She shook her head.

"He hasn't made any attempts to intrude on Frankie's life." Again she shook her head.

"As long as it stays like that, things will be okay." Pearl stopped, turned her body toward the ocean, "Don't you think?"

Frothing water tickled her toes and Pearl continued walking toward the officers' club. Kicking gently, she splashed water about. She had seen Feona, Jay and Fate together as a family. There was no doubt that Jay was captivated by his son and wife.

Frankie, who was always walking to the store or to the warehouse to play basketball with the other boys on the beach, did eventually make his way to the gas station. His curiosity about cars and what makes them go made him a regular fixture there. Eventually, Pearl gave him permission to work a few hours for Jay on the weekends. It seemed enough, or at least enough for Jay, who beamed with pride whenever Pearl drove up for gas.

All that was ever exchanged between Pearl and Jay was a nod and a held gaze of gratitude. It was funny how everything had fallen into place. Everything seemed right and as it should be.

Once again Pearl turned to face the ocean as she thought of the relationship between Frank and Jay. "Thank you," she whispered.

For a Sunday evening in late September it felt quite warm. The sand against her feet as she trudged up the dunes was warm also. As she topped them she found the long brown barracks she called home. Perhaps she would paint the place a brighter color.

CHAPTER SEVEN

"I don't know if she's not being friendly..."

"I know what you mean. She seems like such a pleasant person, I just don't understand why she is so standoffish." Ellie reached for another knife, fork and spoon to wrap in the napkin she held. It was between lunch and dinner time; business was slow.

"You know, she is in a brand new place and perhaps she doesn't feel comfortable. And there really isn't a whole lot for her to do." Pearl rolled the silverware tightly in her napkin, then took another sip of her coffee. "She comes every once in a while to the church meetings, but she's still so quiet."

"Maybe she's just that way. I thought that once she started working here, she would open up and laugh a little—you know, act normal."

"Well, I'm not giving up. But I am going to have to let her go for the off season, it's just too slow and I can't afford to pay her. That is unless you want to give up a couple days a week and let her have them."

"What? I have a kid to raise and old money bags down in Florida hasn't been sending any money to help raise his daughter. I *need* this job."

Pearl nodded. "Okay—just asking. I'll have a talk with her when she comes in Friday morning."

Pearl pondered her decision. She knew Feona would not be happy about it, even though she had never really become part of the group—never sat and relaxed after her shift with them or shared gossip. She simply waited on customers and left when her shift was over, barely speaking to any of the staff.

"I don't know what else I can do to bring that girl out of her shell but I was thinking we could invite her to join us at the seine pull. There'll be lots of people there. And you know Jay, more than likely, will not come. He's always working at the gas station."

"Good idea, Two Shoes, she can bring a covered dish. Who knows, maybe she'll even join in the pulling."

"Now, isn't that something. When I was a young girl, hardly any of us were allowed to pull the seine." Pearl added sarcastically, "I know you sure didn't."

"Pfft." Ellie flipped her hand into the air. "La tee dah, I still am not really fond of roughing up my hands, but I will help hold up the seine."

"My momma gave daddy fits when I did it, and now, all the young girls are getting right in there and pulling."

Ellie twisted her long hair into braids. "And none of this bothers you?"

96

"What?" Pearl quizzically looked at her friend. "What is supposed to bother me—pulling on the seine? Why should that...?" She rubbed her temple. "Now I know what you mean. By *that* you mean Jay, Feona and Frankie. Right?" Pearl grabbed another set of silverware and placed them in the corner of a napkin. As she rolled them up, her eyes looked deeply into her friend's.

"Uh huh, that's what I mean." Ellie raised an eyebrow and sucked her teeth loudly. "I don't get you. No sirree, I don't get you at all, Pearly White. But you aren't me and I am surely not you. So..."

"That was so long ago, Ellie." A glow crossed Pearl's face as she smiled. "I'm over it."

"Well, you might be over it, but for him to come back here just tells me that he's not."

"You don't understand."

"And Frank? This all seems too odd. Frank is yours and Jay's kid."

"I know, he knows and *we* talked— "

"You talked, ha ha. What about the way Feona acts?" It just all doesn't seem right."

"I said we talked, and—"

"And you—"

"Quit interrupting me!" Pearl raised her hand, "Stop!"

"Okay, okay. But it still seems odd."

"We talked not long after they moved here and he started running the gas station. I asked him about Feona and if he had ever told her. I too was worried about her behavior, always so shy and standoffish."

"And?" Ellie pulled a cigarette from her pack and placed it between her lips.

"Jeez, I hate that stink. I wish you'd stop."

Ellie shrugged her shoulders and pulled on the filter tip. "Go on," she beckoned with her fingertips.

"Well, Jay says she's always been that way. That it took him forever to get her to even talk to him, and even longer to get her to go out on a date. She's always been shy." Pearl's lips drew tightly together as she squinted her eyes. "I tell you, Ellie, Jay loves Feona."

"You sure don't see them out much together."

"What are you talking about? Nobody's seen anybody out much together. We just got through one of the busiest tourist seasons I can remember. This whole beach has been busy as heck. Everybody's working. I think that Jay has been so busy trying to make that business of his become successful, that he hasn't had time to get out in the community and introduce his wife. Everybody has been too busy, but now that summer is over, it has slowed a bit—you know, just fisherman—so maybe they'll get out a little more, like the *rest* of us do."

"Alright, alright—you made your point. Maybe she is just shy. Maybe Jay has been very busy. That part is true." Ellie stood and brandished a fork in her hand. "I'll take a stab at all this trust and sunny outlook crap you keep talking about. Maybe I am wrong."

"Won't be the first time." Pearl clucked her tongue, "Tsk, Smelly."

"I know one thing I'm not wrong about."

"Yeah?"

"You're a woman, and sooner or later you're going to need..."

"Need?"

"Want—sooner or later you are going to want a man."

Pearl shrugged. "Maybe."

"Maybe, my butt. You go right ahead and do what it is you think you have to do. As for me, right after fishing season, I'm going hunting—see if I can't catch me a doctor or lawyer in Wilmington."

CHAPTER EIGHT

"What in the hell is the matter with you?" Phil's condescending voice echoed in the front room of his father's house. "This is a fork! Don't you know how to use it?"

Clarence raised his head, his lower lip bobbled and half words left his lips in spurts. His fingers made motions in the air as if he were trying to turn the knob on something.

"You disgust me, you bastard. I ought to..." Phil grabbed the knife next to the plate. His body shook. "Damn, how I hate you, you bastard. Look at you. You can't even feed yourself. You stink; you piss your pants half the time. You ain't no good—you killed my mother, you...you..."

Dropping the knife on the floor, Phil ran from the house, pulled open the door to his truck and sped away. His face red with anger, he spat curse words loudly as his truck bumped onto the hard paved road. After a short distance he turned down a cart path.

From the screened front porch of his home, Jess watched as Phil's truck bounced, kicking up dust before jerking to a stop. Rising from his rocking chair Jess opened the screen door. He didn't speak, but just watched as the young man's chest heaved deep breaths.

Finally, Phil walked over to Jess.

"What you all huffy about?"

Phil shook his head. "Nothing."

"Then why are you coming over here driving like you just learned how and looking like you could spit nails?

Another long heavy sigh escaped Phil's lips. "That bastard..."

"Hey, watch your mouth!"

Pacing the length of the truck, Phil ran his fingers through his hair. "Hey, old man, I came over here 'cause I can't...I can't..."

"Calm down. Just ease off the pedal, Phil. Take a deep breath." Jess stepped from the door and down the few stairs. "I never had a son, but I remember being one. I know I used to get so mad at my Paw that I thought of knocking the living daylights out of him. Never made no sense to me why he used to have me do things. Now I know better."

"I know damn well your paw never beat the hell out of you or your mother. Did he?" Standing next to his truck, Phil leaned and settled his palms against his knees.

101

"Can't say that he did. My daddy was a good man. Had his own ways though—some my maw or I didn't understand. But, nonetheless, Paw never raised a hand to me or her.

"I didn't like it when he made me quit school in the fourth grade...always regretted never being able to finish school or at least getting a few more years of it." Jess stooped to sit on the top step. "And, well, he never would let my maw ride in the front of the buggy with him; that never made any sense to me." He shook his head and grinned. "But there wasn't too much else he could make her do or not do. Strong willed woman—just like my Lottie. He grinned, pulled a small knife from his trouser pocket and began paring his fingernails.

Phil stooped to sit next to Jess, he blushed and lowered his head. "Yeah, you got a firecracker, there. That's for sure."

"You feel like a cup of coffee?"

Nodding, Phil rose and stepped into the screened in porch. "Mind if I sit here?" He gestured toward a chair.

"Suit yourself."

As Phil gazed about the well-kept and manicured yard of the Scaggins home, he relaxed; it was so pretty, peaceful even.

He'd tried cleaning up the yard at his father's house, and it did look better than he could ever remember, but it did not have the welcoming look to it that Jess and Lottie had accomplished through love and labor. Phil figured that too much hate had been spewed at his own home for anything from love to grow.

102

"Here," Jess pushed a steaming cup of coffee toward Phil. "Now, what's the problem?"

Phil's eyes slid upward toward Jess. "Sorry about saying old man and..."

Jess shook his head. "No need, I *am* an old man." He laughed and slowly squatted into his rocking chair. "Son, I know what's ailing you. It's your paw. You got to get away from him or you think you might kill him. And if you ask me, if anybody would have the right, it might be you."

"I don't want to kill nobody." Phil's chest hollowed as slumped forward. "I feel like I got steel grates in my head, grinding and grinding so hard that they won't let me sleep." Slapping the palm of his hand against his head, he repeated louder. "I can't sleep! All kinds of things go whirling in my head. And I feel like I want to hit something all the time."

Phil placed the hot cup on the sill of the screened porch. "It just won't stop and then he—he just sits there staring off into space, smiling at me, even when I kick his chair or yell at him. I don't understand it. Doesn't he remember all the things he did to me, Paul and Maw?"

"Your father is senile, Phil. He doesn't remember a thing."

"It ain't fair! He ought to remember. And he ought to feel guilty for it too."

"So you want retribution? Is that it?"

"I want him to hurt." Phil's eyes shown steely and bright, his mouth was a tense line, pulled down at the

103

corners. "You don't get away with stuff, not stuff like what he did."

"And you want to be the one to dole out the punishment."

"Huh?"

"Do you want to punish your daddy for what he did to you and your family?"

"Beat the hell out of him?" Phil's furrowed brow belied the confusion he was feeling. His eyes questioned Jess as he paused to consider what Jess may be suggesting.

"You think I ought to beat the hell out of him?"

The two men looked at one another for several seconds; Jess leaned back in the rocking chair. "Well?"

"I pushed him one time...just to get a rise out of him. I was thinking that if he raised one hand to me I'd have the right to knock him down. I could do that, you know, he's feeble. He's not strong and quick like he used to be." Pausing, Phil closed his eyes and gritted his teeth. "When I pushed him, he didn't even push back. He just looked at me like he had run into a pole—like it was nothing at all. Now, what in the hell is that? He ain't there no more. He's like twins. He looks like my paw, sounds like him, but he sure doesn't act like him. Hitting him would be like hitting the wrong twin." Again Phil closed his eyes tightly and gritted his teeth. "And I asked him, lots of times, why he hit Maw. You know what he said?"

Jess shook his head no.

"He said his pop would have kicked him from here to Wilmington and back if he ever would have hit a woman." As he shook his head in disgust, Phil kicked at the floor. "Funny, ain't it."

"Umph," Jess nodded.

"I can't tell you how many times he's asked me who I am; most of the time he calls me Paul. I'm telling you, Mr. Jess, beating the hell outta him would be like beating a poor old dog just 'cause he's got fleas and can't stop scratching."

"Part of you feels sorry for him and the other part wants to see him suffer."

"You never said truer words, Mr. Jess. Now tell me what I have to do, 'cause I can't stand being around him anymore. I left him there at the supper table and I don't know what I'll do if I have to go back. The devil is gonna win if I have to."

Rising from his chair, Jess patted Phil on the back. "Phil, I don't know what to tell you to do with your life. That's your business, but you have to make a decision. Since your brother passed I've watched you struggling with your father. I worried about you, believed that you *would* kill him or watch while he killed himself. We all," Jess swept his arms wide, "everybody I know and who knows your family, has been wondering when it's gonna happen.

"Anybody wagering any money on it?" Phil raised his furrowed brow; half grinned, then lowered his head again.

"Yep. Everybody thinks the both of you are nutty as pecan pie. The only reason I ain't bet is because you're kinfolk now."

A puzzled look swept across Phil's face and he watched as the serious expression on Jess's lightened.

"Phil, everyone goes crazy now and then. You think you're the only one?"

"Feels like it."

"Yeah, that's the bad thing about going nuts, you feel like no one else knows how you feel. And so you get more and more into yourself. Well, the whole trick is to *Go*. Go to church, go to a friend, go to one of those head doctors...just go. Whatever helps you, just go to it. You came to me, didn't you?"

CHAPTER NINE

"We just stuck him in the car and drove him on up to Dix Hill. They got trained people there to take care of Clarence."

"He didn't try to stop you?" Pearl asked her father.

"Nope, Clarence is in no condition to stop anybody from doing anything. And he just about can't do anything for himself. Yep, he's better off where he's at now."

"What a shame." Reaching for Emma Jewel, Pearl shook her head. Patting the child's back slowly she sat down with the others seated at the counter of the Sea Gull Restaurant.

"I sure don't feel sorry for that old bag of worms. He hurt so many people." Ellie slid her eyes toward Lottie. "Don't you think so?"

"I don't like kicking a dog when he's down, but that old dog was wormy and stank to high heaven. And he sure wasn't any good for Phil to be around. Now maybe he can get on with his own life."

Carefully applying a coat of polish to her nails, Ellie added, "Well, he's getting out more now. I saw him at Pop's last Saturday night. He was dancing with some little gal from around Snead's Ferry."

"All I can tell you is that I wish him well," Pearl nodded. "I know he's had a hard life."

"Heck! We've all had a hard life. Now, you think about it while I sit over here and feel sorry for myself." Slowly Lottie picked up a large bag of sugar and walked to a corner booth in the restaurant, she feigned sniffles and sang lowly, "I'm so ugly, nobody loves me, think I'll eat some worms." Unscrewing the lids from the accumulated sugar containers she wiped her sleeve across her eyes and sniffled again.

The back door to the Sea Gull flew open as if a gust of wind had all of a sudden burst upon it. A loud clamor introduced children as they entered from the beach.

"Why's Grandma crying?" Frank questioned as he set a bucket full of sand fiddlers down on the restaurant floor.

Billy Burns shook his head, sending sand flying about the room. "Golly, Miss Ellie, Miss Lottie, I sure am sorry, didn't know I had that much sand in my hair."

"There is nothing to worry about, Billy," Lottie grinned. "I don't think there is any way of avoiding the sand around here. And I'm not crying, just pretending."

Shrugging his shoulders, the puzzled look immediately left his face.

Josie and Sarah Butler stumbled through the door next, bumping into the boys. They pressed their hands to their mouths to quiet their laughter.

"Get off my feet!" Frank pushed his younger sister gently.

"Momma, he pushed me!"

"She just about knocked me down...Momma?"

"Get those daggone sand fleas outta here right now! You hear me? They don't belong inside. And y'all, everyone of y'all march yourselves right back out that door and hose yourselves off on the patio."

The children all turned, all muttering "yes ma'am," and exited the restaurant.

"I just got through sweeping this floor." Frustrated, Pearl shook her head and hollered out to the children. "And don't forget to turn the spigot off! You hear me?"

"Yes ma'am," floated in from the outside.

"Gee whiz." Plopping herself back down on the stool she turned to Lottie. "Were we that bad, Momma?"

Before Lottie could answer, Gloria Abbott walked in through the front door with Monroe. A sardonic grin lay across their young lips as the two teenage girls sauntered to the farthest corner booth and sat down.

Pearl watched as they set two bottles of fingernail polish on the table and began filing their nails.

"Mother, may Gloria and I have a Tru-Ade?"

Languidly Ellie pushed herself up from the counter, "This coming summer, young lady, you're going to go to work and you can get things yourself."

"Umph." Monroe whispered an inaudible something to Gloria.

"I'd give anything to be working here next summer. My mom and dad are sticking me back out in the watermelon fields and it's so hot. Then I'll be picking beans and squash—gee whiz, I don't even get to see

109

anybody out there. At least you'll be able to see people." Gloria's eyes grew wide, "Miss Pearl, do you think I could come and work for you next summer? I promise you I am a good worker. You just ask my momma and daddy."

"Oh Lord, now wouldn't that be a sight, those two working here together," Lottie muttered.

Jess laughed. "We got our own Lana Turner and Ava Gardner."

"I'm Ava, I have the dark hair," Monroe pouted.

Gloria'a upper lip curled, "You can have her. Lana's prettier anyway."

"Isn't."

"Is."

"Isn't."

"Is."

"Stop that arguing!" Ellie stomped her foot and turned to Jess, "Now just look what you've started. Those girls are going to be arguing from now until kingdom come."

Sarcastically, Jess asked his daughter, "Are you really considering letting them both work here next year."

"What? I haven't even talked to Gloria's parents. And as for Monroe, I think she'll make a fine waitress, might even learn a thing or too. And if not, there are always plenty of potatoes that need peeling in the kitchen." Pearl turned to Ellie, "Right?"

"Right."

"Mom?" Frank held the screen door ajar. "I guess me and Billy are gonna take these sand fiddlers up to Mr. Jay's gas station. He told me that he was planning on going fishing this afternoon and well, that's what I got them for anyway."

"Go right ahead, Sweetie."

"Hey Mom?"

"Yes son?"

"You seen that big rock Mr. Jay's got on one of the gas pumps?"

"Um hmm."

"You wanna know what he got it on there for?"

"I know you're going to tell me."

"Well, he's got it on there to hold the prices down."

Pearl rolled her eyes. "Hardy, har, har. Very funny. Now you boys be sure to come back here before you get ready for tonight. Okay?"

"Yes ma'am," rang out in unison as the boys' guffawing laughter followed them down to the shore where they made their way to Jay's Gulf station.

"Boys will always be boys." Pearl shook her head.

Ellie's and Lottie's raised eyebrows shot questioning looks to Pearl.

"What? What did I do? He's spending the night—they're going fishing with Jay this evening and then the two boys are going to camp out on the beach."

"Sounds like fun to me," Jess interjected. "I remember doing that as a boy. Me, Earl and Rawl used to do that all the time, sometimes Leon would tag along."

"You boys were always doing something like that. My momma and daddy never would allow me to do it," scowled Lottie.

"Nice girls don't camp out alone," Jess retorted.

"Hey Pearl. Why don't me, you and the girls go camping tonight?" Leaning forward, her chin held in the palm of her hand, Ellie swiveled her shoulders from side to side.

"Yeah, that sounds like a good idea. Momma will you watch EJ for me tonight?"

"If I was younger, my dear, I would say no and beg to go with you. But since I'm an old biddy now, I'd be glad to watch my beautiful Emma Jewel."

The giggling from the corner booth grew louder and louder and finally Monroe tittered, "We want to go, we want to go."

"Of course you can go, girls," Pearl answered.

Leaning into the group sitting along the counter, Pearl whispered, "Gloria is sweet on Frankie and Monroe thinks Billy is the living end—or at least that is how your daughter explained to me."

Ellie nodded her head. "Yep, my daughter has carved Billy's name into every window sill in her bedroom.

****

"I'm not peeing out here now, Gloria, somebody might see."

"There's not anybody around, Monroe! Just go behind a sand dune. You act like a crab is gonna come up and bite you on the hinny."

"I bet those boys walked on down here and are watching."

Gloria rolled her eyes, "You are such a chicken. Come on, wussy girl, I'll go with you."

"Mother, I want to walk back to the Gull so I can pee," Monroe called loudly.

"Go behind a sand dune!" Ellie called back, "there's nobody around." Leaning back on her elbows she stretched her neck and felt her hair touch the blanket.

"But what if the boys have walked down here and..."

"Then when I get hold of them I'll put another crack in their rear end. That's what. Now go!"

Ellie and Pearl watched as the two girls trudged up the dunes and disappeared into a valley.

112

"Oh, how I love this time of year." Ellie bit her bottom lip and turned her head slightly. Josie and Sarah, still in her peripheral vision, sat building sand castles by the shore line. "It's just warm enough and the breeze makes it feel like there's a fan going in front of the refrigerator," she stretched out her legs and turned her ankles until they popped.

"You've always done that."

"What?"

"Popped your ankles. Why?"

Ellie shrugged. "I think my aunt or my grandma in Raleigh told me one time that it would keep my ankles slim."

"Um." Slowly Pearl closed her eyes, stretched her legs out and swiveled her ankles. "Won't do it. Mine won't do it."

"Your ankles always were a little thick." Ellie's lips parted as a 'hiss' escaped them.

"Alright, Smelly." As she shook her head slightly, Pearl reached to throw another piece of driftwood on the crackling fire. "I love this time of year too. And I'm so glad you came up with the idea of camping out."

"The kids enjoy it, and you know, I remember when your parents used to bring you over with Paul and Phil and the Butlers or Wests. Y'all stayed all night."

"We didn't do it very often, usually only the men did it. But Momma pitched such a fit on a couple of occasions that Daddy eventually gave in. But you know just we girls would have never been allowed to do what we're doing now."

"Jo, Sarah—I think the tide is coming in a little, so you better start either building a moat for that sand castle or start building another one farther up toward the dunes," called Ellie.

113

"And I really don't want you getting wet. You hear?" added Pearl.

Faint murmurs could be heard as the two young girls gathered pails and shovels and scurried farther from the incoming tide.

Turning to Ellie, Pearl asked, "You put the hotdogs in the cooler?"

"Yep."

"And I brought some cole slaw and potato salad." Peering into the metal cooler, Pearl pulled out a Pepsi-Cola."

"I put a couple of Seven-Ups in there. Could you hand me one, Pearly>"

Pearl fished around and finally brought out a Seven-Up. "Those girls are taking a long time in the sand dunes. It doesn't take that long to pee."

"What did you and I do when we were that age?"

"Well, I know *you* were always talking about boys...and it's still all you talk about."

Ellie's shoulders shook as she stifled a laugh. "Yeah. My guess is that they are trying to figure a way out to walk down to where the boys are. You know, they're really not that far away."

Looking southward, toward Surf City Fishing Pier, Pearl nodded. "Looks like their fire is getting a little low."

I'll bet you that they're either up on that pier fishing, or those boys walked down here to see the girls."

Pearl pursed her lips. "Maybe."

"Maybe, my butt. Your son is a boy, and he may be a good kid, but he's not the goody two shoes you were. Haven't you seen the way he looks at Gloria?"

Immediately Pearl pushed herself up from the blanket. "I'm going to put a stop to this right now."

"Sit your hinny back down on this blanket." Ellie grabbed her friend's hand and pulled her. "You go hunting after those kids and you're going to make things worse."

Pearl plopped heavily on the blanket covered sand, "Ow! That hurt." She shot Ellie an angry look. "I'm not having deceit going on..."

Ellie's finger nearly grazed Pearl's nose. "Shame on you, shame on you, Pearly White. You're just scared that *something's* going to happen. Stop it now. That was then."

"But..."

"I'll tell you—the more my mother got on me about seeing all the soldiers and trying to keep me from seeing them, the more I snuck out of the house and did it. You were the lucky one, my dear friend. You could talk to your parents when you got knocked up. I couldn't." Her bottom lip quivering, Ellie continued, "I had to marry that jerk and pretend, even to myself, that I liked it."

Pearl watched as Ellie dabbed at her eyes. A new wave of understanding swept over her and she touched her friend on the shoulder.

"So don't you dare make a big deal out of this." She pushed Pearl's hand away. "You've talked to Frankie and Josie about the birds and bees, I hope."

"Yes, with Josie. Tried to with Frank, but he stopped me and said he already knew about all that stuff."

"You're just darn lucky that Monroe and Frankie think they're cousins."

"I had never thought any different." A puzzled look crossed Pearl's face."

"What's the word? Naïve? Yes, Pearly, you are simply naïve."

"I forget."

"You forget? How in the heck do you forget? His daddy, his real daddy, is not even a mile away from where you live—they see each other regularly. How in the world do you forget?"

"I don't know, Ellie. It's like there are two different worlds."

"The truth and lies."

"If that's the way you want to put it, yes."

Ellie smoothed the hair away from her face, snapped the rubber band on her wrist and pulled her hair into a ponytail. "I guess nobody should be pointing fingers at anyone, huh?"

"Nah, not us, anyway." Pearl laughed. "We gotta be thankful for what we got."

Looking toward the boy's flickering campfire, Ellie tittered, "Well, well, well. Look who's walking this way."

Pearl stood as she turned. "All four of them, huh." She looked down at her friend, "You were right."

"Of course, and I bet they're walking this way for one thing."

"Food."

"Yep."

CHAPTER TEN

Feona pulled the white gloves onto her hands. Sighing, she gently placed a lace edged handkerchief in her purse, then snapped it shut.

"Come on Fate." She held out her hand to clasp her young son's. "We're going to be late for church."

One last look in the mirror and Feona smoothed the front of her orange print dress. She touched her left hand softly to her newly permed hair and smiled. *I look okay today,* she thought to herself. *I hope the other ladies like my dress.*

She winked and smiled down to her son. "My, what a fine boy you are, Lafayette Bishop. You're gonna be some kind of ladies' man when you grow up."

The boy's lips parted into a broad grin. "Let's walk today, Mommy."

"Did you pick up all your toys on the floor?"

"Yes ma'am," the boy nodded. "I put them all in my toy box."

Gently laughing, Feona, hand in hand with her son, stepped out the door of she and Jay's oceanfront home to begin the walk to the small Baptist church only five blocks away.

During nice weather it was always a pleasant walk, but lately there had been lots of rain and Feona had chosen to drive. A few times she had chosen not to walk because of wearing high heels. It was so uncomfortable trying to maneuver in the sand next to the paved road. But today she wore her matching orange T-strap shoes with only a one-inch heel. Walking would not be difficult.

Preacher Chambers stood at the double doors of the church greeting his members with an enthusiastic handshake. Still in his twenties, he earnestly welcomed each and every person who approached the doors to his first church.

The long narrow building had been a barracks during World War II, and like many of the barracks on Topsail Island it had been renovated for practical use. He himself had helped with painting and building classrooms. There were still renovations going on, evidenced by the piles of plywood and the sawhorses standing in the lean-to shed next to the church.

Chambers was a tall man with soft brown eyes that often teared during his passionate services. It was not uncommon for him, as he stood before a congregation, to pull out his handkerchief and wipe the tears from his cheeks as they flowed freely.

"My dear Mrs. Bishop, don't you look lovely today. I'm so glad you and your son are joining us this morning." Preacher Chambers beamed a welcome to

Feona and bent in to whisper, "I stopped by the gas station this morning and spoke a few words to Jay. He's a good man, a good man."

"Yes he is, Preacher Chambers. I wish he didn't have to work on Sundays. But there just isn't enough money right now to hire someone, and Sundays can be a busy day. You know we've only been here a couple of years and..."

Nodding, the minister gently encouraged Feona to move along as the line behind her grew. "I'll come by one day this week and talk with you and Jay."

Feona nodded; a faint grin crossed her lips as she moved forward to a pew close to the back of the church.

The service always opened up with a short story of Jesus and his disciples, and then the whole congregation would sing *Jesus Loves Me*. Afterwards they were led through a side door to various classrooms.

Feona watched Fate join the other children and walk out of sight, the door to the classrooms shutting behind them.

Immediately Preacher Chambers asked the congregation to bow their heads in prayer. Feona bowed hers, and then looked up slightly to scan the room. She knew nearly everyone there. However, close to the front sat a young couple she had never seen before. She wondered if perhaps she had simply never paid attention.

Barely hearing the words of Preacher Chambers, her mind raced back and forth. *Why had Miss Janie turned and looked at her? It seemed all the ladies on the island looked at her strangely. Was it because Jay never went to church? Maybe Jay didn't love her anymore. Why didn't anybody like her?*

Still scanning the room she recognized Bella and Francis West. Pearl Rosell was there with her mother, Lottie. Her children would be in the back rooms with Fate, as would be Bella's and Francis's. *Fate is going to have lots of friends,* she thought, *then he won't want to be with me as much. He'll grow up and go away.* She felt nervous as the thought lingered; she took a deep breath to calm herself.

As the prayer ended, Janie Butler moved from her own pew, two ahead of Feona's, to sit next to Feona.

"Are you doing okay today, dear?"

"Yes, thank you Miss Janie." Questioning eyes searched the older woman's. "Do I look like something's wrong?"

"No, no, my dear. I'm just asking. You look so pretty today. You know, orange is one of my favorite colors." Janie patted Feona's hand. "You should come and have a cup of coffee with me sometime."

"Thank you," beamed Feona. "That's nice of you."

Janie moved back to her seat just as the preacher reached for his hymnal.

Lifting her head to listen to Chambers, Feona reassured herself that at least one person liked her.

"I would like everyone to pick up their hymnals and turn to page two hundred and twelve, "*What a Friend We Have in Jesus.*" The preacher sing-songed the title confidently.

Softly singing the words, Feona's eyes fell on Miss Janie who was leaning forward, whispering to Francis West. *Is she talking about me?*

Again the nervousness returned and she frantically looked toward the side door where Fate and the other children had entered. He was the only one she trusted.

120

Even Jay she did not trust. *Jay does not love me anymore.*

The song seemed like a faraway echo, and she felt her breathing become short and quick. Her head felt hot and her mind raced back and forth, wondering why Miss Janie had asked if something was wrong. What was Janie going to do if she had coffee with her? Would Miss Francis be there? Who all was going to turn against her?

She looked once again toward the side door and wished her son would hurry and come so they could walk home.

She felt her breath coming in gasps and felt heat rise inside her head. Where was he?

Placing her hands on her lap, she tried to calm herself as she smoothed the skirt of her dress. *Nobody likes me.* The thought would not leave her mind as she looked about the congregation and noticed how others were smiling and listening to Preacher Chambers. Someone looked her way, nodded their head and smiled. *They're talking about me.* Feona could feel her pulse racing.

"Momma?" Tugging on her dress, Fate looked up. "Are you okay, Momma? You look scared."

Gathering Fate in her arms, Feona kissed his cheek. She could feel calmness returning to her, and all of a sudden felt silly for feeling so frightened. She looked about the room, hoping no one else had noticed that she had not realized that the service was over.

"Sugar," June Finley squeezed Feona's arm gently, "I am so jealous of that dress you're wearing. I simply love it. Wish I was young enough to wear clothes like this."

Tousling Fate's thick locks, June continued. "This boy of yours is smart as a whip. I've been teaching Sunday

121

school a long time, and this young man can rattle off *The Lord's Prayer* like nobody's business.

"Well Miss June, that's the prayer we say every night at bedtime."

"Well, you've done a good job, Honey. He is such a well-mannered little boy." June tousled Fate's hair once again. "Y'all did walk to church today, didn't you?"

"Oh yes, it's such a lovely day, and Fate really wanted to walk this time."

"Do you mind if I walk with you?"

"Oh no, Miss June. That would be just lovely. I don't mind at all." Eagerly Feona stepped away from the pew, excited that someone wanted to spend time with her.

Oh how silly, I've been thinking that no one likes me, she thought as June walked next to her. *June is such a nice lady. They're all nice ladies. And June is the one they all look up too.*

Looking back as they crossed the road, she noticed again the women chatting and laughing. *Maybe I can be like that someday.*

She looked gaily into June's face and listened to the older woman explain how her husband did not go to church often—that he too ran a business that kept him busy on the weekends.

"He's been working at the barber shop since after the war. He gets there every morning around nine and keeps busy right on through the day. Even Sunday, that's when most of those military boys want to get their hair cut..."

Feona listened intently; she noticed how June Finley styled her hair—swept away from her face into a soft bun at the nape of her neck. Her dress was a floral print that fell against her calves' mid-way. *Maybe I should wear my dresses a little longer,* thought Feona.

Feona noticed how June held her handbag in the crook of her arm. It was a nice bag, with brocade along the edges. She thought she would like to have one like that.

"Miss June?"

"Please just call me June. You've been here long enough to just call me by my first name, honey."

Her cheeks reddened and Feona suddenly realized that she had left her handbag in the church pew.

Quickly she passed Fate's hand into June's. "Hold him for me. I'll be right back."

She turned her body, still smiling at June, and without looking stepped into the path of an oncoming car. Feona's body was thrown several feet before it landed on the pavement.

"Oh my God," June called out. Gathering Fate in her arms she tried to shield the boy from the sight of his mother. She called out again as others who had seen the tragedy ran toward Feona who lay sprawled in the middle of the road.

The young couple whom Feona had noticed in church early came quickly to her side.

"Step back," the young man spoke authoritatively. "I'm a Navy Corpsman."

He checked immediately for Feona's pulse. "She's alive." He felt along the limbs of her body and then her torso. "She needs to go to the hospital now. She has broken bones and may have internal bleeding."

Don Roberts lightly brushed the hair from Feona's face. "Is there an ambulance on the island?"

"No." Preacher Chambers stooped beside Feona and held her hand. Bowing his head, he whispered words as tears streamed down his cheeks.

"The hospital in Wilmington is the closest. We have to wait for an ambulance from there." Bart Ralston's wife, Lily, spoke calmly.

"That will take forever. This woman does not have that much time," the Corpsman muttered.

"My station wagon. I've got a station wagon." Lily spoke quickly. "To hell with an ambulance."

"Move her onto a piece of that plywood," ordered Corpsman Roberts.

Several men rushed to the shed and returned with a piece of plywood. Gently the Corpsman and his wife, Bonnie, moved Feona from the pavement to the wood.

Calling his wife's name, Jay came running from a distance. He had heard of the incident and left the gas station open with Frank at the helm.

Running toward the scene, Jay hollered for his wife again and again. "Fe, Feona!" Glimpsing his young son in June Finley's arms, he nodded his head toward her before kneeling down to caress his wife's bloodied face.

"We're going to take her to the hospital in Wilmington, Jay. It would take too long to wait for an ambulance. Don't you agree?" The Corpsman's steady eyes gazed into Jay's.

"Fe, my lovely Fe." Jay pressed his lips against his wife's forehead."

"Sir, I'm going to need for you to step away so we can put her in the station wagon."

Jay stood and watched as the rear door of the station wagon was opened and his wife was slid into the back. He crawled in and lay beside her, stroking her hair and listening to the soft breaths that fell from her lips.

"I am such a fool," he whispered as the car sped toward the hospital in Wilmington.

124

CHAPTER ELEVEN

"We're stringing lights on the outside this year." Pearl looked up at her father as she wiped down a table at the Gull.

"Here or your house or at the Sea Gull?"

"Both." Leaning backwards, Pearl stretched her back and rubbed the small of it.

"That's a lot of work and you know I'm no young buck anymore..."

"Oh Daddy, I don't expect you to climb on top of the house."

Jess nodded and snickered. "Your mom and me are just gonna put up a little tree in the living room. And maybe stockings. Your mother has had the same Christmas stocking for you since you were born. When you and the kids come over on Christmas it will be full..."

"Of oranges and nuts and maybe a pair of warm socks."

Jess laughed. "The usual." He cocked his head slightly, "You planning to string lights the whole length of that barracks building?"

"Yes. The couple renting the end apartment is going to do their part. They're even going to put reindeer on the roof. Isn't that neat?"

"Neat," Jess pondered the word. "I guess it depends on how coordinated the man is, if it's going to be *neat.*"

"Ha ha, Daddy. You know what I mean."

Jess laughed again. "Yeah, I know what you mean. But the *whole* place? That's a lot of work."

Pearl nodded. "And since the middle apartment is empty, we're stringing it too. We're even putting a nativity scene out in the yard. Phil made one out of wood and his girlfriend Sassy painted all the pieces. You should see how good she does, Daddy. She sure is talented."

"That's a lot of work, Sweetie. Who are you getting to help?"

"That Corpsman, Don Roberts, and his wife Bonnie. They're the couple in the end apartment. Frankie is helping...and then Jay said he'd like to help too."

Jess looked about the restaurant; it was nearly closing time and the place was deserted. Of course, this was to be expected this time of year.

"I know it's your business, gal. But I'm still your father and I need to know just what is going on with you, Jay and Frankie. It seems like the boy spends a lot of time at Jay's station, which I guess is alright, but you. What's going on with *you* and Jay?"

126

Slowly straightening her body, Pearl stared at her father; a puzzled expression crossed her face and she slumped down into the booth.

"Daddy, you should see the way he frets and fawns over poor Feona. And it's hard on him trying to raise that little boy, Fate. He's got no time at all to make a go of his business."

"I'm sure it is difficult for him. He has had a whole truck load of woe in his life." Jess lowered his head, shaking it slowly from side to side.

"Yes, he has, Daddy, and I'm not about to take my friendship away when he needs friends the most." Pearl's mouth pursed into a determined line. "I think if it wasn't for Frankie and me, I think he'd be lost, completely lost."

"Maybe he should have stayed in Texas."

"Gee whiz, Daddy. I know he had to tell you what all was going on down there with his mother."

"Yep, but who's to say..."

"Baloney, he was going nowhere. Thank God, his mother decided to move in with Marsha."

Jess chuckled to himself. Just when he thought that he had become comfortable with his grown daughter talking to him as an adult, with her own ideas and feelings, he found himself amazed. She was still his little girl.

"What are laughing about? This is serious. Jay and his family are between a rock and a hard place." Her brow furrowed and eyes sparkled a steely green. Pearl drew her shoulders downward and thrust her chest forward.

"That poor man is just about destitute and he has no one to help him. His own family won't hardly help him."

"You're referring to the home he rents out in Texas?"

Pearl nodded her head. "His mother refuses to sell it, so all he's getting out of that is about forty dollars a month after she gets her half."

"I imagine that she needs money to live on too, Pearl."

"But..."

"Don't be so hard on her. She's made mistakes like the rest of us and if you think about it, she probably did the best she knew how."

Embarrassment reddened Pearl's cheeks and she paused for a moment to sigh.

"She lost her son, or thought she had, and then she lost her husband. That's a lot. Then she turned to her friends who couldn't help her." Jess rubbed his leathery hands together. "I know all about it, Gal. Jay has told me a few things too."

Pearl's eyes met her father's. "You're right, as usual," she pouted.

"I know it's mighty hard on him, gal. And now with the accident, it's got to be doubly hard. You've always had such a giving heart, a kind soul, but you can't save the world, Pearl, and I don't want you to get your heart broken...again."

Jess took his daughter's hands in his own. "He is a married man—married—you know what that means."

Pearl again held her father's gaze. She knew what he was referring to. Instantly she withdrew her hands from his. "Daddy? No! That is the farthest thing from the truth. I'm just trying to be his *friend.* That's all. Nothing more."

Jess raised an eyebrow. There was no arguing with his daughter. She was a grown woman now. Against his own belief he tried to convince himself that perhaps she was simply trying to be a friend to the man. Surely, he did need friends now, and even if there was more to it than simple friendship, it did not mean the man did not need help now. Jess heard the angst in his daughter's voice, the compassion in her eyes. How could he deny her the love she wanted to give?

"Okay, gal. Don't get all riled up.

"Daddy. It's just been hard on him and Feona. I know Jay was planning on buying that little house they live in, but I don't think he can hardly make the payments now."

"He's renting from Carl Burns. Right?"

Pearl nodded. "Uh huh. And Frankie is manning the gas pumps in the afternoons after school so Jay can tend to Feona. Miss Janie, me and Miss Francis have been checking on her too. But Daddy, we gotta do something to help him."

The earnestness in Pearl's voice moved Jess to feel things he had not felt in years. Pleas from his daughter had always wrenched his heart.

He looked into his daughter's eyes. They were the same ones that had begged him to let her pull on the seine—the same ones who had pleaded with him to let her have her own horse—and the same ones that had so desperately sought his understanding when she had found she was carrying Jay's child.

Deep in thought, Jess rubbed his hands. "Let me think on it a bit."

Still in thought, as his eyes focused on a spot on the table; he rubbed his chin. "It's off season...no tourists and only a few die-hard fishermen are hanging on at the piers."

Pressing against the table, Jess pushed himself up. "Like I said, you let me think on it awhile." Turning to leave, he winked at Pearl. "Gal, I like the idea about the lights—makes everything look real Christmassy."

Pearl watched as her father slowly made his way down the stairs. *I could pick him out in a crowd of a thousand by those elbows.* Jess's short-sleeved shirt showed his elbows, wrinkled and hardened by time. They stood out from his body as he swaggered across the hard road to his truck. *He still has that same old walk.* Pearl chuckled. *Oh how I love you, Daddy.*

She knelt into the soft naugahyde cushion of the booth and thought of her parents, of how much she would have liked her life to be like theirs. She had never wanted to be special or important. She had never wanted to be a leader in the church or community. She had never had any desire, like Ellie, to be popular or the prettiest girl. All she had ever wanted was a nice quiet life where she could enjoy the ocean, fishing, and the ones she loved. *Oh, why did it have to be so complicated?*

As she slipped her legs from beneath her, Pearl rose and walked outside to lean against the front patio railing facing the paved road. A stand of scrub oaks mingled with merkles stood catty-corner to the Gull. She stretched her neck back and let the ocean breeze whip through her hair. It felt good, even this time of year when there was a definite coolness in the air.

Pulling her jacket close around her she closed her eyes and felt the railing push against her abdomen.

"Oh my, it has been so long since I felt a man against me."

There was no sadness about Pearl as she let thoughts of intimacy enter her mind. She relaxed into them and felt the corners of her lips turn upward.

"Ha!" She laughed aloud. "It's been so long. She thought of Roger and rolled her eyes. A wave of passion swept over her and the familiar voice of her husband whispered inside her head. She smiled at the memory, no longer aching as she had at one time.

Opening her eyes, Pearl scanned the oak trees and spotted several red-wing blackbirds and waited for their trill.

"Ah, there you are," she spoke to herself as they began returning each others' song. She whistled and tried to make the sound in her throat, as if to mimic their trill. "Never could do that."

CHAPTER TWELVE

Feona blinked her eyes and waited for the grogginess to leave her head. It seemed she was sleeping all the time. Reaching for the drink on the nightstand, she bumped it with her wrist; she heard the plastic tumbler fall to the floor. Shaking her head in disgust, she thought of the sticky cola puddle now by her bedside.

Pulling herself into a sitting position, Feona yawned and tried to focus on the television set. There was a program on now, she could hear the voices. She was just not sure which program it was. Someone must have turned the sound down. *Who could have done that,* she wondered.

Jay had been such a dear after the accident and had gone almost immediately to Boom Town in Holly Ridge to purchase a television for her bedroom. Now if only she could change the channels without getting out of bed. *Maybe someone will come by and take care of that for me,* Feona thought as she positioned herself more comfortably in the bed.

Focusing her eyes on the dresser, she searched for the alarm clock. *One o'clock. Secret Storm is on now.*

"Damn it all." Instantly her hand flew to her mouth and she scanned the room and listened for sounds that may indicate she was not alone in the house. "I've got to stop all this cussing."

Pushing herself to her elbows she considered trying to get out of bed, but the pain was too much. She slunk back against her pillow. "Ooh, this is just too much."

Eying the bottle of pain pills, she shook her head no and grumbled, "I'll just fall back asleep if I take one of those."

The empty chair In the corner of the room, where Janie Butler had sat most of the morning, looked disheveled. Feona sighed; there was nothing she could do about that now. She'd wait until Jay or Fate came in and she'd have them straighten the blanket on it.

A rerun of *My Little Margie* was playing. She'd never liked that show. Oh how she wished Janie would have turned the channel for her before she left. Certainly Janie would have known that she liked *The Secret Storm*.

"Now I'm going to miss all my shows, *The Edge of Night* and *As the World Turns*, oh poop." She swatted the side of her bed and tossed a pillow onto the floor.

She reached for the *Photoplay* magazine on the side table and thumbed through it. Jane Meadows of the comedy television show *The Honeymooners* was on the front cover.

You'd never know her hair was red from watching her show. She ought to dye it brown. Feona studied the picture; she had never known anyone with red hair.

Wetting her forefinger, she turned a couple of pages. Chuck Connors smiled back at her. She really liked him. He stood tall without the props that he wore on *The Rifleman*, his television show. His hair was smoothed back and he wore a blue button-down shirt that matched his eyes.

"Yoo hoo! Hellooo!"

Feona raised her head and quickly set the magazine back on the nightstand and listened to the sharp rap on the front door.

"Mrs. Bishop, are you home?"

Light footsteps sounded on the linoleum floor, and Feona listened as she heard the steps enter the kitchen. She called out, "Who's there? Who's there?"

"It's only me, Feona—Pearl Rosell. I brought dinner and put it in the refrigerator."

"Thank you," Feona lilted. "I'm back here in the bedroom. Please come in and change the channel on the television for me. I want to watch *The Secret Storm*."

Pearl raised her shoulders and grinned as she entered through the doorway to Feona's room. "Yes, dearie, I'll be glad to do that." She stepped over to the small set and clicked the knob. "I'm just stopping by as usual to straighten up a little." Studying the room she noticed the cola spill. "Oh my goodness, don't you just hate it when you spill the Pepsi, I'm always doing it." She smiled. "Soft drinks get so sticky. I guess it's all the sugar. Let me go get a rag to clean that up with."

Feona's eyes bore hard into the back of Pearl's head as she left the room. *You bitch; I bet you think I spilled that on purpose.*

"Now don't you worry none, I'll get this up in a jiffy." Pearl entered through the doorway, smiling as she looked up at the woman and noticed the scowl on her face.

"Oh dear, ha ha, I hope you don't mind me using this?" Pearl held up a torn and tattered dish towel she had found lying under the kitchen sink. "I'll be sure to rinse it out before I leave. Okay?"

Her brow still furrowed, Feona smoothed the blanket across her abdomen. *Why is she talking so much? I can't even hear my show.* "That's alright. It needed washing anyway." Her voice was calm as she replaced the scowl with a smile. "Can you turn up the television a bit? I still can't hear what they are saying."

Pearl looked over to the set where the soap opera continued, the background organ music playing dramatically. "Oh, I'm sorry Feona, I know you really like these shows."

Wiping once more with the rag, Pearl then rose from her knees. "I'm forever spilling stuff, especially when I get in a hurry." She stepped back holding the towel. "Now, Feona, I have to say that you look wonderful today. I bet it won't be long before you're up and around."

"I don't know." Feona's eyes searched the ceiling, then moved back to the television program. "I just don't feel right."

135

"Well, until you do feel better and can get up I'll be here to help you."

"Oh, you're so thoughtful, Pearl. And you're such a good cook. Jay and Fate really enjoy your cooking. But don't worry too much about the house. Fate and Jay can pick up, and besides, the only one making a mess in this house is me.

"You'll be up and around in no time."

A weak smile crossed Feona's lips, but it faded quickly. "Miss Janie just left a little while ago and she was such good company. She changed the sheet on my bed and made me lunch and then we talked a little about things."

Feona glanced toward the chair where Janie had been sitting. "Dear, would you mind straightening the blanket on that chair in the corner. It just plum drives me loony whenever I see a mess. And since I can't do any housework now, it just seems that everything is in disarray."

Giggling, Pearl straightened the blanket and sat back in the chair herself. "I'll make sure I straighten it before I leave. Okay? And I'll straighten up the kitchen after I have a chance to see how you're doing today."

A blank looked settled on Feona's face. Her eyes drifted back to the television show then back to Pearl. Her lips quivered a bit; shaking her head as if to clear it, she spoke. "Uh, um—don't worry about the kitchen. I think Miss Janie just made some sandwiches and that doesn't make much of a mess."

"Good, but I did bring some oyster stew for you, Fate and Jay. Hope you like it. Momma made some cornbread to go along."

"Ah honey, that sounds great. But you needn't have bothered. Um, Jay doesn't like oysters."

"I thought he did, and when I mentioned it to you the other day, you said you would love some."

"Did you hear what I said?" The sound of grinding teeth surprised Pearl, and she must have looked astonished as Feona's mood quickly changed.

"Sorry, I didn't mean to snap at you. I guess being cooped up all the time just makes me edgy, and I was really hoping to be able to watch *The Secret Storm.*

"Oh, I'm so sorry." Pearl settled in the chair and pressed her finger to her lips. "I'll be quiet now."

Feona scowled as she watched the show. She ground her teeth and bit her lip. Finally a commercial came on.

"I do appreciate you bringing over food and helping. Not being able to cook for my own family makes me feel worthless."

"Oh no, Feona. I'm sure that if it were me in your situation, you'd be helping too. It's just what a small community does. Right? You grew up in a small town, didn't you?"

"Yes, you're right." Feona bit her bottom lip again. "I used to live way out in the country—not a neighbor around for a good ten miles. I never did go to town much. In fact, when I started working at the drugstore, it was the first time I had been there without my grandmother. She was always with me when we went to town, and it felt so odd when I started my job and she wasn't hovering over me."

Nodding, Pearl could only imagine how coddled the girl must have been, being an only child. She certainly had been. She thought of her own life and how her parents had fussed over her.

Feona was young, a good ten years younger than herself. She tried to imagine how difficult it must be living in a new place. Still, Jay had said how excited she was to move to the island.

Pearl shrugged and flashed Feona a knowing look. "I remember being so cooped up when I was carrying Frank. Oh, it was so hot and the doctor didn't want me to go anywhere or do anything...and Momma or Daddy wouldn't even let me out of their sight"

Feona leaned forward a bit. "My mother and father died when I was just a baby, and Granny was always so worried that something would happen to me. She hardly ever let me out of her sight. I didn't understand when I was little, and boy oh boy, did it get on my nerves that someone was always hovering over me. I thought I was going to pull my hair out." Grinning, Feona pulled the blankets up to cover her nightshirt. "Would you be a dear and turn the volume up a little bit more on the television?"

The set was nearly blaring but Pearl rose and turned the volume up just the slightest bit. She picked up the pillow on the floor and set it on the foot of the bed. "I like this one too, but since I'm usually at the restaurant,

I hardly ever get to see it." Pearl's voice strained to be heard above the television.

"I watch my soap operas every day. What else am I going to do?"

Pearl thought she heard a touch of sarcasm in Feona's voice, and noticed her pursed lips. "Oh Feona, I know. It's not as if you can do much." Pearl fussed with the blanket on the chair. "I've been thinking of getting a television set for the Gull so that during the slow season I can watch and catch up on all the stories."

Pearl's eyes settled gently on Feona's as she moved away from the television. "Is it warm enough in here for you? You seem a little chilled." Pearl walked to the small gas heater in the corner of the bedroom. "I'll just turn it on a bit."

"You know, that heater has been off since early this morning. I asked Jay, before he left for work, to turn it off. I just about roasted in here last night."

"Well, I'll just turn it on low so you can get warmed up a bit. How about that?"

Without answering, Feona's eyes moved to the pillows and magazines pilled around the bed. "Jay sleeps in the sunroom on the daybed since all this happened. He tried, of course, at first to sleep with me in the room, but he just wasn't getting any sleep with me tossing so much."

"He's always talking about you Feona. And I know he's really worried that you'll be okay."

A puzzled look crossed Feona's face. "Talking about me? Why is he talking to you about me? What is he talking about me for? What is he saying?"

Pearl heard the anxiety in Feona's voice, she heard the fear. "He just wants you to get better; he wishes you weren't laid up in bed."

"Oh. I'm so sorry, I'm so confused. I *do* appreciate all that everyone has done for me, especially since I hardly even know anybody. Y' all have been so nice and I'm sorry if I get edgy sometimes.

"Feona, we all have times when we just don't feel like being nice."

"Hum, I... Feona inadvertently pushed several magazines to the floor as she readjusted her position in the bed.

Pearl could hear the woman's quick, heavy breathing and she saw her wrench her hands.

"Nice? What do you mean? You don't think I'm nice?"

Oh my God. She's twisting everything I say. "Oh Feona, please—yes, you're nice. But maybe I put it the wrong way. I know that sometimes, *I* don't feel like being nice because I feel badly. And I thought that perhaps you might feel that too."

"Oh, I see."

Pearl could feel the tension in the room and sought quickly to change the subject to something light-hearted. "I just love your and Jay's place. How do you like living on the beach, oceanfront?"

"It's *nice*." Nodding, her lips slightly turned upward, Feona added sarcastically, "Everything's *nice*."

"Maybe I came at a bad time today. Maybe I'll come back later." Pearl's puzzled gaze settled on Feona. "I'm sorry if I offended you."

"No, please forget what I've just said. I'm tired. I'm confused. I just don't know. Please come back and sit down."

"You poor thing, It must be horrible to be here all by yourself." Pearl reached her hand to brush Feona's bangs to the side of her face.

"I've been meaning to thank your daddy for talking to Mr. Burns about our rent payments. He's going to let us pay half each month until the summer when business picks up and Jay can pay more toward the house. We really want to buy the place, but with this..." Feona shrugged her shoulders; her lips began to quiver as tears welled in her eyes.

"Daddy will come by soon and you can thank him then. We all know what it's like to fall on hard times."

"Well, since the accident Jay's had to pay doctors and he can't be at the station quite as much as he'd like." She pressed Pearl's hand. "Frank has been wonderful coming to the station and helping out."

"He likes to do it," Pearl nodded.

"It seems we are always short on money. I just don't know what he does with it all." Drying her eyes and biting her bottom lip, Feona's crying turned into sobs. Her words were unintelligible as Pearl sat next to her on the bed and wrapped her arms around her.

"There, there, now. Everything is going to be fine." Pearl stroked her hair as she would a child's and held Feona as she shook.

"Pearl, do you like me?'

"Of course I do."

"I think that you're the only one who does."

"That's not true. Miss Janie thinks the world of you."

"No, no. You should see the way she sits in that chair and looks at me. I hear her whisper things too and she doesn't think I hear her."

"What?" A curiousness filled Pearl. She had never known Janie Butler to act in such a way. She was one of the kindest, most understanding people she had ever known.

"Francis West did the same thing." Feona looked into Pearl's eyes. "Sometimes Jay does it too. He says mean things to me. I hear him talking in the bathroom in the mornings to someone; I don't know who, but he tells them he wishes I would go away—that he can't bear the sight of me anymore."

"No! No Feona, Jay loves you." Pearl looked into Feona's tear-stained, distorted face. The woman was obviously worn out and confused. Certainly the things she was saying could not be true. Pearl could feel the young woman's entire body shaking as she stroked her damp hair.

It was all so very strange. Maybe what some of the women on the island were saying about Feona was true. Pearl had heard from Ethel that worked at Boom Town how Feona had once accused her of laughing at her, and had gotten so mad she had left her groceries behind.

Pearl had never experienced anything like that with Feona. Still, there had been rumors of Feona turning her head when someone waved to her, or closing her front door as someone approached it.

She never asked Jay about these rumors; she thought that most likely they were just small town gossip. Maybe during those times Feona was having her time of the month. Pearl nodded to herself and thought how true that could be.

"Could you get me some Pepsi so I can take my Darvon?" Feona caught her trembling breath and reached for a Kleenex to wipe her eyes and face. "I'm so sorry."

"No need to be sorry, sweetie." Pearl patted her on the back and stood up, "I'll get that Pepsi for you."

As she entered the bedroom holding the tumbler of cola, Pearl noticed how Feona fumbled with the bottles of medication on her nightstand. She couldn't get the cap off.

"Why in the world do they put these on so tightly?"

"Here." As she held out her hand, Pearl read the labels on the bottle—*Darvon*. She took a pill from the bottle and handed to Feona.

"I need more than one of those."

"It says for you to only take one."

"Give me the damn bottle!" She grabbed it from Pearl's hand, and spilled the contents onto the bed.

"Look what you've made me do!"

Standing numb, Pearl started to help pick up the pills.

"What are you doing?" Feona's brow was lined and scowling. "This is none of your business. You and Janie, Francis—all of you are talking about me."

"Oh Feona." In her most soothing voice, Pearl tried to comfort the woman. "I wasn't trying to tell you what to do. It's just that the label says..."

"I don't give a damn what the label says."

"Just relax." Pearl stroked Feona's hand. "I just was curious as to what pills you're taking. I know you have to be on some pain medication."

"You would be too," shot back Feona. "That idiot driving the car crushed my pelvis. I'll never have any more children. He should have been going slower—it was right outside the church and there were people walking to their cars. Why wasn't anyone looking out for me? They don't care. They wanted me to get hurt!"

Her eyes wild and her breathing shallow and fast, Feona raged on. "It's not fair that he got off. They said it was my fault and that idiot driving the car doesn't have to pay a thing. It's not fair."

"No, it's not fair." Again Pearl comforted Feona as she burst into another crying jag. Her entire body shook as she sobbed hysterically.

Pearl held her shoulders and spoke to her as gently as she could, but Feona's eyes looked wildly about the room. She began grinding her teeth, clenching and unclenching her fists.

"Oh my God, Feona. You need some help."

144

"No! No...go away now. I'll be fine. It's you and Janie, you make me nervous."

"We're just trying to help you, honey."

"No. I don't need any help and if you don't get out of here right now, I'm telling Jay."

A surprised and puzzled look crossed Pearl's face, "What? What did I do Feona? I'm sorry if I offended you."

"I'm going to tell Jay that you came in here and stole things. You're always stealing things. And you say such mean things to me, horrible things." She screamed the words again. "Horrible things. You're trying to hurt me—you're trying to burn down this house and with me in it."

"What in the world are you talking about?"

"You are. It's not cold in here and you went over to the stove and turned on the gas. You didn't even light the stove. Now, go! I don't want you in my house ever again! I don't want any of you bitches ever coming in my house again!"

The sound of the racing feet along the porch startled Feona and Pearl. They heard faint laughter filter into the room from outside. The two women looked at one another, Pearl's eyes questioning Feona's, so full of hate. The sound of the screen door slamming shut, followed by the bang of the wooden door jolted Feona and she turned her attention toward her bedroom doorway.

"Fate! Fate! Mommy's in here."

The patter of footsteps became louder as the young boy came running into his mother's room. In one hand he held a staff of sea oats, in the other he held a balled handkerchief. "I got a bunch of rolly-pollys. Me and E.J. have been playing baseball with them." Fate tossed one in the air and swiped at it with the sea oats shaft.

As the boy bounced onto the bed, Pearl noticed Feona wincing, but still a broad smile covered her face. She kissed her son on the cheek and glared at Pearl.

"Hi, Miss Pearl. You look pretty today," the boy spoke innocently.

Pearl watched Feona's brow furrow once again; nervously she raised her voice to a higher octave. "Your mother should be very proud of you, I heard that you got a one hundred on your spelling test. You are such a smart boy."

Pearl stepped toward Fate, but Feona's eyes warned against it and Pearl stepped back.

"Tell Miss Pearl bye-bye, Fate. She just stopped by for a few minutes and has to go now."

****

"Momma, I'm confused, I just don't know. I've never seen anyone act the way she did. And the things she was saying about Miss Janie..."

Lottie arched an eyebrow. "That girl has always been standoffish, always been shy."

"Lots of people are shy, Momma. This is something else."

146

"Why don't you go and talk to Janie? See what she has to say. She's the one that has been helping out more than anyone."

Pearl nodded her head and thought to herself, *Jay must be beside himself.*

She questioned if perhaps Feona had been telling the truth. Had Jay been being mean to her? *Not the Jay I knew,* she thought. *But he was in the prisoner of war camp.* She shook her head defiantly. "No."

She had known Janie, Francis and everyone else in the area her whole life. Never had she heard anything like this before. Oh yes, people gossiped, but not with such maliciousness as Feona described. Maybe she had caught these people on a bad day. Maybe she really did have what her father called 'cabin fever.'

"On the other hand," Lottie interrupted Pearl's thoughts, "remember Clarence, how mean he used to be and how he blamed everyone for anything that went wrong?"

"That was a long time ago. Before they put him away, he was just as sweet and easy going as a dobbie calf."

"Dobbie calf, yep—that's the way he was alright, he was just plain lost most of the time."

"Feona's not like that, Momma. She's very aware of what's going on around her. She just thinks everybody hates her. She didn't act like that before the accident."

Shrugging, Lottie sighed heavily, "Not many of us have spent much time with her to really know that. You and Ellie spend most of your time at the Sea Gull and

147

outside of church; I don't think Feona socializes any at all. I've heard how she sort of ignores people when they talk to her and how she usually has something else to do when you invite her somewhere—or at least that is what she replies. She hasn't joined the choir or come to any ladies meeting. And the few times I've seen Jay at pig pickings, she wasn't with him...except the one Enid had when they first moved here and she was standoffish then. Really, if you think about it, she hasn't had much to do with us."

Pearl nodded.

"If you remember, the one picking she did accompany Jay to, they left very early, and I noticed that she was whispering a lot to him the entire time. I didn't think much of it at then, but well..." Lottie shrugged.

"I don't know what is going on, but I saw those pills she's been taking. One of them is Darvon; I guess it's for pain. Those pills could have something to do with the crazy way she is acting now."

"Could be."

"Some of that stuff will make you cuckoo if you take too much of it."

"She acted like I was going to hurt Fate. I don't understand that."

"Me either. Like I said, talk with Janie. She knows just about everything that's going on around the island.

CHAPTER THIRTEEN

Feona heard the front door close; Jay was home. She wished suddenly that she had not been so sharp with Pearl. What had she said to Pearl? It all seemed as if it took place in a fog.

"Mommy, can I go outside and play in the backyard?" Fate questioned his mother.

"Give me a kiss first."

The boy leaned against the bed as Feona drew him close to kiss his curly haired head. "Daddy will call you in before dark. Don't dig holes by the clothesline," Feona chided lovingly and winked. The dark thoughts had vanished; it was as if nothing had happened.

Jay tousled Fate's curly head as the two passed in the doorway. "Hey Buddy, how's my boy?"

"Momma says you'll call me at dark, Daddy." Fate whooshed by, and both Jay and Feona grinned as they heard the back screen door slam.

"So how's your day been going, my darling sweetie pie?" Jay bent low over his wife and smelled her hair, nuzzled her neck, and then found her mouth for a short kiss. She pushed him away and grimaced, suggesting to him that his breath smelled badly.

"Sorry dear, I'll brush my teeth in a bit."

"Do you want to hear about *The Edge of Night* or *Secret Storm*?" Feona tittered.

"Hardy har har." Jay pulled a chair close to the bed. "I know you must be tired of laying in bed all day, but the doctor said you should be ready to get up soon."

"I just don't know Jay." Feona's eyes sadly searched her husband's. "I just don't feel ready."

"Last time we went to Doc Whaley he said you should be getting out of bed a little at a time. Maybe walking into the living room or even sitting outside. The fresh air would be good for you, hon."

As her body tensed, Feona pulled the cover tightly against it. "If I thought I could do those things, don't you think I would?" She looked defensively at Jay. "Do you think I like lying in bed all day long?"

"No. I don't think you like lying in bed all day. But you need to at least try. Miss Janie and Pearl are supposed to be helping you with that. Now, isn't that neighborly of them to try to help you, dear?"

Feona pulled her lips in over her teeth. Her chest rose with quick breaths., "You have to be crazy if you think I'm going to let either one of those bitches touch me."

150

"Feona! The cussing," he looked questioningly at her. "I've never heard you cuss so much."

"I don't cuss...but I should. They're stealing, you know. They come in this house and bring food, but then they always leave with something under their coat or in their purse. My best gravy boat is gone!"

"Gravy boat? I thought that got broken last Thanksgiving."

"It did not! That Francis West stole it."

Her face looked worn and haggard to Jay. It looked as if she had aged ten years since they had moved to Topsail. He did not understand what was happening to his wife.

"And Pearl!" As she spoke the words, Feona saw something in his eyes. She stopped and her mouth fell open. "You two are in it together aren't you?"

For a moment he thought she knew about Frankie, about him and Pearl during the war.

"What do you mean?"

"You and she are trying to take Fate away from me. You want me to go back to Texas. Don't you? I bet Janie is in it too, she is going to cover it all up for you." Her face distorted as she screamed accusations at him. Feona began throwing the magazines on the bed at Jay. She picked up the tumbler of Pepsi and hurled it at him.

"Get away, get away!"

Jay walked slowly toward his wife, soothingly speaking until he reached her side, then he grasped her wrists and held them as she screamed. "No, sweet

Feona, no." he spoke calming. "Not again. Please. No more. Just relax."

Slowly Feona began sobbing, her chest heaving, and breaths coming slower and slower.

"Shh, my dear, you're tired." He stroked her hair as she relaxed and her eyes closed. Her breathing slowed and became shallower.

Jay lay beside her, holding his wife as she fell into sleep. "Shh, just rest now."

Jay picked up a bottle on the stand. It was for pain. *That* he knew she must have. But hadn't the doctor said that she should not be in much pain now? It had been over two months since the accident. Why wasn't she getting any better? And why was she accusing people of stealing and trying to hurt her or take her child away. None of this made any sense.

Is she losing her mind? The thought made his whole body ache.

****

How many times had he had asked himself if he had made a mistake about moving back to the island? It had all seemed so right in the beginning. He reassured himself, time after time, that it was the right move. Frank was proof enough that it had been a good decision. He and the boy had cultivated a trusting relationship. Frank worked at the station, they fished together, went hunting together. Frank even came to him to talk about girls and problems at home.

It was Frank who had told him of the relationship between Pearl and Roger. Although much of the more personal information was missing, Jay filled in the lines.

This knowledge made him feel even more justified in having made the move back. No, he had no right to tell Pearl who to see, but he was so glad that she had not continued seeing a man who was so obviously using her.

Knowing that it had been Pearl's decision to end the relationship with Roger, reassured Jay that this grown woman was still the girl he had once held in such high esteem.

He knew he had done the right thing for Frank by moving back, but had he done the right thing for Feona? Despite her enthusiasm for the move, once they had arrived she seemed to pull farther away.

He wondered, had his mother been right all along? She had said that Feona was fragile. Maybe she had seen something in Feona that he was incapable of seeing.

He remembered how shy Feona had been at the drug store in Donna, Texas, where she had worked, and how long it had taken him to even get her to look into his eyes. At the time he found her shyness endearing. After all, she was quite a few years younger than he.

She had always been shy, always quiet and nervous in crowds, often unsure when trying new things. He had to prod her into trying oysters, into getting into a boat, and even into going to church. Oh how he'd hoped she would fit in! And why wouldn't she? Feona was a lovely girl, so easy to get along with, always so eager to please. Or at least she had been at one time.

But her insecurity had grown, and she had begun thinking that no one liked her. She thought she did everything wrong. And the cussing? Feona had never cussed. Oh, every now and again he'd hear a soft "phooey" or "dagblastit" whispered from her lips. And if she heard him cuss at all, she'd admonish him, reminding him that he was not raised to be vulgar.

What had happened? She seemed to be changing right before his eyes. Maybe she didn't love him anymore and this was her way of pushing him away.

Jay did not understand any of it. It seemed he could not please her lately. She didn't want him to touch her. She squirmed when he tried to kiss her or nuzzle her. He was certainly not allowed a hug. Feona always angrily pushed him away. Then if he suggested any intimacy, she'd say the strangest thing. "You're not supposed to do that to me."

Once, she slapped his hands away and yelled out that Francis West was staring at them through the window.

How odd, he had thought. But, like everything else, he swept it under the rug, and chalked it all up to having been raised by her grandmother and living so far away from people. Feona had been sheltered.

Now, when she was sleeping, he could hold her. She felt warm against his body and he longed to be close, he longed for the girl he had once known.

Lord knows he loved to see her happy, and he did everything to make that happen. But maybe, just maybe, he had sacrificed his wife for his son. The thought ran through his mind often as he watched her distance herself more and more from the people of the Topsail community. And now, since the accident her insecurities had grown into fears—unfounded fears that he did not understand. He had tried every way he could to include her. He'd spoken with Pearl, Janie, Francis, Lottie and Ellie; they all had made efforts to include her in their activities, but time after time Feona declined an invitation to go to the movies in Wilmington, to join in a pig picking, to go clamming or to just gather with friends at the Sea Gull or Pop's Pavilion.

The short time she had worked for Pearl at the Sea Gull she had complained daily of the hard work there. She was glad when the season was over and she no longer had to wait on people and clean up after them. She informed Jay that she would not go back to work at the Sea Gull in the spring.

Her accident had forced Feona to allow Fate to play with the children of the community. Otherwise the boy would have been still clinging to her skirts. That was the one good thing about all that was going on now. Jay relished the idea of his son playing cowboys and Indians in the sand dunes and climbing the squatty scrub oaks populating the island. It was a wonderful place for children to grow up.

Jay looked at his wife sleeping soundly in the bed. She looked haggard, so much older than the girl he had married in Texas. He kissed her forehead and touched his cheek to hers. *Why was all this happening?*

Lost, he felt lost, and who was there to go to even ask for advice?

He wished it could have been Jess. They had once been like father and son. Now, he needed someone he could trust, someone who would offer sound advice. Jay laid Feona's arms down by her side as he tiptoed from the room. He sat down in the sofa in the living room and dialed the number.

CHAPTER FOURTEEN

The thought of taking his wife to a psychiatrist was terrifying to Jay. Wasn't that where crazy people went? And when Jess first mentioned it, he was insulted. Had it come to this? Did the old man dislike him so much that he would insult him and his wife?

Jess must have read his thoughts and he reached to pat the younger man's shoulder. "Sorry, son."

Jay had not heard anyone call him "son" in such a long time. That role had long ago passed with the death of his father, and the acquisition of his own role as father.

Yet he remembered Jess calling him that more than sixteen years ago. It had meant a great deal then—as a young man going off to war, he needed the reassurance that a father could give. At that time he had been so uncertain, so confused and afraid—not of being killed, but that he would lose everything. And he had. Now, this new battle, he understood this one even less. What was it going to bring? And was he strong enough to bear what it brought?

"Sorry, son," Jess repeated. "That's the only thing I know to tell you. If everything you're telling me is true—and Pearl and Janie told me a few things, too—well, sounds to me like your wife has had some kind of breakdown."

"When you lose someone or something bad happens, a woman can have a breakdown." Lottie nodded. "Sometimes you feel like the whole world is falling apart."

"I saw some things in Germany—men all cracked up, beating their own heads against the wall until they were bloody and passed out. I saw men take their own lives, blow their own brains out. It was the war. But Feona? She's not had anything bad happen to her. What could be the problem?"

"Don't know. Maybe all the moving around...leaving Texas."

Jay shook his head. "No, she was anxious to move. I don't think that would be it."

"What about her grandma? Does she ever hear from her?" Lottie brushed a gray strand of loose hair from her face.

"No. Her Nanny died a few months back before Feona's accident."

"And she didn't go down for the funeral?"

"That was a funny thing, odd. She didn't get a phone call about Nanny until two weeks after she passed on. Her old boss at the drug store called and said he thought she should know." Jay looked perplexed at the couple, hoping once again that their understanding and caring was as real as it had once been.

"Do you know much about her Nanny?" Lottie fidgeted with the loose strand of hair.

"Some, I guess. She was always around when I went to the farm where they lived. At first she didn't allow us to be alone, but after a few months she did. She was always nice, always polite. And I guess you might say *protective* of her granddaughter."

"Sounds normal to me." Jess nodded.

"Nanny didn't talk a whole lot. She cooked when I went there for dinner, and she'd listen to the radio with us. She was always nice." Chuckling to himself, he added, "But they sure did live out in the boonies. It took me a good half hour to get out to her place—with all the windy roads and woods." Jay considered his last words. "But they weren't poor. I think Feona's mother and father left her enough so that life wouldn't be so hard."

"Really?"

"Not rich, just not poor."

"Um." Lottie rubbed her back as she sat in the rocking chair on the porch.

"After Nanny passed away, Feona received a check for a couple hundred dollars. She mentioned that the check should have been for more, but then she never mentioned it again. She didn't act very upset about it, but I know she missed her Nanny and wished she had been able to go to the funeral. Nothing seemed out of the ordinary, if that's what you're trying to get at."

"No!" Jess and Lottie spoke simultaneously.

"I was just asking. You just never know, son."

There was the word again: son. Jay relaxed, feeling once again that the Scaggins were people he could trust and who cared about him.

The corners of his lips drew upward. "Feona and Nanny just weren't showy people. I guess in a lot of ways, the way they lived reminded me of y'all. "

"Nothing wrong with that." Jess joined his wife and sat in the other rocker. "I think we're mighty fine as people go."

"I can tell you that she rivaled your biscuit-making skills, Miss Lottie." Jay laughed and leaned against an old soda pop crate as the older couple rocked in the wooden rockers.

"So her parents died young?" Jess asked.

"I asked her about her family one time. She said she really didn't remember them much; she was so young when they died."

"How did they die?" Lottie's eyebrow rose as she leaned into the conversation.

"Nanny said they were both killed in a car accident when Fe was only a baby. Feona was thrown from the car and survived."

"How sad." Lottie bit her bottom lip.

"She also said that she was the only one on either side of the families that would take the baby in."

"Well, I ain't no doctor and no psychiatrist. But it doesn't sound like she had it too bad. She may have had some misfortune in her life, but that builds character." The rocking chair moved slower and slower; Jess rubbed his stubbly chin. "All I can offer is my opinion. Like I said, it sounds like she may have had a breakdown, but you'll need a doctor to verify that. I'd suggest you taking her to see Dr. Stuart in Wilmington—he's the one that diagnosed old Clarence."

"She's not crazy like Clarence!" Jay regretted raising his voice as soon as the words left his lips.

"I'm not suggesting that she is, son. It's just that Dr. Stuart is a doctor of the brain, a psychiatrist –he's going to know all about situations like this." Jess's voice was calming. "And if he doesn't, he'll know who to send her to." Jess's eyes met and held Jay's. "Something ain't right, if she's thinking that anybody around here is trying to spy on her or hurt her."

****

"Your daddy was right. Dr. Stuart says she has had a nervous breakdown and that she just needs to rest. She's gone to stay with some friends in Texas for a few weeks." Jay's eyes implored Pearl's as he leaned into the car window.

"Should I come over and help you and Fate while she's gone? "

"No, no," he said quickly, searching Pearl's eyes. Could there be some way she could know the truth, the real problem with Feona? Pearl had always known his heart.

He felt a tug, a needy desire to reach out to Pearl for solace. Numbness flew through his body as the thought entered his mind; instantly shame made him brush the thought away. "No need for you to come over. But I wouldn't mind if your momma and daddy let Fate come and visit at the farm while I'm at the gas station." He stood straight now, no longer leaning against Pearl's car. "I'd really appreciate it if they could. I'm sure it won't be for long; maybe a week or two and Feona will be back." Jay's lips turned slightly upward. "When she gets back I'm sure she will be just like her old self."

Pearl nodded, and though she felt something was amiss, she did not ask. Jay had seemed nervous, distracted, but she had no right to pry into his life. What passed between Jay and Feona was their business, not hers—he was a married man.

Weren't these her mother's words...*married man*? Pearl felt her face redden. Why did she even think of it?

"We're friends," she spoke aloud as she drove across the air hose; the loud 'ding, ding' exploded in her mind interrupting her thoughts. "I just want to help a friend."

"How long has it been, Pearl?" That was the question Ellie had asked her not two weeks ago.

162

At the time Pearl had scoffed at the question. It seemed intimacy was the only thing Ellie ever had on her mind.

"Sex," her mother had whispered. "I don't like the word." She had winked, "but it's not bad." Pearl had seen the sexual play between her parents her whole life. Even now, when they were nearly seventy years old, there was still flirtatious behavior between the two. She smiled and her heart warmed knowing that the two people that meant the most to her knew true love.

"How long has it been?" Ellie's question repeated in her mind.

The tug of desire, the yearning for physical pleasure, had disappeared after Hurricane Hazel. She had been disgusted with herself about Roger, and after dismissing him she had engulfed herself in working the Gull and raising her children. Those two things kept her very busy.

Oh, there had been that thing about Phil. She shuttered as she thought of it. *Oh God, he must have thought I was nuts.* "I should apologize to him," she spoke softly as she nodded. "I bet I made him feel really uncomfortable."

Pearl smiled to herself, *oh what a fool I can be, have been. I hope I don't do anything so stupid again.*

She remembered the last time she had seen Phil. He was with the same girl she had seen him with the time before. Pearl hoped he had found someone to love. She hoped he had finally found peace now that his father had been put away.

What an odd way of saying it: Clarence had been put away.

Ellie had said he needed to be put away a long time ago. Lottie had said the same. Both women refused to show any sympathy for the man. He had, after all, according to the two women, caused too much pain in the lives of loving people.

That was another thing that was odd these days: Ellie and her mother agreeing on things. That didn't seem right. So much didn't seem right.

Snickering, Pearl shook her head as she recalled days when Ellie would holler back at a drunken Uncle Clarence. And times when Lottie would stand up to anyone who threatened her daughter's well-being. She guessed that they were both forceful women.

I've never been like that. I don't think I ever had to be that way—someone else was always taking my part. A striking understanding of herself swept through her. "Darn, I've been blessed."

"So that's who I am. So that's why Ellie has always called me Goody Two Shoes."

Over the years she and Ellie's relationship had advance to a different place. There was less manipulation and less petty rivalry, and more understanding and acceptance.

Pearl had grown to understand her friend, maybe not always accepting Ellie's choices, but then again, not being so judgmental. Maybe Ellie knew more about her than even she suspected.

'How long has it been?' Repeated in her mind again, Ellie's words. And why now? Why not a year ago or six months ago?

"Humph—odd." It made no sense to Pearl, but—well—even though Ellie was her friend she knew she would never divulge the fleeting thought she had just had about Jay.

"What a coincidence," Pearl spoke aloud as she drove up to the Sea Gull Restaurant. Ellie sat wrapped in a brown cape she had purchased during a trip to Raleigh where her mother now lived. Cigarette smoke billowed above her like a halo as she exhaled.

Her Grandma Portman had passed away a few years back, and Ellie's parents had sold their home at the sound and moved to the old Portman home estate in Raleigh.

"Much against Father's wishes," Ellie had chided. "Poor Father, he would have stayed here and lived like a farmer all his life if it hadn't of been for Mother." Ellie guffawed; still believing that her mother's way of life had been best for her father.

Pearl studied her friend's face as she spoke, *the old bat took him away from what he loved, that's why he died up there in God forsaken Raleigh.*

There was no use in arguing with Ellie; she saw her parents the way she wanted. And, as Lottie had said, 'if he didn't want to be with the woman, he would have left long ago.'

Pearl wasn't too sure if she believed that. She had seen repressed and manipulated people struggle in relationships that only kept them down. She thought of Josie and Clarence. Time after time Josie had been offered the opportunity to leave him, but had never done so.

"Ahh! Too much. I think too much." She sighed and reprimanded herself. "Daddy always said that you can't save the world." Pursing her lips with determination, Pearl pulled her car into the parking space at the Gull, then exited, striding toward the stairway to the restaurant.

"I can smell that stinky cigarette all the way down here," she hollered to Ellie.

"No you can't."

"That gorgeous cape is going to smell just like cigarettes."

"Ooh, I like the smell of cigarettes." Ellie sucked a deep drag from the Winston she held between her fingers. "Mucho bonito fumar." Ellie cocked her head to the side. "I think that's the right way to say it? At least that's what Raul says."

Pearl shook her head and grinned. "The one from Cuba?"

Ellie nodded, untying the scarf wrapped to hold her hair back, She shook her dark mane free, and slipped her hand through her locks seductively. Standing, she drew the cape across her face to where it only allowed her deeply eye-lined eyes to show. "It makes me mysterious," she cooed. "Don't you think?" She moved the cape to take another pull on the cigarette, then covered her face again, smoke escaping through the woolen cloth of the cape.

"Aucha, aucha," Ellie coughed as she slung the cape from her face. "Oh God. I think it got in my eyes. That smoke got in my eyes!"

"When are you going to quit that nasty habit? Look at yourself. You're hacking away like crazy and you look like a raccoon."

Ellie dabbed at her eyes, smearing them even more. "Darn!" She stuck her face toward Pearl. "How's it look? Did I mess it all up?"

"You still look like a raccoon, Smelly."

"No I don't."

"Ha, ha, well then you look like a panda. Either way, you've got smudges all around your eyes."

"Shit!"

"Ellie, watch your mouth. Not so loud. Customers might hear you."

"It's winter time, Two Shoes, the place is dead as a doornail."

"Well, I really don't want you to get in the habit of cussing around here."

"Yeah, don't want to sound like Feona Bishop. Now, that gal sure has a potty mouth on her."

Ignoring Ellie, Pearl walked past her and opened the door to the restaurant.

167

Ellie followed and found her handbag behind the counter. Pulling out a jar of face cream, she slathered it around her eyes. "How is she doing, anyway?"

"Jay says she's gone to Texas to stay with some friends for a while."

"Really? Hasn't she been lying on her butt the last few months? What does she need a rest from?" Without waiting for an answer, Ellie continued. "She has been one of the rudest people I have ever met." Ellie dabbed at her eyes with a napkin. "Ever since she moved here, I have tried and tried to get to know her. I've invited her to come to the beach with me and even asked her to go clamming with me. I told her she could bring the kid along." Ellie rolled her eyes.

"Half the time she turns her head like she doesn't even see me, and the other half she just says in that prissy little way of hers, 'I don't think I can do that right now.'" Ellie caught her hands beneath her chin and fluttered her eyelashes. "Daggone Pearl, she won't even let that kid out of her sight."

"He's just a little boy, Ellie."

"Oh, you know what I mean. She hovers around him. I don't think she would have even let him go play with the kids next door to her if she hadn't been hit by that car and been unable to chase after him."

"I'll agree with you there. She is overprotective when it comes to Fate."

"And that little boy is a dreamboat, with that brown curly hair and dark blue eyes. I just hope his momma doesn't ruin him."

168

Pearl shook her head. "I don't think Jay is going to let that happen. I know that since the accident, and especially since Feona's *problems,* he's been taking him fishing more, and he's even had him out to the farm. He plays really well with Bella's kids and Emma Jewel." Turning her face aside, Pearl tittered, "You should see the way Emma Jewel fawns after him. She gets her little brush and brushes his hair and she follows him nearly everywhere he goes."

"Oh lord, another heartbreaker, just what we need around here." Pausing for a moment, Ellie shifted her eyes from the counter to meet Pearl's. "Just like his father, huh?"

Color rose in Pearl's face quicker than she would have liked.

"What are you blushing for?" Ellie taunted.

"You're just not going to let it go. Are you?"

"Hey, this is the first time I've said anything about Jay. Anyway, the first time in a very long time."

"We're just friends, you hear. And yes, I do care about him. I care about him and Feona. The problem is that *you* have never understood how I can care about anybody unless I...I... You know, let them get in my britches."

"Look. I'm just telling you that you're setting yourself up. You're getting involved with someone *who* you once bayed at the moon for—but this time he has a wife."

"You don't understand."

"No, Pearly, y*ou* don't understand. You can't go feeling all mushy gushy for people, especially a man, and not expect him to *want* something more 'physical' from you."

"But Jay and I are friends. We understand one another, and we know that we can't get involved that way."

"Oh, so you've talked with him about it?"

"No, we don't need to talk about that." Pearl glanced at Ellie then quickly looked away.

The tapping of Ellie's fingernails against the counter seemed to echo through the room as Pearl tried desperately to hold on to her denial.

"Stop it, just stop it. You don't understand!" The words flew from Pearl's mouth with such vehemence that it shocked her. "What Jay and I had and were back before the war is gone. It left with Paul and my babies. Do you understand that Ellie?"

"Can you honestly tell me that you don't think about him when you look at Frankie?"

A quietness filled the room as the two old friends stared into one another's eyes.

"That was a long time ago."

"Answer my question."

"I look in the mirror and I no longer see that naïve girl I used to be, but I'm still me. All that is in the past. I'm different now. Oh, I resemble that little girl with all the dreams, but now my dreams are for my children."

"Well, I'm dreaming of a cheeseburger and French fries." Frankie strode into the Sea Gull from the beach entrance. "It's cold out there. I need something nourishing for my growing body. Got any hot chocolate, Mom?"

"Have you been listening to our conversation, Mr. Smarty Pants?"

"Um, let's see. Something about Mom looking in the mirror and not seeing a little girl anymore," the teenager snidely answered. "Geez Mom, I hope you're not a little kid anymore. That would be kinda sicko."

Frank turned his winsome gaze to Ellie. "Don't you think so, Miss Ellie?"

"In lots of ways, Frankie, your mother and I are still young—at least I am." She flipped her hair and sashayed behind the counter to grab a handful of frozen fries. Placing them in the basket, she lowered it into the bubbling oil. "We're not old, sonny boy, we're in the prime of life."

Rolling her eyes, Pearl added, "I was just talking about being young at heart, my dear. You'll understand when you are older." The door to the cooler creaked as Pearl opened it to retrieve a raw burger patty. Slapping it on the grill she turned the flame higher.

CHAPTER FIFTEEN

Locking the door behind her and turning the sign to closed, Pearl rolled her neck to the side and heard a slight 'pop.' It had been a good day. Most days were good days now.

The lines near her eyes crinkled a bit as she smiled to herself. She liked living at the beach. It was close to work—and the nice thing about that was that work didn't feel like work at all.

So many of the customers were friends or had become friends through the years. Many had been coming to Topsail Island since the late 1940s when it opened for development. Each summer vacation and fishing season brought them back, so that each season was a kind of reunion between she and the tourists.

"How have you been?"

"Did you have a cold winter?"

"Did Joe graduate?"

"Oh, I see you have a new little one now."

172

A relationship had developed between those that worked at the Gull and those who visited each season.

Pearl loved being at the Sea Gull; she liked being there even more than being at home—even more than being at the farm. Everything she wanted was there at the Gull. It offered so much—companionship, fun, food—and the ocean was right out the door.

She thought bringing up her children around the place was good for them. It offered them the chance to socialize, to learn to get along with others—things she felt she had missed out on as a child. They would not be as naïve as she had been.

Summer after summer, fishing season after fishing season, the same people came back, and came back again. The clientele had grown and expanded beyond what Pearl had ever dreamed, and it seemed like she had everything she needed.

In the nearly eight years since opening the doors for business, the reputation of the Sea Gull Restaurant had grown, not just with a larger customer base, but physically as well. The patio area had been rebuilt and extended, and tables were added so that customers could eat outside if they liked; the summer months were especially busy and the inside was so packed that there was no room; the only option was to offer outside dining.

Little by little improvements had been made—a roof over the dining area of the patio, screening in the area, wider stairs to the roadside entrance, a brick fireplace and grill for roasting oysters in the winter months, and more picnic tables outside along with wooden swing sets for children. A lifeguard stand had also been built to provide a feeling of safety for the swimmers. Pride welled inside Pearl as she thought of all that had been accomplished.

Her children were certainly living a different childhood than she had. She had nothing to complain about—hers had been perfect. But for her children she saw a better future and she was delighted by the ease with which they became friends with vacationing children. And she loved the way they took instant pride in being part of the operation of the Gull.

E.J. liked helping Mommy and Aunt Ellie roll silverware.

Josie liked waitressing, and saved all of her tips to buy her own clothes.

Frankie, who usually got off the school bus at Jay's gas station, when he did come to the restaurant, always helped clean the grill and stock the shelves in the back.

Life was good. Pearl was certainly not going to mess things up by getting romantically involved with anyone. Roger had been a lesson.

And though innuendo about her and Jay having feelings for one another abounded amongst her family, she staunchly denied any such thing.

They were not the same people they had been in 1941. Pearl had been so naïve then, so full of dreams and happy endings. Time had proved otherwise, and she had found real love, strong, unshakeable love, with Paul. She told herself that even though she was sorry that Jay had gone through so much hardship, she did not feel that she was the one to ease his pain.

Evidently he had found solace and peace with Feona. Pearl was very happy for him and wished nothing but joy for him and his family.

Still, it only seemed natural to have a friendship with him; he was Frankie's father. But anything more than that she brushed away. He was a married man and from all she could tell, a happily one at that.

Most evenings, if she had been in the kitchen cleaning up after a long day, she'd open the side door and lean against the railing, watching the sun set. Pearl had to admit that those late summers and autumns when the muhly was in bloom she did think of the days when she and Jay were young. Often she felt a stirring, and then, if a red-wing blackbird would trill, it would pull her to a place that made her feel warm and contented.

A time or two Pearl had suspected that Jay would not have dismissed her if she had presented herself. But then again, perhaps he was just looking for someone to understand, especially since his wife's accident. Pearl knew that since then he had seemed a bit sadder than usual. He was going through a difficult time with Feona. But Pearl was not about to get involved in that.

Still she chatted with Jay at the Gulf Station when she stopped for gas, but only light conversation. It seemed he always had his mind on other things when he spoke, as if he was holding something back. But Pearl never questioned it. Over a year ago he had spoken at length with her about his wife's condition. Once again, he had come to her car window as she stopped for gas at the station. His eyes had searched hers as he explained what all the doctor had said.

"A nervous breakdown, huh," Pearl spoke sympathetically. "My old friend, I'm sorry." She held out her hand to touch Jay's and she squeezed it tightly. "I hope she gets better soon."

She thought, *Being at the end of my rope. Wanting to pull my hair out. Screaming until my throat is raw. Denying the truth. Yessirree, I've had that happen before...is that what you call a nervous breakdown. Humm."*

Recalling the conversation, Pearl shook her head, confused with just what sent people over the edge.

She walked over to the juke box and leaned against the chrome exterior, her eyes perused the lists of songs and singers,
"Chantilly Lace...Kisses Sweeter Than Wine...All Shook Up...Chances Are." She liked that tune by Johnny Mathis, and she slipped a coin into the slot and selected it along with *Walkin' After Midnight*, the song by the new singer, Patsy Cline. It played first and Pearl swayed her hips as the alto belted out note after note.

She imagined herself walking down the beach at night, her bare feet being tickled by the waves and sand. The thought brought a smile to her lips, and she followed the thoughts as they led to a mysterious someone who might come into her life.

"Ha ha ha." Laughter trickled from her throat and she found herself on the patio overlooking the ocean; the loud speaker still blared the music. As the tune ended she heard the faint whir of the juke box as it moved along the 45 records for the next selection.

'Chances are if I wear a silly grin...' Johnny Mathis crooned.

Pearl closed her eyes to the silky voice and breathed in the salty air. 'In the moonlight when I sigh, hold me close dear.'

Her eyes still closed, she pictured the stranger she would meet as she walked during midnight, as the previous song suggested; he stood atop the sand dunes and turned. It was Jay.

"No." Pearl rolled her eyes. "No, no, no," she said emphatically.

"No?" A voice from the ocean side of the patio startled Pearl, and a small gasp escaped her lips as Jay stood before her.

"Who are you saying no to?" Jay asked. "I haven't even asked you anything yet."

Pearl fumbled with the words. "I uh, it's, well, I just was, but, now..."

Laughing gently, Jay touched Pearl's shoulder. "Hey. I'm sorry. I didn't mean to interrupt your moment alone. I know after a busy day at work it's nice to get outside and just think or...not think."

He laughed again. "All these romantic songs I hear coming from the loudspeaker—I guess you're thinking of a new boyfriend." His eyes met hers. "Huh?"

Regaining her composure, Pearl grinned, "No not really."

Jay shrugged, "Well, it's none of my business anyway."

Pearl didn't speak; she avoided Jay's eyes as she moved back into the kitchen. She held the door open for him and he followed behind, closing only the screen door.

"I was just walking—had to get out of the house for a while."

Pearl nodded. "Fate...is Fate at home?'

"When I left he and Feona were watching *Walt Disney* on television."

There was silence for a few moments, then Pearl asked, "Is this about Frankie?"

"No, no." Jay moved closer to her, his shoulders slumped a bit. "I really need to talk with you."

Oh my gosh, Pearl thought, *he wants to be with me.*

"Jay, I can't, I mean...you're married."

"What? What are you talking about?"

A puzzled look crossed her face, "I'm sorry, I just thought..."

The corners of his mouth curled a bit as Jay shook his head. "No, no Pearl." He chuckled. "No, I'm sorry if you thought that. I guess I have been acting a bit sheepish the last few months, but other than your father, I haven't felt like I can confide in anyone. I never wanted to bother you with any of this, and believe me—if I would have known that Feona would have...well, problems, I never would have moved back here."

"Confide?" A furrowed brow belied Pearl's confusion, and Jay felt a bit of annoyance in her tone. "What have you been confiding in my father?"

"When things began happening," Jay struggled with the words and closed his eyes, "when things got bad I went to your father. He's the one who told me to take Feona to a psychiatrist."

A knowing look of relief crossed her face as Pearl sighed. "Oh, Daddy has always been the one I can go to. He always keeps a calm head." Pearl moved toward a chair and motioned for Jay to sit.

"Can I make you a cup of coffee?"

"Only if you're making one for yourself."

Rising to turn on the coffee pot, Pearl grabbed a couple of mugs. "Little cream, right?"

Jay nodded, "Yep."

As she stood by the gurgling pot, Pearl examined the man sitting so patiently. She always looked at him when they talked at the gas station, but tonight she saw things that she'd overlooked in those chats. He had a touch of gray near his brow—only on the right side. The scar he had gotten during the war above his eye was dark and thick. Why hadn't she noticed how hard it had become?

They had never *really* talked since he had moved back to the island. There had been an understanding without words—maybe a word or sentence about how to deal with this or that situation, like ideas on how to get Feona more involved in the ladies groups or about Frankie working for him, but nothing too detailed or involved. Everything just seemed to naturally fall into place—as if they were moving along as they should. It seemed that instinctively they knew parameters of their relationship.

Suddenly Pearl realized that the trust was so intrinsic that a part of what they had so long ago had never left. It was evident in the way they communicated about their son. It showed in the way they respected each other's lives.

She looked at him curiously, not as if he were strange, but as if something wonderful had suddenly appeared. The feeling startled her.

"I think the coffee might be ready, Pearl," Jay spoke, capturing her attention. "Never was much of a coffee drinker until I moved here."

Pearl handed the steaming mug to him as she took a sip of her own. "I never liked it either until a few years ago."

"I guess we're getting older, growing up," Jay chuckled. "Isn't that what grown-ups do, drink coffee?"

Pushing Pearl's chair out for her with his foot, Jay sighed. "Well, I hope you don't get upset with what I'm about to ask you, but I really need a woman's point of view."

"I'm listening."

Leaning back in his chair he studied the woman before him. Her arms were crossed across her chest, her brow was furrowed.

"You, Miss Janie, Ellie, everyone has been so much help to me since Feona got hit by the car."

Her mind still trying to wrap around this new feeling inside her, Pearl leaned back in her chair. "Is that when the nervous breakdown happened?"

"I don't know." Jay cocked his head sideways, not understanding why Pearl was bringing that up.

He began again. "It's just that everyone was so nice and helpful, that..."

"When I would go over to your house, sometimes Feona would be very nice and we'd laugh and have a good time. And then other times she was cool toward me and accused me of such horrible things, Jay. I don't understand how a nervous breakdown would cause her to accuse me of stealing and of trying to hurt her."

This is not where he wanted the conversation to go. He had come over tonight to ask Pearl if she would like to help organize a party for Feona's birthday. That was all he wanted. He did not want his wife's condition to be known. Hope was all he had, and his trust in Pearl was tied to that trust. She was the one who might help him get Feona back to normal.

Pearl watched as a sullen look gradually covered Jay's face. "I'm sorry, there's so much I don't understand. I know she had a nervous breakdown and I assume she is doing better." Her eyes questioned Jay's.

Jay's gaze slid to the floor, his mouth tightened. "I didn't come here to talk about my wife's *condition*. I came to ask you if you would get one of those oyster roasts or pig pickings together—I want to try to get Feona out among people. I want her to be happy, to have a good time."

His anger was evident in his tone as he stood to leave.

"Good Lord, I'm so sorry Jay. I don't know what I've been thinking lately."

"The worst." He spat the words as he moved toward the screen door.

"You're right. I'm sorry. Please come and sit back down. I'd be happy to talk with you about a party for Feona. She's had a horrible year and one would really make her feel better."

"She doesn't think any of the women around here like her. She thinks they all make fun of her, and that she was so stupid for walking out in front of that car."

"Why in the world does she think that, Jay?"

Settling back in his chair Jay shrugged. "Beats me. I don't know where she gets half the ideas she comes up with. All I know, Pearl, is that I love her." This time Jay's eyes meet Pearl's. They could have bored holes in her with their intensity.

"I love my wife. She was there for me when I felt my whole world crumbling. I would never hurt her. But after this, well, I don't understand."

Jay continued searching Pearl's eyes. She didn't know how to respond; she didn't know what he wanted from her.

"Jay, I..."

His gaze fell away as he rubbed his hands against his thighs. "There are days when I really don't know who she is."

"Has it been like this ever since she came back from Texas?"

Pausing, Jay closed his eyes. "She never went to Texas."

"What?"

"She never went to Texas. I lied. I didn't want everyone to know that I had checked her into Cherry Hospital."

"Cherry Hospital? Jay, that's where they put crazy people."

"She's not crazy!" Again Jay stood to leave.

"Daggone it, Jay, sit down, talk to me. What is going on?"

"Feona never had a nervous breakdown, Pearl. She has a mental condition."

CHAPTER SIXTEEN

"I think we need to have a pig picking *and* an oyster roast." Ellie pulled an emery board from her apron pocket and began filing her nails as she leaned against the counter. "I mean, it's slow as molasses this time of year and we need to liven things up."

"If we have it here at the Gull we'll just ask everybody to bring a covered dish and we'll do everything outside. It's still nice outside now, and I don't want to have to clean a bunch of mess up inside the restaurant." Lottie stood, her hands on her hips, "You know what will happen if we open those doors and let people into the restaurant. They'll think it's a free for all and won't bother to clean up after themselves. We'll be cleaning till morning. Best if it's outside."

Pearl nodded. "Yeah, you're right, Momma. And Ellie, I think you have a good idea there. It's already January and I haven't had the first oyster." She settled into one of the stools at the counter and swiveled from side to side, "It's not like it used to be, huh? It seems just about every week, back before the island was opened, that someone was having an oyster roast or pig picking. Now, we're lucky to go to one every month or so."

"Will Pike is still playing, isn't he?" Lottie questioned.

"He plays at Pop's nearly every weekend." Ellie cooed.

"I guess that shows how much I get out these days." Lottie fumbled with the bandana holding her hair back. "I just can't do like I used to."

"Oh, Momma." Reaching to stroke her mother's wrinkled hands, Pearl winked. "Momma, you do more than any other seventy-year-old women I know."

Lottie grinned and winked back at her daughter. "Seventy-one, sweetheart, and it won't be much longer and I'll be seventy-two."

"Geez Miss Lottie, you sure do not look your age." Ellie walked near to Lottie, leaned in and hugged her gently. "I never thought I'd ever say this to you, but I think you're a really good lady."

Returning the embrace, Lottie quickly pushed Ellie away. "Enough of this mush around here." She straightened her back and mugged for the two younger women. "We have a feast to plan, and if we're going to do it we better get cracking."

"So this is supposed to be a party for Feona? She hasn't been to any of the pickings, except for that one when she and Jay first moved here. What makes you think she's going to like this?"

"No, no—it's not a party for Feona. Jay just wanted me to get some folks together because he's trying to get Feona to get more interested in the community. He wants her to make friends and quit being by herself so much. I'm just trying to help him out. He says the doctor thinks it would be good for her to be around people and to quit worrying so much about the little things."

"After a nervous breakdown, I'd think she would need some peace and quiet." Ellie pulled a cigarette from her pack and placed it between her lips. "Being around people would be the last thing I'd want to do if I was nervous."

Lottie held a match to light Ellie's Winston. "They're doing all kinds of things these days with people. They've got all kinds of new ideas and medicines. Used to, if you couldn't hold yourself together they threw you in the loony bin."

"Miss Lottie, that reminds me—I went up with my cousin Phil a couple of weeks ago to see Clarence at Dix Hill. Boy oh boy, that was some sight. He had no idea who I was or who Phil was. I don't think he even knew who he was. "

"That surprises me, Ellie. I would have never thought that you would ever want to visit your uncle. It's never been a secret how you feel about him."

"I wouldn't have gone, but Phil had to sign some kind of papers up there and Jay said he was too busy to take him up there again, so he asked me if I'd take him. Said he didn't like driving in the big city. Heck, I drive in Raleigh all the time so it was no big deal to me."

"So Jay's been taking him, huh?"

"Just a couple of times as a favor. Phil said this was the last time he was going, though—said he was done now with the old man and that his conscience was clear—something about making his peace."

Pearl looked questioningly at her mother. "A few Saturdays ago, Frankie worked at the station all day by himself. He said he was glad it was slow, because he'd never had to run the place alone before. I never questioned it."

"So what's the big deal if Jay is driving Phil up to see his father?"

"Nothing," Pearl answered too quickly.

Ellie smashed her Winston into the ashtray and snickered. "You two are so cellophane." Propping her feet up on an adjacent stool she swiveled her legs back and forth. "Y'all are hiding something," Ellie sing-songed.

"I don't know what you're talking about Smelly," Pearl spat.

Changing the subject back to Clarence, Ellie began talking about the one-time trouble maker.

"You wouldn't recognize him."

"What a shame," Pearl sighed.

"Shame, schlame, I still don't feel one bit sorry for that old coot. If you ask me he got what he deserved. But I will tell you that I took no pleasure in watching him—made me kind of sick to even look at him. He was drooling and had this glazed look in his eyes. He's skinny as a rail. They propped him up in the bed so we could talk, but I think I did better by talking to the wall."

"Do you think they're treating him right up there?" Pearl asked.

A sarcastic grin appeared as Ellie slid her eyes to look at Pearl. "Are they treating him right? Now that's a good question." Ellie drew a deep drag from her cigarette, "Right—according to whom. Whose definition are we talking about?"

Pearl rolled her eyes, "We've gone over this before, so I'll just ask you this way—I'll make it easy for you. Would you let your dog stay up there?"

"Well, he gets fed and he doesn't stink, so I guess it's not too bad."

Pearl's fingers tapped across the counter. "So you think he's where he ought to be?"

"Yeah, the place didn't smell bad and I saw others around that seemed okay. I just think Uncle Clarence is gone, baby, gone. Pshew." Ellie's hand pointed to space and she repeated the sound. "Pshew."

A knowing glance passed between Pearl and Lottie.

"Okay, you two. What was that?" Ellie's eyes widened. "I saw that look between y'all. Now what's up?"

"What do you mean, Smelly?" Pearl crossed her arms defensively.

"Ha, you can't fool me Two Shoes, you and your mother have this look between the two of you when you have *a little secret.*"

"Well, if you know it's *a little secret* what makes you think we would share it with you?"

"Ladies, y'all know I'll find out sooner or later." Ellie crinkled her nose and stuck out her tongue. "So why don't you just make it easier on everybody and let me in on your *little secret.*"

Ellie watched the two women, their arms folded as they feigned wide eyed innocence.

"I have no idea what you're talking about," the older woman sucked her teeth. "We're just talking about *your* lunatic uncle."

"Momma, don't be so mean." Pearl reached her hand to touch Ellie's. "Sorry."

As she studied the two women's faces, Ellie unwrapped an unopened pack of cigarettes.

"Haven't you heard? They're saying now that smoking is bad for you." Pearl touched her friend's hand again.

"No, it's not. I saw an ad in *Look* magazine the other day with some doctor smoking a cigarette and he was saying that the ones with filters are fine and dandy...thank you." Ellie held a cigarette between her fingers and smiled.

"Hmmm, don't try to change the subject on me now." She squinted her eyes at the women and paused,

"Ah ha! I've got it. Y'all must think I'm stupid." She looked at her wristwatch. "It took me about five minutes to figure out your little secret."

Pearl and her mother puckered their lips and grimaced.

"What secret is that, smarty pants?" Lottie asked.

"Jay is going to put Feona in the loony bin."

"Nope, Jay would never do that to Feona. I can tell you that for sure."

"Well, it's something to do with Dix Hill or the loony bin and Feona." Ellie pulled her long hair back and twisted it, securing it with a rubber band from around her wrist. "Tell me I'm wrong," she added defiantly.

Exhaling a long breath, Pearl calmly spoke. "You're wrong, Ellie. Jay would never do that."

"Maybe he should. She has always acted a little strange." Satisfied that she was on the right track, Ellie continued, "It's something to do with this nervous breakdown, something else is going on. But for right now, I'll drop it. Okay?"

"Yes," Pearl agreed. "Let's drop it and just concentrate on planning this party for Feona. Let's try to do something nice for her. She has been through a lot. Jay has been through a lot. *Okay?*"

"Humph," Ellie pouted. Thinking, as she discussed plans with her friends, that Pearl was the same old Pearl she had always been—acting like she always did— like nothing was going on when it was so obvious that something was.

190

CHAPTER SEVENTEEN

Will Pike stood at the corner of the patio holding his fiddle tightly against his chin. He plucked its strings with his middle finger, listening as the notes rang out. A young woman stood by his side; she too held a violin.

Listening as he tuned the instrument, she followed his lead and after a few moments the two together slid their bows across the strings introducing the first notes of *Nobody's Darlin' but Mine*.

Dropping the instrument to his side, Will smiled as he nodded to the audience.

"It looks like ol' Jess and Lottie have outdone themselves this time. Couldn't ask for a prettier view than this, as my daughter Sassy plays with me tonight."

Will explained that although it was an old song, it was his daughter's and her beau Phil's favorite one.

"Ever since she was knee high she's loved this song, and I do believe it was the first one she learned. I'm right proud of my Sassy, and I hope you folks will enjoy this evening as we play a little music with our friends Enid, George and Jimmy." Smiling from ear to ear, Will Pike leaned into the microphone. "Oh yeah, forgot to tell you, my little gal likes to sing, so I hope you brought your earplugs." Will moved away from the mike and guffawed.

"Oh, Daddy." His daughter blushed and looked to her left where Phil sat watching her.

Enid laughed aloud and strummed harder on his guitar as the other men in the band nodded their heads in good-hearted fun.

Will lifted the violin to his chin once again, and drew the bow across the strings as he joined in rhythm with his daughter.

Sitting at one of the tables was Enid's wife, Bella; she bounced her youngest child on her knee while the band warmed up.

"Come lay by my side little darlin'," Sassy sang thinly. *"Come lay your hand on my brow."* She sashayed over to Phil and flounced her skirt. He looked up at her, obviously pleased and proud of his soon-to-be wife's singing voice.

Everyone around the patio seemed to be having a good time. Many sat at the tables that had been moved against the walls of the Gull to make room for those who wanted to dance. But many mingled near the stairway that led to the beach.

From the grill came the pungent smell of roasting pork. Just the other side of the patio, another grill, a make-shift grill, made of cinderblocks, held a pile of merkle bushes; they crackled and glowed. As oysters in burlap sacks were placed on them, a hissing and sizzling noise burst forth.

Above the sizzle and laughter rose the words of the song; *"Be nobody's darlin' but mine, love. Be honest, be faithful be kind.*

Jay had never forgotten the words. He did not want to be reminded of them now. The song had been his and Pearl's song so long ago.

No, he thought as he moved his arm to around his wife's shoulders. She looked up at him, her eyes wide— and then he saw the scowl on her face. She pulled away and set her gaze on the burning merkle bushes.

Pearl watched as Jay dropped his head and sighed.

"And I'd rather be somebody's darlin', than a poor boy that nobody knows."

What was that she felt pulling? An invisible tug like the sea behind her was drawing her to forgotten places. As she leaned against the railing, something from the past called. It was so recognizable, yet not recognizable at all. She too listened to the words of the song that had played the night that Jay had been called to war.

Jay turned his head to meet her gaze and he felt numbness consume his body.

Pearl's lips parted and her hand rose to her throat as she felt a flush of heat move from her chest to her face. A tiny sigh left her lips as if to release something that had been bottled up inside. All at once she felt the ocean breeze move across her body and she saw that same breeze tousle Jay's dark hair.

It seemed like such a long time that they held each other's gaze, though it must have been only seconds; Will Pike screeched his bow against the strings as the tune played on and Sassy began repeating the last verse of the song. *"And I'd rather be somebody's darlin' than a poor boy that nobody knows."*

It was in his face...in his eyes...the sadness could be seen even in the way he held himself. Jay dropped his eyes to his wife and rubbed the side of her shoulder even though there was no response from Feona.

He turned again to look at Pearl; she had never quit looking at him.

Now it was plain as day; Pearl saw his pain and disappointment. Surely he was hurting from not only their lost love but from the absence of it with Feona.

At that moment Pearl knew she wanted to offer her love to Jay, though she did not know how—and she did not know what all it would mean. Still, there it was; it had to be. Perhaps it had all been destiny. Their love was meant to be since the first time they met in 1940, when everything was so young and innocent and beautiful.

Ashamed of her feelings, she turned away from Jay and his wife and looked at Phil, who was rapt in watching his fiancé sing and sway for the one she loved. It reminded her of she and Jay, but there was also something that reminded her of her time with Paul. *Our love...its peace...its belonging.* She smiled broadly, *Oh, where is all the magic coming from*, she thought as she closed her eyes and let the smells and sounds of the night encompass her. Turning toward the ocean Pearl opened her eyes; a thin lace of white foam edged the incoming tide; the rolling water sparkled with flecks of moonlight. Above, the stars twinkled; she could feel the salty breeze as it tickled the hairs on her arms.

"Hey Pearly White," Ellie rubbed up against her friend. "I've been watching you."

"And?"

"I know what you're thinking." Ellie flipped her hair to the side and leaned against the railing.

Pearl smiled, "I don't care." She searched Ellie's face. "What makes you think you're right about it?"

"I know I have been wrong about some things, and I know I can do the wrong things." Raising an eyebrow Ellie threw back her head and tittered gently. Leaning in so as not to be heard, she whispered to Pearl. "I know a lot about what goes on below the waist, Pearly."

Another song had begun and the crowd of people raised their voices and clapped as *Kisses Sweeter than Wine* rang out. Sassy belted the tune, surprising the crowd that she could also sing strong and raspy.

Pearl stepped on the first step of the stairway that led to the beach. She looked at Ellie and gestured for her to follow.

They walked silently for a short time, both having removed their shoes, leaving them at the stairway bottom step.

"I don't know why in the world I keep calling you Pearly White when you have set your sights on a married man." Ellie moved in front of Pearl and walked backwards along the shoreline. Facing her, she smirked. "Goody Two..."

"Shut up! Shut up! I've not been doing any such thing. Jay and I are friends—that's what I want us to be—just friends. Can't you get that through your thick head?"

"Then what was that I saw pass between the two of you? It sure as hell wasn't gas."

A laugh fell from Pearl's lips and she shook her head. "Ellie, I don't know what in the world it was—and no, it wasn't gas. My lord, you have always had a way of *describing* things. But you are right, something did pass between us. We do have a son that we share. We were once in love—but gee whiz, Ellie. We were so young, so naïve."

Reaching out to grab Ellie's arms, Pearl stopped and stood face to face with her friend. "If he had not come back here..." she stopped and looked skyward. "If Paul had not died... if Feona were well."

"My daddy always said "if" was a big word."

Pearl nodded and released Ellie; they continued walking toward the old officers' club where now a new fishing pier stood—Barnacle Bill's. "But all those things happened and I've come to understand that I can't change a darn thing that happened in the past. All I can do is move forward and be the best mother, the best daughter...the best friend I can be."

"Oh God, you're getting religious, aren't you?"

"I don't know. I hardly go to church at all. Miss Janie or Miss June picks the kids up every Sunday. But one thing I do know is that I have no alternative. There is no other way for me, Ellie. I have to reach out to Jay. He is miserable, and he has no one to talk to."

"Then he needs to find some male friends."

Pearl pondered the suggestion. "Maybe. Maybe that is what he needs."

"But that is not what he wants, Pearly. He wants you."

"Oh, wonderful! What is it about him and me? It seems that we are destined but at the same time doomed."

"If you get involved with him, what do you think it would do to your parents?"

"I think Daddy would have another heart attack."

"And what do you think it would do for your reputation around here?"

It was quiet for several seconds, then Pearl answered. "I have no idea. But it would not be good for the kids."

"I've never had a good reputation around here or anywhere I've lived, Pearly. So my flirting and occasional 'messing around' is, well, sort of accepted. I guess I'm just not expected to be put up on a pedestal. But you, well, you may have fallen a bit when you got married early to Paul. But no one ever doubted that Frankie was Paul's. You still are held high on that pedestal. "

Pearl nodded and reached down to grab a sand dollar.

"You have a long way to fall. It could hurt you in more ways than one."

"I'm tired of being on that pedestal."

"Roger tried to pull you down."

"Yeah, but that was my fault. All I had to say to him was 'no' and that would have been the end of it."

"If y'all had been carrying on right here on the island I think the jig would have been up. But you were out there on the farm where nobody could see you."

"Yes, I did try to keep it hidden—not one of my best moments." Fumbling with the sand dollar, Pearl shook her head, "I still can't believe I was so stupid—geez, he was such a jerk."

"You know he's gone back to working at The Ark in Jacksonville? I can't believe he is his age and still flipping burgers."

"What's wrong with flipping burgers?"

"Not a thing. It's just that he had his sights set on flipping his *own* burgers—not somebody else's."

"Right once again, Ellie. Even Momma tried to tell me he was after the Sea Gull."

The two had reached Barnacle Bill's Fishing Pier and restaurant; like the Sea Gull it was closed for the season. Still, lights glared from the corners of the building and from the end of the pier. Picnic tables sat facing the ocean there too, and Ellie and Pearl sat on one of the benches facing the big plate glass windows of the building.

"I was surprised that the Dine-a-Shore Restaurant didn't hurt our business at the Gull."

"Well, they get mostly fishermen from the pier and we get more young folks." Pearl shrugged.

"They're getting a lot of the people who come in the summer, too," Ellie spoke slowly.

Shrugging again, Pearl spoke. "But I think we have enough tourists to go around. We're about a mile away and...

"Oh my goodness, we need to start heading back." Pearl rose and grabbed her friend's hand. She looked north toward the Gull; she could hear the faint sounds of music and laughter echoing across the sand.

"I don't think they even missed us," Ellie snickered.

Pearl did not answer. Her mind was on Jay and Feona. Surely he had noticed her absence. "But Feona," Pearl began...but all she could think of was having left, not being there to help Jay. She should have been making some kind of effort to help Feona enjoy the gathering. She should have been talking with her, something, anything—Jay was counting on her.

"His wife is not your responsibility."

Pearl did not respond to Ellie's comment.

"What do you plan on doing? Just tell me how you plan on befriending Feona *and* being Jay's lover?"

Pearl's toes grabbed the sand as she broke into a run. The hard packed sand stung the soles of her feet as they pounded against it. *Damn you, damn you,* she thought as she ran. The cool night air was chilly, still she broke a sweat as she ran, her lungs burned as she breathed heavily.

199

In the distance she heard Ellie call out her name but she did not stop. She felt her hair sticking to her forehead and sides of her face as she neared the Gull and slowed her pace.

There sat Feona, still gazing into the burning merkle bush embers, exactly as she had been when Pearl has left. She scanned the crowd, *where was Jay,* she thought, then she heard his voice.

"I don't give a damn what you think. I'd have to respect you for that."

He sounded angry and Pearl felt anxious as she neared the stairs hoping that no trouble had started. Topping the stairs she noticed a small crowd had gathered in the corner near the band; Jay stood there, hunched over, his broad shoulders heaving as he breathed heavily.

Pearl walked closer, but stopped next to Feona and sat down next to her. Taking Feona's hand, she patted it. "Everything is going to be okay," Pearl smiled, then rose and made her way closer to where Jay stood; he still hovered over the man who lay sprawled on the floor.

Surprised by the feeling of her heart welling with pride, Pearl stifled a smile and instead feigned a stern and concerned look. She shook her head, "Tsk, what is he doing here?"

Bella Abbott leaned in to whisper. "You should have seen it! That man that used to work for you came walking up the stairs, drunk as a skunk and started calling out your name, then Ellie's name. Jay got up and tried to talk to him quietly but that man just got louder."

Pearl's lips pursed and she grew angry. Still she kept calm. "Did you hear anything else?"

"He said something about thinking that he shouldn't have gotten fired back then—that he wanted his job back...and then some things were said that I couldn't make out; that's when Jay punched him in the face."

Pearl was glad her parents were not there to see the spectacle. It would have really upset her father, who had been ailing lately. He certainly did not need any more excitement in his life.

The music had stopped and Enid, Will and George had gathered Roger and were taking him out to the front of the building, where he would either sleep off his drunk or endeavor to drive home. Stretch Morrison would probably follow him back to Verona in his squad car, or he'd make sure Roger crawled into the back seat of his Rambler.

Pearl was glad to see him go; she certainly did not need him hanging around reminding her of her indiscretions. Why in the world he hung around the area was beyond her. Roger seemed to have no scruples or sense of integrity and only bad could come from having him involved in her life in any way at all.

As the musicians returned from depositing their load, Pearl caught Jay's gaze. He looked irritated but in control as he raised an eyebrow and shook his head.

"Sit with Feona for a few minutes while I go and talk to Jay," she whispered to Bella.

Bella nodded. "Sure thing, honey. I never did like that ol' Yankee you had working here. He always acted like his poop didn't stink."

Pearl laughed lightly and grinned. "Sometimes you just don't know about people until you *know* about people. He sure had me fooled—guess I should have listened to my momma and daddy."

Giggling, Bella nodded and walked to Feona's side. She too reached for the woman's hand as she sat beside her. She looked to Pearl and raised her brows in sympathy.

Pearl nodded back as the musicians began strumming their instruments. Already the intruder seemed to be forgotten as the music began. Will pulled his bow across the strings introducing his most favorite tune, *The Orange Blossom Special*. It never got old and always brought the crowd to their feet. Pearl moved in closer to where the band played and looked gratefully into Will's eyes. She smiled, and Will winked an understanding look in return. Pearl mouthed a thank you and turning, she bumped directly into Jay. "Oh," Searching for her composure she started. "Sorry that had to happen."

"Don't even give it a second thought." Jay rubbed his swollen and torn knuckles. "Man, that jackass has a jaw like a rock."

"I heard some of what he was doing, but you tell me—just what happened to make you hit him?" She looked up into his eyes—waiting.

"I sort of remember him from back during Camp Davis—not much. I just know he was a show-off, acted like he was better than anybody. He was always walking around puffed up like he was important. He had a reputation for...being with young girls and..." Jay caught himself and turned away.

"I know," Pearl sighed.

"I know about you and him. I don't blame you, and I don't judge you. Times were hard—I'll leave it at that."

Changing the subject quickly, Pearl gestured toward Feona who, though sitting next to Bella, still sat mesmerized by the burning merkle bushes.

How odd, thought Pearl.

"I don't think this was a very good idea."

"I wouldn't say that, Jay. I think everybody had a good time, and the fight kind of added a little excitement to the night," she tittered.

He agreed, nodding and chuckling. "Yep, the band is wonderful, everyone is having a good time. The food is delicious and..."

"Sorry about Feona, Jay. I wish I could tell you what to do—I wish I could help you with her." Her eyes held concern and sympathy for Jay but she turned them away quickly to observe Bella as she sat next to Jay's wife.

Pearl nodded to Bella and in response Bella shrugged and raised her hand in a modest wave.

Jay leaned into Pearl and taking her arm, guided her to a table near the beach railing. "When I was a kid growing up in Donna, down in Texas, there was a man and his wife that lived across the road from us. I always wondered why that man was always sitting on his porch rocking and looking so forlorn."

Pearl listened intently as Jay continued.

"He always looked so sad, but when I would pass by his house, he'd always wave and smile to me. Every once in a blue moon he would offer to play catch if he saw me in my front yard. Sometimes he'd holler something funny to me from his porch. But usually he would be sitting in his rocker looking like he bore the weight of the world.

"I hardly ever saw his wife, but when I did, she'd be just as nice as could be. A few times she acted strange though, and once she grabbed me and told me that people from Belgium were visiting her at night and scraping the paint off the walls in her room. She said that her husband kept them locked in the cellar during the day."

"What?" A puzzled look crossed Pearl's face and she didn't know whether to laugh or frown.

Shrugging, Jay gave a half-hearted laugh and continued. "I was just a kid, and this lady had never said anything like that to me before. And her husband was always so nice, so I went to my parents. My mother told me to forget it, that they were just odd people and to leave them alone. But my dad told me that the lady was sick, that she had a disease in her brain and that I should be nice to her."

CHAPTER EIGHTEEN

"Why? Why can't I kiss that boy? There's nothing wrong with him. I've seen him around the beach." Monroe stood perplexed as Nadine Abbott pulled her into the kitchen, away from the young teens sitting cross legged on the floor. "His daddy fixed our sewer last fall."

Nadine Abbott sighed and rolled her eyes. "In the first place I didn't even ask you to play with us—you're way too old and..."

"Your momma asked me to chaperone y'all to make sure you behaved yourselves..."

"I don't need chaperoning and I wished you'd never come. Why in the world do you want to play spin the bottle with us for anyway? You graduated high school with my sister Gloria."

Sarah Butler walked into the kitchen and grabbed both girls. "You two need to hush, now. Wade can hear you." She jerked hard on Monroe's cashmere sweater.

"You are too old to be playing kissing games with us; you're eighteen years old, Monroe."

Monroe smoothed the wrinkled sweater; her hands gliding softly over her waist and hips. "That kid there," she nodded toward a tall blond boy sitting next to Wade; he winked and smiled broadly. "That's the kid who wanted me to play and I had no idea that he was only fourteen years old."

"He's not, he's sixteen. He flunked first and fourth grade, but holy moly, Monroe, it just ain't right for you to play kissing games with us."

"Well, if he's sixteen I'll kiss him instead of Wade." She crinkled her nose and winked. "Wade is only fourteen, right? But his feelings will be hurt if I didn't kiss him." Genuine concern filled her voice as she leaned over to search the group of teens seated on the floor.

"I know Miss Bella wants you to watch us, but I'm sure she didn't want you to be trying to kiss the boys."

Monroe tossed her long wavy locks and placed her hands on her hips. "He sure is cute for sixteen," she winked back at the boy and licked her lips. "I sure wouldn't have minded if the bottle would have landed on him." She grimaced once again at the two girls admonishing her. "What's his name?"

Sarah and Josie rolled their eyes.

"Why don't you just go on home. Momma and Daddy ought to be back from the New Year's party pretty soon." Nadine stood next to her friends; they all glared at Monroe.

"Glad to." Monroe's hips swiveled past the group of young teens sitting on the floor; the blond haired boy stood to follow her.

"Bobby!" Nadine called out. "It's not even twelve o'clock yet. It's not 1960 yet!"

Sarah put her arm around Nadine. "Let him go, honey. If he likes her then, he ain't good enough for you."

Nadine wiped away her tears while Josie turned her attention to the record player and changed the 33 rpm album of Pat Boone to a 45 rpm—Neil Sedaka's *Oh Carol*.

Josie grabbed Wade's hand and pulled him up. "Let's dance."

Most of the other teens joined in, though Nadine stood talking with Sarah about how cruel it was for Monroe to steal the boy she liked.

The evening continued until nearly twelve thirty, when Enid and Bella walked in the front door, each wearing a brightly-colored party hat and blowing a party favor.

"Happy New Year! Happy 1960!" The couple hollered out in unison. Enid called his daughter Nadine to his side and hugged her tightly. "My best girl, the best girl in the world." He looked to his son, who was sitting alone by the unlit Christmas tree. "Boy, I love you too." He looked around the room. "Where's my Gloria? And Arlo?"

"Come on, Enid, let's go on to bed." Bella bent to kiss her husband's head. "We've had too much fun tonight."

Protesting as she pulled him along, Enid could be heard, as the two moved toward their bedroom. "I'm going oystering tomorrow whether or not you like it, hear me, woman."

"Yes, dear." Bella replied.

"Now I mean it, sugar, whether or not you like it."

"Yes, dear."

"And I ain't taking no for no answer, ya hear me?"

"Yes, dear."

Nadine heard her father walking back up the hall, and his slurred words. "You kids need to get on home now. You that's walking, don't fall in the ditch. And those that got your mom or dad picking you up, don't fall in the ditch—uh—no—said that—don't, well..."

"Come to bed, Enid," Bella beckoned.

"Yes dear."

****

"Can you believe it's 1960," Rawl West leaned close to his wife, nuzzling her neck. "I tell you, old Bart Ralston can near about make liquor as good as old Clarence used to."

Francis giggled softly as she held her husband's body close to her own. "You think he got the recipe from him?"

"Or old Clarence came back from the grave to make a new brew," Rawl laughed. "But that was one of the best parties I've been to in ages."

"Miss Williams sure knows how to throw a party, and she really is nice. She's fixed the Mermaid Bar up real nice, with all those glass globes hanging from the

208

fishnets and those paper lanterns. It looks real nice in her place."

"Yep, sure does. I like that old broad."

****

Phil Rosell put his arm around his new wife, Sassy. "How's it feel to be Mrs. Rosell?"

Sassy threw herself into Phil's arms and kissed him long and deep. Caressing his face, she looked deeply into his eyes as she drew her hand to her throat. It was warm, as was her whole body. She pulled Phil close to her again. "Paw said that I better make my wedding day a date to remember, he's always forgetting him and maw's anniversary." She giggled and kissed Phil quickly on the lips. "Now you don't have any reason to forget the first day of the year, 1960."

"No sirree." Phil picked up his bride and walked through the door of their new home.

****

"I can't believe it's 1960," As he laid down on the quilted mattress, Leon snuggled up against his wife, Carla. Been a pretty good year fishing. I think I'll build you a sewing room."

"No need to. Donny will be grown and out the house in a couple years."

"I'm building myself a sewing room then, how 'bout that?"

"Suit yourself. But I could sure use a place to put my fabric and sewing machine."

"You're plum ornery. You know that?"

"Ain't that the pot calling the kettle black?"

Leon rubbed his arthritic fingers. "Humph."
He rolled closer to Carla and kissed her cheek. "Night dear."

****

Art Finley shut the door as silently as he could, took off his shoes and padded across the linoleum of his living room. A dim light filtered from beneath his bedroom door. "Damn," he whispered.

June Finley laid the book she was reading in her lap, "Happy New Year," she spoke sarcastically.

"Happy 1960," Art answered as he crawled beneath the covers of one of the matching twin beds.

******

Jordan and Tillie Butler and Ron and Janie Butler Burns sat gathered around the kitchen table. Tillie yawned. "I just can't believe it's 1960."

"Me neither," her husband Jordan added.

"Like I was saying earlier, cousin, we need to pull the rest of those old trucks out of the warehouse so it won't interfere with the boys playing basketball." Jordan took another sip of the iced tea before him.

"Nobody's got hurt yet." Ron responded.

"Our boys and the others around here sure do like going there." Jordan paused for a moment and scratched his ear. "So, what do you think?"

Ron nodded his head. "Alright, I'll set it up on Monday." He took a sip from the tumbler before him, "I still can't believe it's 1960."

"It'll be that for a whole year, cousin."

"Yep."

Pearl stood at the door of Josie's and E.J.'s bedroom. She could hear her youngest daughter's light breath as she breathed slowly, in and out. Josie was out with friends, though it was nearly two in the morning.

She didn't worry about her daughter; she trusted her and thought to herself how wonderful a childhood her daughter was having. There were so much more things to do than when she had been a teen. Josie was even a cheerleader at Topsail School, something that she would have never had the nerve to even try out for when she was young.

Josie was always in a happy mood and had lots of friends with whom she enjoyed all kinds of activities. She went to the movies in Wilmington just about every weekend, and she attended dances and sock hops at the school. Now, she knew her daughter was out having a good time. More than likely she was out with her friends collard stealing. Pearl laughed to herself, remembering how as a teen she wanted go with Paul, Ellie and Phil while they drove their cars—lights turned off—to farms and silently raided their collard fields. It seemed like so much fun. It was the one activity, other than going to the banks for picnics, that she really enjoyed. Her farm had been victim to several collard raids, and she recalled how casually her parents accepted the prank.

She remembered Mrs. Sarah Burns bringing over a big bowl of collards one evening and remarking, "I think these came out of your garden last night. Cooked them up and they turned out pretty good."

Pearl remembered how they had laughed about it, and how she had reminded her mother how collard stealing was all in fun.

When her parents had visited earlier in the day, she and the children had enjoyed a bowl of collards and black-eyed peas—a staple for every New Year's—it was bad luck not to have them on New Year's.

Shutting the door to the girl's bedroom she moved past Frank's; faint snoring escaped from behind the closed door.

He would be joining the Navy by the end of the month. She was sure that his decision had been influenced by Jay, and she was a bit angry with him about it. But she recalled how Jay had explained it to her. "It was peace time," Jay had said. "A good time to get serving one's country out of the way. And it would offer Frank a chance to see the world, and afterwards he could go to college on the GI bill."

Yes, it was a good idea. But thoughts of her baby boy leaving home tore at her heart.

Her father always had the right words, and when she related her feeling his response was, "a good momma bird teaches her babies to fly."

Pearl could not argue with that, and she made up her mind not to cry, not to act unhappy, but to support her son in every way.

Pulling her legs beneath her as she sat in the big soft chair she had bought at Boom Town, Pearl brought a steaming cup of hot chocolate to her lips. It tasted sweet and it warmed her. Closing her eyes she felt secure and proud of herself, her children and the thriving business she had built. Life had been good.

"I can't believe it's 1960." She placed the cup of chocolate on the end table and pulled her robe closer around her body. "Twenty years," she sighed. "Twenty years ago this fall; it will be twenty years since I met Jay."

****

Lying in bed, Jay turned his body to lay on the left side. Maybe he could go to sleep, but he had been thinking about the year it was and what it meant. *It had been nearly twenty years since he had come to area— since he had met Pearl.*

The light from Feona's bedside table flickered on. "What's the matter, drink too much booze tonight?"

Jay didn't answer as he heard his wife adjust the pillow on her bed. "So this is it, 1960." Feona scoffed at the thought. "Here I am in beautiful Surf City, Topsail Island, and it's the middle of winter, cold and damp as hell. 1960, it's going to be a hell of a year."

Jay held his hand out to grab hold of Feona's. "Dear, we could have gone to a party tonight if you would have liked."

"I think *you* had enough for both of us."

Ignoring the accusation Jay restrained from the inclination to disagree. "We could have gone out, dear. You would have had a good time. These people..."

"These people around here are strange. I don't like them and they don't like me. And besides, all they do is drink. I'm sick of seeing drunken people and I can't stand people who drink."

"A beer now and then doesn't make someone a drunk."

"The last time you went to the Mermaid Bar you came home drunk."

"I wasn't drunk."

"You smelled like a beer factory."

I will not get angry, I will not get angry, Jay thought as he listened to his wife.

Today had been a bad day. She had complained about one thing or another since the time she woke up. He wondered if she had been taking her medication.

"I'm not going to argue with you, dear. It's past both of our bedtimes and I have to open up the station tomorrow." Jay looked at the clock on the wall and corrected himself. "I have to open the station in four hours."

"Don't expect me to make you breakfast."

Jay turned his back to his wife and pulled the cover over himself tightly.

"You heard me, didn't you?"

"If you get much louder, you're going to wake up Fate."

He heard her muttering under her breath as she turned out her bedside lamp. In a few minutes he heard her raspy breathing. Closing his eyes, Jay prayed silently, *please let this be a good year for my family."*

214

The hardwood flooring felt cold on Lottie's feet as she made her way to the kitchen. She'd had a difficult time trying to find sleep this night, as she still felt consumed by the excitement of visiting with her daughter and grandchildren earlier in the day.

Maybe a hot bowl of grits will hit the spot, Lottie thought as she filled a pot with water and turned on the gas stove.

Pouring the grits into the bubbling water, she stirred slowly then lowered the heat. Still stirring she reminisced about the day. Oh, how her grandchildren were growing. It made her happy to see them so healthy and carefree. And Frankie, well, he had turned into such a handsome young man. He did have Jay's eyes and his thick dark hair, but he had the facial features of a Scaggins. They had lucked out there. If it had been otherwise, there would have been no fooling the community.

Sometimes she wondered about that; if they really had fooled those folks who had been around in those days, nearly twenty years ago. Did Bella or Enid know the truth? If they did, they had never given an inkling as to it.

But would they have? She knew there were some secrets in the community that were simply accepted. She knew there were babies conceived out of wedlock—most just laughed about that—the "early arrivals."

There were a few things, like Ray Lloyd's drinking problem, that was frowned on, but because Ray was usually such a loving and giving father and member of the town, it was overlooked, never mentioned—simply accepted as one might accept diabetes or a club foot.

Was that how Frankie was accepted? Lottie had often pondered these questions. But she could not deny that the arrangement with him and Jay had turned out well. Frankie had been working for Jay for nearly five years. They had grown close and she knew that despite his encouragement for the boy to join the Navy, Jay was simply encouraging his son to do what he thought was best for him.

Josie had turned out well, too. She was a blossoming young woman, more mature than Pearl had been at the age of fourteen.

Maybe we did shelter her too much, she thought.

Still, Lottie was mighty proud of her daughter, and the way she had taken over the Sea Gull Restaurant after Paul's death and made it such a success. She was proud, too, of how Pearl had conducted her personal life. *Well, Roger,* she thought with a frown. But that had been years ago. Now Pearl was over all the pain in her life and was moving forward.

Lottie did hope that someday her daughter would meet another man and fall in love. She was simply too young to live alone and she had so many years ahead of her that could be filled with love and joy. The children would be grown and gone in a few years.

"Ah, Emma Jewel, E.J.—our little princess." Reaching for a bowl from the cabinet, Lottie shook her head, recalling the last time she had seen her youngest granddaughter. She had been lying on the back porch of the apartment building Pearl and her family owned, and she was stroking a hairy stray dog that had wandered into their lives only a few weeks before. Nursing at its teats were six puppies, which E.J. bragged she had helped deliver into the world.

"She just came up on the porch, Granny, and laid down right in front of me and started having puppies. I helped pull the first one out of her and the second. And she let me do it, Granny. She's just a poor old tired dog."

E.J. had laid her head against Julie and closed her eyes, telling the dog she loved her.

"Y'all get in here and sit at the table with Grandpa and Granny," hollered Pearl to her children. "And be sure to wash your hands."

Lottie loved her little granddaughter, and she knew she spoiled her with too much sugary treats and allowed her many more freedoms than she had with Pearl.

Pearl. Lottie's mind drifted back to Pearl...and Jay. She had become used to him living on the island and it seemed he had not interfered in her daughter's life, but lately there had been little things that made her question just what was between the two. An affair with a married man would simply not be tolerated by either she or her husband, and Lottie was sure that Pearl understood that. "I will not allow that to happen."

Pulling a chair out from under the kitchen table, Lottie sat and dipped her spoon into her bowl of creamy grits.

"1960, I think this is going to be a good year." From the bedroom she heard her husband, Jess, call out, "You up eating again, sweetie?"

"No."

"Yes, you are. You're going to get fat, old woman. What do I want with a fat old woman?"

"The same thing you want with a thin old woman." Lottie chuckled loudly. "Go to sleep, sweetie, I'll be in as soon as I finish my grits."

A few more spoonfuls and Lottie finished her food and placed the bowl in the sink. She ran water over it and left it for the next day's chores—something she would have never thought of doing even five years ago. But at the age of nearly seventy-three, she figured she could relax about tidiness; after all she'd been chief, cook and bottle washer nearly her entire life.

Turning off the kitchen light, Lottie slowly moved into the breezeway. It was cool but not bad for the first day of January. She wrapped her robe closed and tied the belt. She could hear Jess snoring lightly from their bedroom as she gazed into the starry night sky.

"1960. Oh my goodness how time flies." A chill ran through her and she rubbed her feet against the legs of her pajamas. "All the things that have happened in these years." She closed her eyes. "Thank you Lord," she whispered. Opening them, her yard looked like something one would see in a book of fairytales, with the trellis and flower bed, all devoid of any vegetation, but still magical in the moonlight. The clank of the boats at the dock added music to the scene before her, and it came alive as she pictured the numerous pig pickings and oyster roasts there, the games she had played with her daughter and grandchildren, the horses tied at the post no longer there, and the sight of destruction Hurricane Hazel had left as she passed through.

She heard Jess as he moved to his side in bed. "Be in soon," she said quietly, as if not to wake him if he was asleep.

She worried about him, this man that had been with her since her teen years. He had always been there for her—always her rock, always making things right or palatable. How could she make it in life without him? She could not imagine going on if her beloved Jess was not by her side.

He had not been feeling well lately and she worried that his time was near. Lottie sat in a rocking chair and let the ache leave her body. She had never dealt well with loss, and the thought of losing her husband brought back those feelings that had drowned her in her youth. The children she had miscarried and the loss of her only son, Billy. Even after all these years, these decades, she wanted to scream at the thought of that loss. She closed her eyes and rocked, tears streaming down her cheeks.

"Sweetie? What's wrong? Why are you crying?" Jess stooped to caress his wife's swollen cheeks; he kissed her eyes and held her head close to his body.

"Oh, nothing, just thinking of the year and getting sentimental, I guess." Lottie wiped her tear stained face with the sleeve of her robe. "I'm just a big old baby. Old—big." Lottie patted her tummy."

"We've all put on a few pounds over the years. But I tell you one thing, my dear; you still have a figure to beat the band—now, tell me what you're crying about."

"Oh, you'll just laugh at me. You'll just say something like you always do."

Jess pulled the other rocking chair beside Lottie's. He smoothed her unruly hair and kissed her lips gently. "I love you, I've always loved you and I love pulling your chain...and you love pulling mine. Now, tell me what are you crying about."

"YOU! I'm crying about *you.*" Tears streamed down Lottie's cheeks. "I can't stand the idea of living my life without you, you old buzzard."

"What makes you think I'm going anywhere?"

"You've been weak lately, you haven't been feeling like your old self, you aren't eating like you should. That's what. That's why."

A scowl crossed Jess's face as he leaned back in the rocker. He removed his hand from Lottie's and blew a long breath from his lips. Turning to look at her, he wiped a tear from his cheek.

"I ain't going to live forever, sweetie. Neither are you. We're both in our seventies—that's old, Lottie.

We're old. Neither one of my parents lived past sixty-five."

"My momma lived to be seventy-one."

"Well, you know what I mean."

"And my granny lived on up into her eighties."

"You always got to argue, don't you?"

"Sorry, dear. I've just had this feeling lately. And you know it scared me back when you had your heart attack, but not like this. Back then I *knew*, for some reason that you were going to be okay."

"Are you telling me that you're having some kind of premonition—some kind of omen—an owl hoot in the wrong tree or something?"

Lottie threw back her head and laughed aloud, "Lordy, Jess. I guess I'm just all amazed that it's 1960. Who would have thought that we would have lived to see 1960 and television and airplanes that go around the world and cars that..."

"It is amazing, I'll agree—scares me sometimes too, all the new-fangled contraptions. Enid's got something on that new car of his called power steering—makes it real easy to turn. And Carl has a pacemaker, you know." Looking at his wife reassuringly, Jess patted her hand. "You see, if my heart gets bad I can always get one of those things put in my chest to make my heart beat— just like Carl, whose got to be close to eight years older than me—hell, he'll probably live to be a hundred."

"Sorry, I guess I just worry too much. I worry about you and your health."

"What will be will be."

Lottie wrinkled her nose and grinned recalling the song by the same name sung by Doris Day. She sang the chorus, "*Whatever will be, will be. The future's not ours to see, que cera cera.*"

"It's in the Lord's hands, sweetie." Jess leaned against his wife and nuzzled her hair. "You still smell as sweet as you always did. And I'll tell you another thing. I feel pretty good—pretty frisky." He winked and nodded toward the bedroom."

"Really? You know how long it's been since we did that?"

"Few months?"

"A year?"

"Not that long, sweetie."

"Then you've been dreaming about it."

"I always dream about you. The love of my life."

The couple rocked a few more quiet minutes then Jess spoke.

"Do you know why I married you?"

"'Cause my daddy would have blown your head off if you hadn't."

"That too...but why do you think I wanted to marry you?"

Before Lottie could answer, Jess continued.

"I loved you from the moment I saw you. And I saw you from afar. You were helping your daddy pull in on the seine. You had that look on your face—that determined look, like nothing in the world was going to stop you from what you had to do."

222

"Well then, you should have known then that I was stubborn."

"That you are. But I knew that I needed a woman like you in my life—someone who wouldn't let me be shiftless, someone that would want me to be a good man. I knew that when need be, you could be strong enough for both of us. I needed someone who wouldn't settle for half-way. I knew you were the part of me that God left out—you completed me."

"Ah, Jess, why are you telling me this right now, when I've been fretting over you so much?" Lottie rose from her rocking chair and pulled Jess from his. "Let's go to bed."

Slowly the couple walked to their room. Lottie pulled the covers over Jess as he crawled into his side of the bed. Leaning over she touched her cheek to his feeling the coarse stubble of his face; she kissed it, and then kissed his lips gently.

Jess drew an arm around her waist to pull her closer, "Get into bed," he whispered.

Lottie got into her side and snuggled warmly against her husband. Both their feet were cold and they both giggled as they rubbed them against each other's.

"My love, my love, you complete me too. That little girl you saw helping her daddy was so alone and scared, always trying to fit in. Helping my daddy made me feel like he needed me. You have always been my salvation, never judging me and always making me feel important and always, always loved."

"We've had a good life, my beautiful Lottie. And 1960 is going to be even better."

"Prove it."

"Jess kissed Lottie long and softly. His hands felt her body through her night clothes and he closed his eyes, "I love you."

She felt his sigh and warm breath escape against her neck once, and then she felt it no more as it left his body.

"I love you, too."

CHAPTER NINETEEN

"He would have been seventy-three this coming June." Lottie winked at Janie Butler. "I sure do miss my dear Jess. He was my rock."

Janie reached her hand to cover Lottie's. "He is surely going to be missed by everyone. And I know it has been painful for you, dear."

Lottie wiped a tear from her cheek and smiled. "It's been like pulling my intestines out through my nose."

"My goodness," chuckled Janie. "Now if that doesn't sound like something Jess would say, I don't know what does."

As she reached for her cup of coffee, Lottie chuckled as well. "He knew how to make everything better."

"I know my Ron often went to visit him when needing advice, or sometimes just to complain about me." She laughed. "Everybody needs someone to tell their troubles to, and Jess was one of the ones that could be trusted with your secrets."

"Ain't it funny how things work out?" Lottie posed the question rhetorically. "I would have never thought I would ever leave my farm. And I would have never believed that this old spit of an island would amount to anything."

She leaned closer to her friend. "Don't you remember Janie? This place was all merkle bushes and squatty oak trees and sand—rolls and hills of sand, and now just look at what has come about in the last twenty years. And that's all it's been, twenty years."

"It sure has flown by fast, hasn't it?" A reflection of her youth sparkled in Janie's eyes. "Yessirree, we had some mighty fine times on this island when we were young. But now, Lottie, it's still a fine place to be."

Lottie nodded.

"Just look at all your daughter has done. My goodness, she has turned out to be some kind of business woman. Now who would have thought that little gal who never wore any shoes would turn out to be such a success?"

Beaming with pride, Lottie laughed. "I know, I know, my little gal is doing so well. She always said she wanted to have an oyster bar or some kind of restaurant on the island, and here she is all on her own, without no man, doing a heck of a job running the Sea Gull. You know Janie, I sure am proud of her, and you know that gal has been through some rough times."

"Losing Paul like she did must have been hard on her." Janie leaned back against the dark print fabric of her rocking chair. Her hands curled around the swan-sculpted handles. "Nobody finds any fault, Lottie, with what sorrow often leads us to do."

This was the first time anyone had made an allusion to Pearl's affair with Roger. At least, this is what Lottie believed Janie was alluding to. For a moment she felt defensive. Janie must have sensed her feelings and reached again for her hand. "I don't mean no harm, Lottie, I just want you to know I love you...and well, it's kind of like—all of us that have been raised around here—we know each other, we protect each other and we might fuss a little, but it's like brothers and sisters. In the end, we're all going to take care of one another."

Releasing a long held sigh, Lottie snickered. "You are so right about that, Janie. We do watch out for one another. And I do worry about my girl; she's been alone for a long time and I sure do wish she could find someone to love. I sure do wish she would get remarried, but I guess all that's up to God."

"She's got to work a little at it, too; it's a different world that we live in now. When you and I were coming up there was just farm boys around, but now we have all these servicemen, Marines and sailors from Camp Lejeune coming over here. I tell you, I sure do worry about my Sarah Elizabeth. If I ever caught her over at Pop's Pavilion I would tear her butt up, and if Ron ever caught her over there, well, there's no telling what he'd do."

227

"Some of those boys are pretty rough, Janie. I know that. But some are really nice boys—away from home for the first time, and they're just looking for somebody to be nice to them."

"We have a few military families renting a couple of our cottages, and yes, they are very nice. But I still am going to keep a tight rein on Sarah, and you ought to keep a tight rein on that little granddaughter of yours, Josie. She's blossoming ahead of schedule, if you know what I mean."

"Lord knows, she sure is. Not a bit like her momma in that way. Pearl could have cared less about boys when she was Josie's age. All she ever did was wallow around in the sand and pick that darn purple heather."

"I remember that gal always carrying some of those weeds like they were a bouquet of roses. Ha ha, that was such a sight. Yes, Josie is a lot different from her. When she and Sarah get together all they want to do is listen to Elvis Presley and do this new dance—the twist. I tell you, these young people are something."

"It'll be easier, I guess, to help Pearl keep an eye on the kids with me living over here on the island. Now, Janie, you should see the apartment Pearl has fixed up for me. She had Frankie use the pickup truck; he and Jay brought over a lot of the furniture from the farm house. But some of the things are so old, Janie, that I simply figured I'd leave them behind. That old bedroom suite of mine was my momma and daddy's, and it was falling apart anyway. So Pearl went and bought me a new one."

"Your daughter sure is taking care of you."

"Pearl has an electric range in the apartment, and a nice new Frigidaire and even a new washer. I feel like I just struck gold. You remember how poor we always were, Janie."

"Yes, we all had to struggle back then before they opened the island up for development. I guess there's good and bad about it. I just don't want to see it grow up like Myrtle Beach, or like Miami, Florida."

Lottie agreed, and like a little girl at Christmas she continued telling Janie of all the new things she was getting.

"She bought me my own television set, and last night I watched *Wagon Train* with Ward Bond. He's a good actor. And then she wanted to get me one of those new dryers but I just wouldn't hear of it. I like my laundry smelling like the outdoors."

Janie leaned back in her upholstered rocking chair and listened to her friend go on and on, knowing all the while that deep inside Lottie was aching for her beloved Jess. This was just her way of pushing sorrow out of her life. She'd always been able to do that—to make lemonade out of lemons. But what else was she supposed to do? Janie herself had lost a teenage son only a few years before, and Lottie's adage, 'like pulling my intestines out of my nose,' was exactly how she had felt. But she went on. She looked for the sunshine and prayed for God to help her make it another day, and then, another day until she could smile again.

Janie pushed herself to a standing position. "Ooh, these old bones are creaking and aching." She sucked her teeth a moment then walked to the kitchen and called out. "I'm listening, just keep on talking."

Returning with two saucers of bread pudding, Janie handed Lottie a cloth napkin and set a saucer on the end table next to her. "It's good, I just did finish making it this morning."

Placing the napkin in her lap, Lottie pressed a fork against the pudding and cut off a substantial piece. "Umm, that is mighty fine. You are going to have to give me the recipe for that, Janie."

****

It had been a week shy of three months since her father's death. During those long winter months, Pearl had busied herself preparing the Sea Gull for reopening in late March when the fishermen would be returning to the island. Her daddy had always been there this time of year to help with painting the outside of the building or mending broken rails and replacing stair steps. True, he had been slower in the years since his heart attac, and even slower in the last few years. But he had been there and his absence was palpable. His absence not only caused pain, but it changed the rhythm of her life.

Most days her father had been at her home on the island to greet the children as they came off the bus. Sometimes the bus driver would deposit them at the farmhouse if Jess had any specific chores or plans with them. But now things were different, and Pearl made sure the bus driver dropped the children at the Gull. Of course, Frank had graduated last year and was working at the gas station with Jay. She wasn't sure just how much longer he would be there since he had been talking seriously about joining the Navy.

Her heart ached at the thought of her son leaving home, but she knew he had to start his own life, and as Jay had explained, the military offered so much for young people. It would be a shame to not take advantage of it.

Pearl sighed as her thoughts ran to her youngest, Emma Jewel. How happy she was that E.J. had gotten to know her grandfather. He had been there to escort her to school the first day and subsequent days and he had spent lots of time with her explaining fishing and the ocean, farming and all the things that Grandpa Scaggins had held of value.

"He was such a good grandpa," she explained to Ellie. "He taught all the kids how to clean a fish, bait a hook; he even taught Frankie how to build a good boat. That's something he hadn't done in years and years. But I know he thought it was important enough to teach Frankie." Pearl leaned back against the padded seat of the booth. "They built one together, you know." She looked over to her friend relaxing, her legs sprawled across the cushioned seat. "They went fishing in it at least every couple of weeks—sometimes Jay went."

"I miss your daddy a lot." That was all Ellie could say before she broke into sobs.

Pearl comforted her. "I know."

"I'm just daggone tired of people dying around here." Ellie dug a tissue from her purse and wiped the black watery stains of mascara from her eyes. "And it's always the wrong people." She looked perplexed as she shifted her gaze to Pearl.

"Look at old Clarence; he lived too long if you asked me, and other than being nutty as a fruit cake, he was as strong as a horse up there in Dix Hill. It just ain't fair."

"I don't understand a bit of it, but I surely am not going to try to figure out any more about what is fair and what is not or what is right and what is wrong. I just have to go with what is in my heart, Ellie."

Ellie straightened her shoulders and flipped her hair to the side. "Well, I just know I have to get away from here for a while. We've scrubbed the heck out of these napkin holders, and I don't think a bird could find a single crumb in the crack of these booths." She placed her hands on her hips. "I say we deserve a little time to ourselves and we should go scooterpootin'."

Pearl rolled her eyes.

"Jump in the car and just go driving around—scooterpootin'—don't you ever listen to your daughter? That's what the kids call it today."

CHAPTER TWENTY

The sound of the bell tinkled loudly, and Jay moved from behind the cash register and hurried to the car parked in front of the gas pumps.

"Fill 'er up," the young Marine called from his open window.

Jay nodded and placed the nozzle in the gas tank, then asked the young man to pop the hood so he could check the oil.

"Don't worry about the windshield, bub, I can see just fine. Don't really want anything obstructing my view right now."

Jay followed the man's gaze. Walking in his direction, about fifty yards away, were Pearl and Josie.

"Now, that is what a woman is supposed to look like," the driver of the car snickered.

"I can tell you right now, sir, that little gal is not quite fifteen years old."

"I'm not talking about the kid, mac—I'm talking about the momma. That woman is built like a brick outhouse."

"That woman is spoken for, *MAC*." Jay held his hand out for the cash. "Three dollars and sixty cents."

Jay watched as the car pulled away from the pumps and moved slowly past Pearl and Josie. "What in the world did I say that for," he asked himself. "I've got no claim on her."

Immediately he thought of Feona. *Geez, I just don't know if I can take much more of this. She accuses me of everything under the sun. Says I cheat on her, that I steal things from her, that everybody is stealing something or other from her and that nobody likes her.* Shaking his head in disgust he watched as Pearl and her daughter neared.

"Hi Jay." Pearl waved and walked toward the entrance to the gas station. "I sure could use a Pepsi about now. It has got to be around eighty degrees already and it's not even June yet."

"Who's minding the store?" Jay called out. "I've never seen you outside of the Sea Gull this time of year."

"Oh, just out for a mother-daughter walk with Jo."

Crinkling his brow, Jay finally nodded. "I see."

Pearl waited until her daughter was inside the gas station, and saw her open the refrigerated drink box. "She's been talking about some young boy she was supposed to meet at Pop's, and I thought I should tag along." Lifting her head to meet Jay's eyes she continued. "Josie isn't as shy and naïve as I was at her age, Jay."

"I've noticed that, Pearl. But you were really naïve for your age."

"Hey, so were you, Mr. Man About Town."

"Yeah, we were both pretty..." *Just where is this conversation going to go,* Jay thought. He surely did not want to go back to when they were young and in love before the war.

"Times sure have changed since then, huh?" Pearl responded quickly.

"So, did you meet the young man?"

"Sure did."

"And?"

"Can't you tell? She's madder than a wet hen, Jay." Pearl shook her head, "That *boy* was a Marine. I'd never let Josie go out with a Marine. Not now. She's barely fifteen years, and certainly not old enough to date Marines."

"She does look quite a bit older than that, Pearl."

"I know, that's what worries me."

"But you raised her right, and she's not going to do anything she shouldn't do."

Pearl raised an eyebrow and pursed her lips. Her eyes looked deeply into Jay's and for a moment she lost her train of thought.

"I meant to say that you are doing the right thing, watching out for just who she sees." Jay could feel his palms begin to sweat and he felt fidgety.

"She's been waitressing at the Gull most days and stays busy with that, but the *afternoons* are when I worry about her—when she gets off work. She's got to find something to do besides think about boys. She's just too young."

"I've seen her with Janie's daughter, Sarah."

"Sarah's not as boy crazy, she still plays with a doll." Watching as Josie popped the top from a Pepsi-Cola, Pearl shifted her body to lean against a gas pump. "What in the world is this?" Her hand felt the smooth contours of a large rock set atop one of the pumps.

"Oh that? Some of these service boys have been complaining about the prices of my gas, so I set that up there to hold my prices down." Jay grinned.

Pearl's neck stretched backward as she let out a loud laugh.

Jay's eyes followed the length of it to the top of her blouse where he could see the tan lines of her swimsuit.

Pearl blushed as she felt his eyes upon her, and she turned her face and met his; their eyes held for a moment.

"Momma, I want to go. I want to go to Grandpa's farm." Josie interrupted the moment.

"We'll go in a few minutes. I want to rest for a bit." Pearl walked toward the bay window of the gas station, where an old car seat sat on cinderblocks. Locals usually sat and chewed the fat there, so to speak, as they visited Jay on slow days. Pearl and Josie sat down, taking turns sipping from the Pepsi bottle.

"I guess it will always be Grandpa's farm." Jay placed his hand on Pearl's shoulder. "He'd be able to give you just the right advice you need."

"What advice? Are you two talking about me?" Josie smirked and rolled her eyes.

"Yep, he sure would have." Pearl laughed and held her hand out to touch Jay's. "Thanks." Their eyes held for a second more; then she turned to her daughter.

"Let me have another sip of that, young lady."

Jay watched as Pearl leaned her head back, pressing the bottle to her lips and swallowing the cold drink. A familiar feeling ached in the pit of his stomach and he could feel his heart beating a little faster.

"Mr. Jay, I've been meaning to ask you if you'd mind if some of us girls had a car wash here to raise money for new uniforms for the cheerleading squad for next year."

Jay leaned against the door frame of the gas station. "Cheerleading, huh? That's right, your momma told me that you got picked to be on the cheerleading squad next year. I'll be darn."

"Would it be okay, Mr. Jay?"

Scratching his head, Jay rubbed his hand across his jaw and winked at Pearl. "I can't believe your young'un is a cheerleader."

"Just as long as she keeps those grades up. Schools not even out yet..."

"Three more weeks, Momma."

Josie and Pearl both looked to Jay. "Well," they spoke simultaneously. "What do you think?"

"If you're going to do it, it better be soon. I don't need a traffic jam here, because as soon as school's out you know how busy it gets."

"Yippee, that's what we want, Mr. Jay. We want lots of cars stopping by. We need brand new uniforms and pompoms, and we want a banner that reads, 'Topsail Pirates'."

Chuckling aloud, Jay instructed Josie to use the empty lot next to the station, where he would be sure to provide a water hose. "Just be sure to bring your own sponges and rags. I don't have those to spare."

Josie jumped up from the car seat and wrapped her arms around Jay. "Oh, thank you so much, Mr. Jay. You are the best."

Pearl leaned back against the seat and watched her daughter as she hugged Jay. She was glad her daughter was more outgoing than she had been as a teenager, and glad that she was part of a group. Jay's smile was infectious; something that time and all the wrongs of the past could not take away. That smile was just as it had been when they were young. Pearl smiled back at Jay, her heart beating faster.

"Jo, why don't you go on over across the street to Butler's Snack Shack and grab a burger?"

Josie held out her hand, rubbing her fingers together. "Dough?"

"Where's your tip money?" Pearl asked.

"Momma, I'm saving that for a bathing suit."

As she dug into her short's pocket, Pearl grinned at Jay. "Nice to have her buy her own clothes."

He smiled back and tossed a fifty-cent piece to Josie. "Get yourself some fries with that burger. Okay?"

"Thank you, Mr. Jay." Josie turned, nearly losing one flip flop from her foot. "Oops," she called, laughing as she skipped across the road and pulled open the screen door to Butler's Snack Shack.

"I think she's sweet on Junior Butler. I knew she'd jump at the chance to go over there and see him."

Jay sat down next to Pearl, leaving plenty of space between them. They both looked over to the Snack Shack and watched as a few more customers entered.

"He may not be there," Jay said wistfully. "He might be over at the warehouse playing basketball with his cousins, Willie and Pete."

"You know that was awfully nice of Jordan to turn that old warehouse into an activity building for the kids around here. I worried for the longest time that with the kids might get hurt on those old trucks and machines left from the war."

"Oh, you worry too much, Pearl. Those kids had a ball climbing on them."

"I don't know about that. Little Louie Robbins fell off of one of those trucks and cut himself up pretty badly."

"Well, he's a bit younger than most of the boys that go there. He's fine though, and they got most of the gear out of there now except for that old Jeep. I've been thinking of getting hold of that and fixing it up as a wrecker." Jay turned to Pearl and raised an eyebrow. "What do you think of that? I'm gonna paint her bright red and paint *Surf City Mobile Wrecker Service* on her."

239

"What we need here is an ambulance."

Jay nodded his head. "You're right about that. Last summer, when that boy from Kinston had a wreck at the end of the island, we sure could have used one. I think he would have made it, too, if we would have had some sort of breathing apparatus available."

Both he and Pearl sat with heads held low for a few moments. Jay broke the silence. "I got a postcard from Frank the other day." He brought his hands to his knees and rubbed them back and forth. "Guess you did, too."

"He's not liking it too much up in Illinois at the Naval Training Center," Pearl tittered.

"That's what he wrote me, too. But what is there to like?" Jay laughed. "Boot camp is no picnic."

"I'll be glad when he comes home."

"Does he know yet where they're shipping him out to yet?"

Pearl shook her head. "I don't know, but I sure am glad that there is no war going on anywhere. I don't think I could bear it."

"I think it's rougher on the parents than it is on the kids. I was so excited about joining the Army when I was young. I couldn't wait until I could see the world." Jay turned to search Pearl's face. "I had no idea the ache it caused my parents." His hand reached toward Pearl's but she drew it back.

"Jay, no, not here."

"Then where?" Jay heard himself say; immediately he regretted it. "I'm sorry."

Rising from the car seat, Pearl felt herself redden. Her hand flew to her chest and she felt light, as if she was going to pass out. Her mother called it swooning.

"Are you alright?" Jay asked, as Pearl's eyes fluttered and as she reached for the side of the building.

"I just think I stood up too fast," she answered. "And all I had to eat today was that Pepsi."

"That's not food, Pearl." He motioned for her to sit back down.

Pearl shook her head no. "You're right. Pepsi is not food."

"Let me get you a pack of Nabs." Jay quickly walked into the gas station office and lifted the lid from a glass container of Nabisco peanut butter crackers. He opened the package and handed Pearl one.

"Thanks," she mumbled between chews. "I needed that."

"I've noticed you've been getting thinner."

"I haven't been feeling very hungry lately, and I've been so busy trying to get ready for the tourist season. And with Daddy dying, well, it just has been an odd year so far."

Studying her face as she spoke, Jay recognized the sadness written not only in her eyes but on her entire face. He could almost feel her loneliness and he reached out his hand once again.

"Jay." Pearl shook her head and lowered it. In nearly a whisper she spoke. "We are in broad daylight. My daughter is across the road. And if you haven't noticed, you have a ring on your finger." She lifted her head and

241

drew a stern gaze directly into his wanting eyes. "This is wrong."

"Just let me talk to you sometime. Please." Jay pleaded. "I just need someone to talk to. I don't know how to cope with Feona. I don't understand. I don't want to hurt her."

"Then don't." Pearl's lips drew a taut line across her face. "What do you think I am? Your whore?"

Jay stepped back quickly, astonished at the word. "What?" Now, he grew angry, his jaw clenched and his face reddened. "Where in the world have you been living the last few years? What have I done to make you think that?"

"All these *puppy dog* looks you've been giving me, and last fall when we had the oyster roast for *your wife* and the way you looked at me."

"What do you mean, *the way I looked at you?* You were the one who couldn't take your eyes off me. And it's not my fault...the past. It's not my fault and don't you try to make it."

Pearl felt her chest rising and falling. She could feel the hotness in her face. Looking about, it seemed that everyone must be watching her but there was no one. A few cars were parked across the road at the Superette, and one or two had passed by in the last few minutes. What was she thinking? This, in the open, in the middle of town, she was having an argument with a married man.

"You're right. We need to talk." Calming herself, Pearl ran her fingers through her shoulder-length hair.

242

She had let it grow out; feeling the rubber band around her wrist she gathered her locks in her hands and fashioned a ponytail. "When?"

"Where?" Jay asked.

"How about at my parent's farm. Momma will be there."

"Okay. When?"

"When is good for you?"

"How about Monday? It's always slow on Mondays, or it will be until school is out. I'll take off around ten in the morning. That okay for you?"

Jay nodded, "Leo Weldon's son, Dan, has been filling in for Frank since he left. Nine should be okay."

They both nodded in agreement, then Pearl, familiar with where the key to the restrooms was kept, leaned into the doorway and grabbed it.

Jay did not watch her as she turned the corner toward the lady's room, instead he watched as a Chevy pulled in front of the gas pumps. The familiar 'ding, ding' of the air hose rang out and he briskly walked toward the customer.

Pearl looked in the mirror above the bathroom sink and studied her face. Except for the redness of her cheeks and forehead, she was pale. Splashing cold water on her face she pulled a paper towel from the dispenser and patted it dry. She raised her hands to her face and almost immediately tears poured down her cheeks. They would not stop and she splashed more cold water on her face. But each time she patted it dry more tears flowed. *What is the matter with me?* She thought. *Why did I say that to him? I know he doesn't see me as a whore. I know that. Why did I say that to him?* Pearl leaned against the cool cinderblock wall of the restroom. "Oh, how I wish Daddy was here. I miss him so much." She thought of talking to her mother about this. Maybe she could shed some light. Maybe she would know why she felt the way she did.

Pearl looked at herself in the mirror once again. Her eyes were puffy, as were her lips. Her face was pale all over now, except for her nose. It always turned red when she cried. She laughed. Watching herself laugh, she touched her hand to her throat. "I don't look too bad for a thirty-seven-year-old woman." She felt her waist, slipping her hands above her hips. "Gotten a little thick, I suppose, but not too bad, never was skinny." She leaned forward and peered at her reflection, her fingertips touching the lines gathering about her eyes. "Too much sun." Fluffing her hair she wetted her lips with her tongue. "Would a man be interested in me?" She leaned in even closer, gazing into her own eyes. "Does Jay still want me?"

Quickly her hand flew to cover her face and she felt it redden and felt her eyes well with tears. "Enough! Stop it." Pulling her hand to her side, she wiped the tears away with a wet paper towel. "We'll talk on Monday," she reassured herself. Straightening her shoulders and lifting her chin, Pearl unlocked the bathroom door and stepped out into the bright sun.

"What is the matter with you?" asked Josie. "You have diarrhea or something? I've been waiting out here forever and I heard you saying something." Josie slid her eyes to look more closely at her mother's face. "Have you been crying? Your nose always turns red when you cry."

"Don't be silly. Yes, I've been on the pot for a few minutes—just wait till you're my age and you'll understand more the workings of the female body."

"Icky!"

Pearl wrapped her arm around Josie's shoulder. "Come on, we have a long way to walk if you want to go to Grandpa's farm."

"Why don't we just walk to the house and pick up the car?"

"I like the walk and it's not that far."

"Where y'all going?" Jay asked as he watched the two pass by the plate glass window.

"We're going to the farm." Josie laughed back at him. "My momma is making me walk all that way. Now, wouldn't you say she's a mean ol' woman?"

"Long as I've known your momma, she's loved walking that road."

It's where we met, my dear Jay. Pearl thought as she turned from his gaze. Without turning back she hollered, "Ya know, Carl Burns let me, Josie and EJ walk up to the top of the swing bridge the other day. It sure was a pretty view. We even got to ride it as it turned to let the boats through."

"Ain't nothing like it," Jay hollered back.

Mother and daughter walked arm in arm toward the swing bridge, past the Chase Brothers Bait and Tackle shop and ice house, past the Mira Mar Motel and past Butler's Trailer Park. They walked across the steel frame swing bridge and past Firth's Tackle shop where the shrimp boats were moored. Pearl loved the sight of a shrimp boat, especially when it was on the ocean with its doors open.

CHAPTER TWENTY -ONE

"Pearl, why in the world do you want me to go out to the farm with you?"

"I just thought you might like to drive out and see how things are looking. You know you haven't been out there for a long time. Is that because going there reminds you of Daddy?"

"Oh honey, everything reminds me of your daddy." Lottie closed her eyes; a broad smile crossed her lips as she opened them again. "I miss your daddy, he was my life, my whole life. But I'm not dwelling on what he and I did when he was alive. I'm carrying him with me while I do things without him." Sadness passed quickly from Lottie's face and she chuckled. "We sure did have one hell of a life together on that farm."

Pearl looked at the clock. Ten, two and four; the large letters of the clock blinked. A plastic bottle of Dr. Pepper flashed next to the ticking hands of a clock. It was nine-thirty. *What can I say to get her to come with me? I don't want her to know that I'm meeting Jay. I just want her to be there when he drives up. She'll stop it. She'll keep us from...*" Aggravated, Pearl clucked her tongue in disgust.

"What's that all about? What's got you going this morning?" Lottie's eyes narrowed. "You have something up your sleeve, young lady. Now, tell me what it is."

"Nothing, Momma, I just thought you might like to get away and relax for a while. In a couple of weeks we'll be so busy you won't be able to take a breath. And you're no spring chicken..." Biting her tongue, Pearl regretted the last statement.

"Ahh, so that's it. You think I'm going to croak, just like your daddy." Lottie moved from behind the counter, untying her apron as she walked toward her daughter.

"Gal, I ain't going anywhere. Your daddy had been ill for a long time, and it should not have come to any surprise to you that he passed on." A smile came to Lottie's face as she lifted her head. "God knows he was a wonderful husband; he made my life fun." She stood, hands on her hip, taking a long deep breath. "He was an outstanding father, the most loving, giving, gentle and generous man I've ever known. I miss the bejesus out of him." She drew Pearl close and kissed her cheek. "But honey, it was his time to go. And while he's waiting for me up in heaven, I'm not going to sit around that old farmhouse and moan and cry—I'm living my life like he would want me to."

"You are something else, Momma. How did you ever put up with me and my whiney self when I lost my man?"

"Everyone grieves in their own way, my dear. And you did what you had to do. You turned everything around to your advantage. You did your grieving and went on. No difference between you and me except age and wisdom. Wait till you're my age. You'll understand."

"Wise old owl, huh."

"Yep, and besides I'm taking the rest of the day for myself. Me and Janie have plans for today."

"What?"

"She and I are driving to Wilmington and going to Greenfield Lake. We're going to spend the day *relaxing* by enjoying all those pretty azaleas. I wish you would have gone with us to the Azalea Festival. You know who the Queen was, don't you?"

"Linda Christian, she was in a couple of Tarzan movies back in the 40s." Pearl released a heavy sigh. "Okay, okay, I'm not going to try to stop you and Janie..."

"Honey, you should see downtown Wilmington." Lottie's eyes brightened as excitement built in her voice. "It's getting so big. Why, they're almost finished with the new Wachovia Bank, and Kingoff's Jewelers is moving downtown into another big building. They're almost finished with it, too."

"Okay Momma, you and Janie go ahead and enjoy yourselves." Pearl patted her mother on the shoulder. "You have a good time with Janie in Wilmington. I'll hold down the fort here. It's slow as molasses."

"I still say you got something up your sleeve, gal. But I'm sure it will surface sooner or later, and when you're ready to tell me about it you will."

Her bag held firmly in the crook of her arm, Lottie opened the screen door of the Sea Gull and turned to wave good-bye to her daughter. "See you in the funny papers."

Gentle laughter escaped her lips as Pearl waved to her mother. "It's about time she started enjoying herself," she spoke aloud as she plopped into the soft cushiony seat of a booth. "Why oh why did I tell Jay I would meet him today?" She looked once again at the Dr. Pepper clock; it was a quarter to ten. "Ellie! I'm off, be back in a bit," Pearl hollered toward the kitchen.

Waiting for a response, Pearl grabbed her purse from behind the counter. "Ellie," she called again. Impatiently Pearl stepped through the swinging door and noticed the kitchen door propped open. From her viewpoint all Pearl could see was Ellie's hind end bent over, her tight white shorts cut into her tanned legs as her hips swayed from side to side.

Slowly Pearl made her way toward the opened door and leaned against the frame. Years ago she may have gasped at the sight, but now the image of her friend leaning over with her arms wrapped around a young man standing on the steps did not surprise her. She listened for a few seconds to the smacking of lips kissing and to Ellie's over-exaggerated moans. Pearl placed her hand over her mouth trying to stifle the laughter. She waited a moment to regain her composure and cleared her throat loudly. "Ahem, ahem, I say Ellie, I think if those shorts were any tighter they'd split apart at the seams."

Ellie straightened and turned her attention to Pearl. "Oh, hi there, Goody." Turning to the young man, she ran the back of her hand across his cheek. "This is Staff Sergeant O'Brian. Isn't he a cutie?" She leaned and gave the young Marine a quick peck on the lips. "I'll see you tonight, sweetie." Ellie winked and gently pushed him away."

"Ellie, he's a boy. He's at least ten years younger than you."

"That would make him nearly twenty-eight years old, Two Shoes, and I believe that is what you call a *man*, and what a man he is."

"Gee whiz, I don't have time to argue with you, Smelly." Pearl flipped her hand in the air as she turned to leave. "I'm going to be gone for about thirty minutes. Think you can stay inside and wait on any customers we might have?"

"I'll just park my pretty little self out here at the counter and wait for the crowd to appear. Does that suit you?" Ellie replied sarcastically.

Pearl laughed, "I love you, you are one of the most consistent people I have ever known."

Ellie pulled a stick of Juicyfruit from her pocket, and slid it into her mouth.

"What, no cigarette?"

"I'm trying to quit. Mitchell says that smoking will make me have lines around my mouth." Ellie's fingertips smoothed the skin around her lips; she rolled her shoulder. "Gotta keep those young boys happy."

Shaking her head, Pearl stepped out onto the porch and walked down the stairs to her car. "She's going to be eighty years old and still trying to pick up those young Marines." Laughing to herself, Pearl opened the door to her car. She sat still for a moment and took a breath, then looked in the rearview mirror and smoothed her hair and applied a light coat of pink lipstick. *What am I doing,* she thought. Brushing the thought aside she placed the key in the ignition, it started immediately. Her hands placed on the steering wheel, Pearl noticed them shaking.

"What am I nervous about?"

You know the voice in her head answered. *You know what you are going to do.*

Pearl willed her hands to stop shaking. She met her eyes in the rear view mirror, tightened lips glared back at her. "Yes," she replied aloud. "I know what I want."

****

The two-toned blue and white Ford Fairlane bounced along the rutted path to her parent's empty home. Pearl could feel her heart pounding; it echoed in her head and felt as if it would burst through her blouse.

Nearing the front yard, she spied Jay's white and gold Plymouth Fury.

Still dressed in his Gulf uniform, he stood next to the steps of the screened porch. He was still lean and his hair still dark except for a few strands of silver around his brow. As she approached the yard she watched as he moved ever so slightly, shifting his weight from one side to the other.

Walking toward the car as she slid the gear into park, Jay grasped the door handle and opened it. Pearl did not feel her feet touch the ground as Jay slid his hand into hers and helped her from the car. She looked wantonly into his eyes; there was no more denying, no more hiding. She reached her arms to encircle his neck as he drew her body tightly against his.

Jay's lips covered Pearl's, their tongues touching, warmness consumed their bodies. A flood of passion weakened them both as Jay pushed Pearl against the car. He could not hold her close enough. She could not kiss him deeply enough.

Finally, their lips drew apart, and their warm breaths fell against the other's neck. Their eyes searched one another's and they fell into another long kiss.

****

Jay's tanned arm rested beneath Pearl's head, her hair spread in a tangle against the white sheets. Pulling her into the curve of his body he gently stroked the nape of her neck and kissed her shoulders.

Pearl turned to face him. In his eyes she found peace and acceptance. Against her skin his body felt strong and safe. She was not going to think about what was right or what was wrong. Nothing at all mattered except that what she knew right now, at this moment, was everything she had been longing for, everything she had been needing, was being given back to her. She felt whole again. Why had she not noticed that those parts of her had been missing? For the last several years, one thing after another had taken bits of her away. Now, in this bed with Jay there were no doubts, no questions, nothing but an overwhelming feeling of yes.

"I know." Jay whispered against her neck and sprinkled kisses here and there till reaching her jaw line. "I know. This must be heaven."

"Yes, it is heaven being here with you." Pearl pressed her lips against Jay's and smiled. Her lips still against his, she giggled. "In my bed. I can't believe we're in my bed.

"Your momma would have a hissy fit if she knew. She'd get the shotgun after me."

"Umm," Pearl nodded. "After both of us, I think." She giggled and wrapped a leg around Jay's thigh. "Momma seems to really like living at the beach. If it wasn't for her working those few hours a day at the Sea Gull, I don't think I'd see her at all. She's always busy doing something and she hardly ever comes out here since Daddy passed. I don't think she wants to be reminded...I just think she's taken that part of her life and locked it away somewhere. She said something like that to me one time—about locking hurt away somewhere where you don't have to look at it every day.

"I know what she means." Jay pressed his cheek against Pearl's.

"Nobody's been out here to clean or anything since she moved next to me at the apartment house. Just look how dusty everything in here is." She shook the sheet and watched the dust spin and float through the air. "See."

Jay kissed Pearl's still moving mouth.

"Yep. I think since Daddy passed she's been finding ways to not think about him. She says that while Daddy is waiting for her in heaven she is going to enjoy her life like Daddy would want her to."

"She's right." As Jay drew her closer he buried his face in her hair. "Do you want your momma to sit around the house and be sad. Mourning your father that way would kill her."

"Yes, I'm glad she has found a way to have a good life. It's nice to see her happy and with friends. She and Janie have really become closer now that both their husbands have gone. They're always going to Wilmington or forming some kind of committee for the town—naming streets, planting flowers on the corners."

"She always did like growing things. Too bad the farm is left to seed. Is no one working the land?" Jay leaned his head against a propped hand.

Pearl nodded. "Phil and Sassy are renting my house and working the crops and tobacco on Daddy's and my land, but this old house—Momma and Daddy's place—has been empty since Daddy passed. I hate to see it stand empty—an empty house will go to waste if no one lives there."

"Mm hmm," Jay nodded.

"But my house, well, Sassy's fixed it up real cute and Phil has built a garage on the side of it. He's pretty handy like that, like Paul was."

Pearl lowered her eyes, then raised them to meet Jay's gaze. "I loved him very much, Jay. He grew in me to become such a part of my...my soul."

Jay caressed her face with his hands. "I'm so sorry you lost that love. Paul was a good man. I always liked him and never felt bad about...you know. It was good for Frankie. Coming back after the war, I was a mess. I wouldn't have been a fit father." He stroked her hair gently, the corners of his lips rising in a smile. "What happened was right for you and Frank. I'm glad Paul was there for you." Pausing for a moment, Jay breathed in deeply; letting it escape slowly he continued. "When I came in '49 I saw what you two had between you. But I was not jealous. I knew in my heart that you had found love, real love, and I wanted you to have that."

"But I know it hurt you." Pearl's eyes teared.

Jay nodded. "If Paul had not...gone, I would have never come back here. I swear Pearl, I came for Frankie. I was concerned for him...and I guess I was feeling sorry for you. It must have been so hard."

Pearl nodded and bit her bottom lip. "I was such a mess after that, you know...Roger and..."

256

Jay pressed his fingers against Pearl's lips to silence her. "No need." He pulled her hand to his lips and kissed her palm. "If there had been no accident—if Paul had lived, Feona and I would have moved somewhere else. I would have never moved back here. I had been thinking about getting away anyway—Mom and I and the whole situation in Donna was just not working out."

"How are your mom and sister doing?"

"Marsha is good, she's been married to a really nice fellow. She's still a nurse. Mom lives with her and Arnold and I think things are pretty good all around." Chuckling, Jay added, "She is healthy as a horse. Like Lottie, your momma, she's on the go with Marsha all the time. And according to Sis, Mom's doesn't even meddle in their affairs."

Giggling lightly, Pearl asked, "That's where you go every fall, isn't it?"

Jay nodded. "Yep, and I plan on going out for a visit with her this coming October."

"Was Feona...a nervous person in Texas?"

"I didn't notice that, Pearl. Well, I knew she was shy and that she had been raised by her grandmother who sheltered her a lot. They lived so far out in the country—at least ten miles from town and I don't think they had any neighbors. I don't think she ever learned how to *be* around people. I just don't think she ever had the chance to interact. But I don't think that is why she has *her problem.* Doctor Stuart says it's some kind of chemical imbalance. It would have happened no matter where she lived."

"I'm sorry about you two." Pearl pulled her fingers through Jay's short wavy hair. "You told me once that she had been at Cherry Hospital. What is the matter...what kind of chemical imbalance does she have?"

"The doctor says that Feona is mentally ill and that she will never get better, and that the only way she will even seem normal is if she stays on medication. She takes Mellaril and Elavil now, and a couple other pills, but I'm not sure what. Sometimes she refuses to even take them. That is when things get really bad for her."

"Did it start with the accident she had a couple of years ago?"

"This has nothing to do with the accident. The doc said that it may have been some kind of catalyst for the disease, but that she has always had it. That it just has blossomed or started showing itself more since she got hurt." His lips trembling, Jay clenched his jaw. "I don't even know that much about the medicine—I just don't know anything. And I feel so badly about not being able to help her."

Pearl rubbed her fingers across his brow and temples. "I'm so sorry this has happened."

"Half the time I don't even know who she is. When she's on the medication she acts like a robot—she slobbers and her eyes are glassy. She's not the person I married." Jay looked sternly into Pearl's eyes. "Have you ever known anyone like that?"

"Clarence, maybe. But I think that was different. He went senile, and Feona is not senile."

Nodding his head, Jay continued. "I don't know what to do. When she's on her medication, it's like I said, she acts like a robot. I can't even have a conversation with her."

"The Elavil and Mellaril?"

"Yes, when she's on that she acts that way. But right out of the blue she'll stop taking it and then it starts all over again. Her saying such bizarre things—I just don't understand." Bewildered, Jay' face grew pale as he searched Pearl's eyes. "And sometimes she lies about taking it."

Feeling his body tense and hearing the anxiety in his voice, Pearl rubbed Jay's shoulders.

"She won't let me touch her," Jay shrugged. "Like this—since even before her accident. And she accuses me of things that, like I said, are bizarre—that make no sense."

Pearl raised an eyebrow.

"Last week she swore up and down that I was on the roof and was listening to her conversations on the phone with Janie."

"Why in the world would you do that?"

"Yes, why would I do that?"

"She stares at me sometimes and I could swear she is mouthing the words, I hate you."

"Oh Jay, I'm so sorry."

"I don't know what to do. We have another appointment at a psychiatrist in Wilmington next week. Last time we went he said it would be good to get her out of the house, get her involved with things and people."

"She doesn't..."

"I know. The ladies here have asked her numerous times to join the choir or go to oyster roasts, I know. She just shuns everyone and then talks like they are mean to her."

"We'll keep trying."

"She's going to start working at Barnacle Bill's this summer as a waitress. At least she says she's going to, but I don't know how that is going to work out."

"Maybe she'll do it. Maybe it will be good for her. Maybe it will keep her mind off of *those* things—things that aren't real."

Jay leaned back on the pillow; dust flew in the air as he plopped his head down. "Yep, this place could use some dusting," he laughed.

"I think I'll plant a little garden outside in the old spot where Momma and Daddy used to have one. Not as big, mind you, just enough to grow some tomatoes, summer squash, onions and maybe some cantaloupe."

"I love squash, I love cantaloupe."

"I love you Jay."

"I never stopped loving you."

CHAPTER TWENTY-TWO

"It was so nice of you to buy all these fireworks, Phil." Pearl grasped her brother-in-laws hand. "I know this had to set you back a bit."

"Not at all, I was glad to do it and what would the Fourth of July be without fireworks?" As he picked up the crate of assorted rockets he walked down the stairway to the beach and southward toward a group of people a few hundred feet away.

Pearl could hear him as he called out, "Okay all you little kiddies come grab your sparklers. Stand back though while I set this stuff up in the dunes."

Sassy, Phil's wife, approached Pearl. "Sweetie, this is our way of paying you back for letting us rent out on the farm and charging us so little. I think we are finally going to have enough money to buy a new car." She leaned in to kiss Pearl on the cheek. "The old Buick is just about on its last legs and I don't think we could get around very well on the tractor." Sassy laughed and reached for the Sun Drop she had placed on a nearby table. "You're the sweetest person in the whole world." She threw her arms around Pearl and hugged her tightly.

"I'm just glad to see the place producing. And I know Paul would have wanted Phil to work it. He's a good man, too."

Sassy turned to join her husband, kissing her fingers and pressing them against Pearl's cheek, "Thanks again."

Leaning against the railing of the patio, Lottie surveyed the growing crowd of youngsters. "Geez, can you believe all these kids? Where in the world did they all come from?" A long and heavy breath escaped from Lottie's pursed lips. "I don't know half their names."

"Well, there's all our kin and then the Butler's—both families, the Burns, Abbotts, Chase families—both of them and then a couple of military families are here— the Morettis and Schneiders; they're pretty new here on the island. I think they got here about a year ago— husbands are in the Marines."

Wrapping her arms around herself in a hug, Pearl stretched her neck backward; a broad grin covered her face. "Oh Momma, I just love it and I sure do wish Daddy was here to enjoy this."

"Mmm, me too. But golly gee, where did they all come from?" Lottie scanned the patio and shoreline where most of the crowd had gathered. "Not ten years ago, there weren't thirty people on this island—near about."

"Everybody's had kids and then it seems that at least one or two of the families from Camp Lejeune always end up setting up house here every year.

"We ain't feeding all them for free are we?" Standing with her hands defiantly placed on her hips, Lottie shook her head.

"It's just hot dogs and potato chips, Momma. And nearly everybody else brought a covered dish. Don't get so upset. It isn't much and these folks give us a lot of business throughout the year."

"Um, well maybe you're right." Lottie smiled her familiar smile. "Sorry dear, sometimes I forget that the Gull has made you a rich woman."

"I'm not rich, far from it. This restaurant skimps through the winters just like everyone else's business around here. I'm just doing my part for the community. Jay puts on a nice barbeque every winter at his gas station, and Enid and Bella always have a pig picking, the Butlers usually put on some kind of fish fry or something..." As she spoke, Pearl turned her attention to Jay as he walked onto the patio with Feona; Pearl could feel her face lose its color.

"You need to learn to not look so long at him." The sharp, sarcastic tone of Lottie's voice surprised Pearl. She slid her eyes angrily at her mother.

"I've known for some time, my dear. And I suspect others on the island do also. One of you needs to find a way through the woods to your Daddy's and my old farmhouse instead of driving your very recognizable cars."

"I don't want to talk about this right now, Momma." As she turned to walk away, Lottie caught her by the arm.

"You never stopped did you?"

"I don't want to talk about it now." Pearl pulled her arm gently from her mother's grasp and walked toward the stairway to the beach. Lottie's accusatory tone echoed in her head. She could feel her heart beating loudly against her chest.

"'*Of all the gin joints in all the towns in the world HE walks into mine,*' that's how your face looked when you laid eyes on Jay walking in here with Feona, just like Sam in *Casablanca*, except you're Ingrid Bergman not Humphrey Bogart." Ellie stood at the bottom step of the beach stairway. "I knew you'd be heading this way once you saw lover boy come in with his wife."

"They've been here for years, Ellie." Pearl shot her friend a harsh glance. "I don't know what in the world you're talking about."

"I don't either. It's not like he hasn't been here since '55 and not been married to his little sweetheart from Texas. You oughta be used to seeing them together by now. But that look on your face beats all I've seen. It was as if you hadn't seen him since 1941. What's going on Pearly White—or are you one of those *black pearls?*"

Pearl's feet could not move fast enough down the stairway to the shore; she walked northward toward

Ocean City Fishing Pier. Her hair whipping about her face, she angrily pulled it behind her ears. "I swear I'm going to either cut this mess off or grow it long and stick it on top of my head," she yelled loudly.

"Your hair looks really bad when you wear it short." Ellie ran against the beach breezes to catch up with Pearl. "Honey, everybody knows, they just ain't saying anything. Just like with Roger. Did anyone ever come up to you and wag their finger in your face about Roger?"

Pearl spun around quickly and drew her face close to Ellie's. "No, no one has ever wagged their finger in my face, but I have gotten some rotten looks from some of these fine church going folks around here."

"Then they really need to be in church—the old judgmental, bags of worms."

"Oh hell Ellie, what do you know about church."

"Nearly every Sunday Mother dragged me to the Barlow Vista—same as you. In fact, I know we went to church more than your family." Feigning a curtsey, Ellie twirled around. "I used to love getting all dressed up and wearing those pretty dresses Grandma Portman in Raleigh used to buy for me."

Plopping down on the warm sand, Pearl sat cross legged. "Oh Ellie, you always did look pretty in your fine clothes. But I don't know if going to church did you a lick of good."

"Really? Do you think I'm a bad person because I wore pretty clothes to church? Huh, Pearl?"

"You have done some questionable things, but no, I don't think you are a bad person for wearing pretty clothes to church—but I think you're...selfish. Yes, sometimes I think you are selfish. And sometimes I think you really hurt people's feelings."

"I'm not a saint and I've never said I was." Ellie grabbed both of Pearl's shoulders. "Listen, I don't want to be a saint and I never pretended to be. But I tell people what I think, I don't try to hide it or pretend that my poop doesn't stink...and I don't steal, haven't killed anybody and I usually don't lie." Ellie removed her shoes and set them beside her as she sat in the sand.

"Usually?" Pearl joined her friend, sitting only a few inches from her.

"Well, I lie to certain people."

Pearl chuckled and leaned back on her elbows. "I knew that being with Jay and seeing him was the *rightest* thing in the world until I saw him walk onto the patio tonight with Feona. And now, well, I don't know. This is the first time I've seen him out with her since he and I...you know, have been together."

"Funny how love makes you feel. Huh?"

"It just seems that I can't ever have what I want and he can't ever have what he wants.

"Who does?" Ellie laughed. "Whoever gets everything they want? Listen here, Pearly, you have to take what you want."

"But Jay's married. What about Feona?"

"He needs to leave Feona."

"But she is sick."

"She didn't look that sick tonight. Did she?"

"It's not that simple, Ellie. It's not like she has diabetes or is missing a limb. What she has is not visible and she can't help it."

"Everybody knows she's nutty as a fruitcake."

"That's a horrible way to put it."

"That's the difference between you and me, Pearly, I don't care if it's horrible. It's the truth."

A starburst explosion appeared in the night sky followed quickly by another; white and yellow sparkles floated downward.

"I think we ought to head on back to the Sea Gull, they've started with the fireworks and I don't want to miss being there with the kids." Pearl rose from her feet and held her hand out to help Ellie.

"Yeah, I'm getting hungry." She turned to Pearl and wiped the sand from the back of her friend's legs. "Who makes that seashell macaroni salad? Every time we have one of these shindigs, somebody brings this wonderful salad and I just can't get enough."

"Bart Ralston's wife, Lily, makes it."

"Last time I was down at the VFW she made a really big bowl of it and I swear I had to have eaten nearly the whole thing."

"Yeah, I've been trying to be polite about how tight those short shorts of yours are getting. Maybe you have been eating too much of that macaroni salad. You know what they say, 'too much of a good thing can be a bad thing.'"

"Oh, you can never have too much of a good thing."

****

Tammy, the youngest of Jordan and Tillie Butler's children stood in the very corner of the patio; her hips swayed round and round as she moved a bright yellow hula hoop against her waist. Even as another burst of fireworks exploded in the sky she kept her concentration; the hula hoop seemed to even circulate faster.

Emma Jewel sat as close as possible to Tammy, her eyes glued to her friend and the hoop, only to be distracted when another rocket burst against the night sky.

Fate Bishop, Jay and Feona's son, sat next to Emma Jewel. E.J, as she was usually called, leaned against him. "I wish I could do that as well as Tammy does," she whispered in his ear.

"Huh," the boy, lost in the glow in the night sky, responded.

E.J. turned her face to Fate's. His dark wavy hair hung nearly over his ears. "You got pretty hair for a boy." She leaned in closer and touched it.

"Stop it." Fate scowled as he brushed her hand away. "I want to watch the fireworks."

As Pearl and Ellie approached the stairway from the beach to the patio, Pearl jostled her friend. "Hey, look at that little stinker," she motioned toward her daughter, E.J. "Look at her leaning up against Fate. I swear she is so sweet on him. Every time I go over to the Jay's gas station, she stands there like a post staring at Fate."

"Good googa mooga, Pearl. Just what is going to come of all y'all, I'm telling you—you make me look like a saint. Here you are fiddling around with Fate's daddy and E.J. is sweet on his son. If you want the town to talk about something, well, you sure are giving it to them."

Pearl stopped for a moment, lost in thought, "Oh my gosh, you're right." Her eyes twinkled as she let out a suppressed laugh. "That sure would be something, now wouldn't it?"

One of the military wives new to the island, Uta Schneider, leaned over the banister and in her thick German accent hollered down to the women. "Vell, vell, vell. It's your party und no one can vind the hostess." She laughed, her bright green eyes twinkling. "All den kindern are really enjoying the feuerwerk and there is no momma."

"We're coming up right now, Uta."

Edie Moretti and her children, Burt and Nora, sat on the floor of the patio next to Uta's children Robert and Marla. Most of the children from Surf City were gathered there as well and they all expressed their delight with oohs and aahs that echoed along the beach as the fireworks exploded in the sky.

Edie's husband, Mark Moretti, Bart Ralston and Phil Rosell took turns setting up the fireworks. Phil was grateful as the two former Marines lent a helping hand.

Like so many of the local families on the island, Phil had ambiguous feelings about the number of military taking up residence on Topsail. So many of them seemed to look down their noses at the farmers and fisherman and small town store owners. He had heard comments on occasion about stupid southerners and how slow and behind the times they were; Phil did not care much for that attitude. But Moretti and Ralston did not appear to be of that ilk. Immediately they had shown an interest in becoming part of the community. It took hard work and dedication to endure the part of the year when business was slow. And it took a desire to form bonds with others to see the way through those times.

Of course, Ralston had been there since the early 50s, and had set up shop as a dependable handyman and mechanic. Moretti, who came with his family just in the last year or so, had purchased one of the old firehouses on the island and renovated it, and made into one of the island's restaurants. Everybody enjoyed the laid back atmosphere and superb food sold there.

Phil and the other two men stood far back as they watched another rocket scream into the sky. Although the Sea Gull had closed for business at nine that night, tourists had come to join the locals on the patio, eating hotdogs and spilling out onto the beach front and into the dunes for the Fourth of July celebration.

Surveying the growing crowd of people, Pearl looked for Jay and Feona. She could not find them.

"He left not long after you and Ellie went down on the beach." Lottie pulled her daughter down into the empty bench where she sat. "As soon as that first rocket went screaming into the sky, Feona covered her ears. I never saw such a thing, she near about jumped out of her skin and I heard her telling Jay that it sounded like someone was killing a hog around here and she wanted to go home."

Her hands on her hips, Ellie snickered. "They left Fate?"

"No. He's staying with Arlo, Enid and Bella's boy— one more ain't gonna make no difference." Lottie wiped a smear of ketchup from the corner of her mouth. "At least that's what Bella says. And Jay didn't want him to miss out on the fireworks."

"I bet that must have been something trying to pry that boy away from Feona; she fawns over him like he was still a two-year-old."

"It didn't look too hard. I watched Jay say something to Feona, and she shook her head no, and then I saw him whisper something in her ear and she went ahead and let the boy stay."

Ellie sat next to Lottie, scooting close to make room for Pearl. Looking up to her friend she smiled. "Before you sit down why don't you go and get me one of these fine looking hotdogs? I'll take mine all the way with mustard, onions and chili." Grinning snidely at Pearl, she added, "That is, while you're up."

"Do I look like your waitress?"

In unison Ellie and Lottie responded. "Yep."

"I'll have another one of those too, Miss, and could you bring me a sweet tea with that?" called Lottie.

"And a Pepsi for me," followed Ellie.

271

"Josie and Sarah are still hard at it inside serving up the food I assume." Pearl pretended to write down an order. "Is there anything else I can get you two *ladies?*"

"Naw, that'll do fine ma'am, but mind you put a little spark in your step and make sure those dogs ain't cold when you bring them out."

Pearl tuck her tongue out. "Thusst." Pulling the door to the restaurant open she perched herself on one of the stools at the counter. She could see her mother's and Ellie's heads bob and move about as they spoke. *Surely they're talking about me,* she thought. *I don't care; we all know each other's business anyway.* Slapping her hand against the counter, she startled the two girls lost in chatter as they stood next to the hot pot of water sitting on the grill.

"Hey, I'd like some service over here, or are you two too busy?" Pearl scowled as the girls turned to face her, then burst out laughing as she watched their astonished expressions.

"Yes ma'am. What'll it be?" Josie sputtered.

"Let me have one hotdog all the way and then another with just ketchup...and I guess you may as well make me one, too, but I want mayo, slaw and cheese on mine—two teas and a Pepsi." Pearl watched as Josie fished out three hotdogs from the boiling water. "I don't think you're going to have to add any more to the water. Soon after the fireworks everyone will probably go home."

"Yes ma'am," smiled Sarah. "This is fun. I like being in here late at night when hardly anybody comes in."

272

"That's okay for now, when we don't have any paying customers, but tomorrow I expect things will be different."

"Miss Pearl." Sarah leaned against the counter, her eyes already pleading.

"Yes dear?"

"I was wondering if the next time the juke box man comes I could have a couple of the records he leaves behind."

"Of course, I thought you and Josie were sharing anyway." Pearl slid a questioning glance toward Josie. She watched her daughter shrug and then quickly turn her back to fill the drink cups.

Outside on the patio Lottie and Ellie's conversation continued, but it was not on the subject of which Pearl had suspected.

Over the last few years the two women had become closer and much more tolerant of the other. Lottie rarely criticized Ellie's choices in clothing or her relationships with men, and Ellie made room for Lottie's opinions. They often agreed on things, especially when it came to Pearl, though it may not have been for the same reasons.

Tonight though, Lottie was concerned about Ellie's daughter, Monroe. After graduating from high school she had been spending more and more time in Florida with her father, Chuck Bridge. To Ellie's dismay she rarely received letters from Monroe and found herself initiating most of the phone calls between the two of them.

"Most of the time, when I call down there, Chuck says Monroe is out for the evening, I know she's boy crazy, Lottie, she always has been."

"When's the last time you talked with her, Ellie?"

"It's been over a month, Lottie. Normally I wouldn't think anything of it. But it's been so long, and I just don't want her to get knocked-up; I don't want her to have to get married like I did."

"She's a lot like you were when you were her age, footloose and fancy free. But in a lot of ways she isn't." Settling her hand on Ellie's shoulder, Lottie continued. "Now, don't take this wrong, but she's always had more heart than you."

"You mean she's not as selfish."

"Well, let's just say she's concerned about other people and doesn't like hurting their feelings."

"She's like my father. He didn't have a real strong backbone. And he was always giving in to my mother. But like me, when I was her age, I never used to even tell my parents if I was coming or going. I rarely told them if I was coming up here to visit and sometimes they didn't even know I was here—not for a day or two."

"Yes, you were a problem child."

"No, I understand that young people want to have their own lives. I was just an independent child." Ellie grinned and winked. "And Monroe is that way too," she paused for a moment, "sometimes."

"Is that what you think Monroe is exercising—her independence?"

"I don't know. I just have this strange feeling. Like something is going on—something important."

"That feeling is motherhood, Ellie. You miss your daughter."

"I guess so, but I can't help feeling that she needs me, that she's in trouble with something and if I know her, she will not go to Chuck. She doesn't like to talk about her problems, she keeps things all bottled up and then." Ellie pointed to one of the exploding fireworks. "She's like that."

"Got a temper on her, huh?" commented Lottie.

Ellie nodded. "And I'm pretty sure she won't talk to her father about things. I just don't want her to get herself into trouble and not have any help."

"Do you want her to go to Chuck?"

"He's no help. Whatever it is he'll only tell her what a failure she is."

Reaching her hand to squeeze Ellie's, Lottie motioned toward the screen door as Pearl maneuvered her way holding the food.

"You can tell she's a waitress, can't you Ellie?" Lottie asked rhetorically. "She knows how to carry three of everything without dropping it."

Holding the Pepsi, tea and hotdogs in her hands, Pearl opened the screen door with her foot. "I could use some help, please," she spoke loudly.

Ellie reached upward to grab her soft drink and Lottie's tea.

"Thanks a lot." Pearl settled herself on the bench next to her mother. "I swear..."

"Not nice to swear, dear," Lottie admonished her daughter.

"Gee whiz." Pearl rolled her eyes and shaking her head continued, "*I suwannee,* is that better?"

Lottie nodded her head as she took a bite from her dog.

"I suwannee, I think my little Josie takes after the Rosell family."

"And what is that supposed to mean?" Ellie questioned sternly.

"It means that she is exhibiting selfish traits."

"Damn, what is all this about? All of a sudden I'm considered the most selfish person in the world. I'm not Hitler. I haven't killed anybody. So knock it off with the *selfish* stuff. Okay?"

Lottie shot Ellie a disapproving glance then turned her attention back to Pearl. "What did she do now?" asked Lottie.

"I specifically told her when she started working this spring that when the juke box man came to change out the records, that if he left any behind she was to share them with Sarah."

Drawing the straw to her lips, Ellie sucked lightly on her Pepsi Cola. "And she's not?"

"Nope." Pearl sat on the edge of the bench and scooted against her friends making more room for herself. "I swear Ellie..."

Lottie shot her daughter an angry glance.

"Tsk, okay...I suwannee Ellie, if your butt gets any bigger I'm going to have to build bigger benches for out here."

Lottie looked about the patio and seeing that most of the people had made their way to the beach, she slapped her hand down on the table. "Now, I want to know just what in the heck is going on around here. All this swearing and picking on one another, well, I know there is something behind it. You two never pick on one another unless there is some underlying *something* going on. Fess up ladies!"

A flip of her ponytail and a raised eyebrow directed at Pearl suggested that Ellie was waiting for her friend to begin talking.

Lottie leaned forward and looked her daughter in the eyes. "Well? It ain't Josie being selfish and it's not Monroe not calling and it ain't the growth of your rear end, Ellie. All of these things I'm sure are important and worthy of being concerned about, but I know there is something else going on around here and I'm sure it has something to do with Jay." Lottie sat fidgeting in her seat. "You two think I'm too old, huh, to understand. Don't you?"

"Momma..."

"And I'm getting hot here, over this." She grabbed Pearl's fingers as she reached to grab her cup of iced tea. "You been seeing him, more than seeing him. And he walks in here tonight with his wife and you're embarrassed—not sure he loves you."

"Momma, it's complicated."

"I held my tongue with Roger and he wasn't even married. But this is just plain wrong. I will not hold my tongue any longer. You are having carnal relations with men who...who..." Lottie's anger overcame her as she stumbled to explain how she felt. "I did not raise you to be like..."

"Like me?" Ellie leaned back against the corner wall where they all sat along the wooden bench.

"Shut up, Ellie." Both women glared at her.

She could feel the anger and tension between the two as they argued; it was almost palpable, and Ellie felt that this was a discussion about something more than the carnal relations Pearl was having with Jay. She leaned back and listened as the people closer to her than anyone else continued their heated discussion.

CHAPTER TWENTY-THREE

A few hundred feet outside her father's home Monroe Bridge sat parked in her yellow Corvair. The windows rolled down, she could feel a slight breeze as it wafted through the trees of a nearby cypress pond. The air was full of the scent of orange blossoms and she breathed in the sweetness only to reach into her handbag and pull out a pack of Tareyton cigarettes. Holding a slim lighter to the tip of one, she sucked deeply, drawing the nicotine into her lungs. Exhaling through her nostrils, Monroe bit her lower lip then breathed in the contrasting smells of tobacco and orange blossom. This time of the year was when she would have preferred to be in North Carolina, but her father had bought her a new car and a new stereo and so she simply could not resist the temptations that kept her here in Florida.

Hidden amongst the trees of the orchard, she could see through the plate glass window of the living room. She could make out her father and his wife, Mona, as they sat watching the television. It was Sunday night; they must be watching *The Ed Sullivan show*.

Mona stood and walked from the room as Monroe continued watching. "Probably going to get a bowl of ice cream for his majesty." Monroe made a loud kissing noise, punctuating the statement.

In a few minutes, Monroe snickered as her guess was confirmed, and she slumped in the car seat as she watched Mona hand a large bowl to Chuck and another smaller bowl to their son, Ossie, who sat swallowed by the big oversized chair in the corner of the room.

Mona then quickly walked to the television set and turned the channel, lifting her head intermittently as she listened to Chuck's instruction. Finally she stopped and returned to her own chair.

"Oh yassaw, Massa Bridge, whatever you wants Massa Bridge," Monroe muttered in her best southern Negro dialect. "He always gets what he wants." She looked down at her fingers; nearly every one had an expensive ring on it. On her wrist was a solid gold wrist watch; the face encircled with diamonds.

All the new gifts and toys she had been promised by her father if she stayed one more month—then it was another month and now it was nearly August and she was still in Florida. "But why does he even want me here?" she muttered.

Monroe recalled her father's trip to California in June that lasted two weeks, and another trip in July to South America that lasted another two weeks. "I hardly ever see him and he sure as heck doesn't include me on any of those excursions."

When she had shown any interest in the business side of the orchards, Chuck discouraged her by remarking that women did not belong in business.

"Pearl runs the restaurant on Topsail and she's doing great at it."

"Peanuts, that's peanuts. That ain't no business— that's a part time little nothing and if I had it I'd turn it into a statewide operation. That little snipe isn't capable of doing that. I remember her. A little washed-out looking farm girl."

Monroe sucked her teeth and closed her eyes against her father's remark. She flipped the butt of her cigarette out of the window, knowing that her father would be furious with her for doing so. He hated trash on his land, especially cigarette butts. She grabbed a sales receipt from a bag on her seat, crumpled it, and then threw it out the window too. "There, how do you like them apples...oranges?" The words bit like acid as they escaped her mouth. She had come to hate the smell of citrus and despised herself even more for being under her father's spell. There was nothing she couldn't ask for that he did not get her and nothing she could do to please him.

It made no sense, him wanting her around. And it made even less sense to her why she complied with his wishes. At one time memories of her childhood growing up with all the pretty cloths, dolls, and new toys— whatever she wanted, conjured up happy thoughts and good times of going to Tampa and the city, but that seemed so long ago and at times felt as if it had all been a dream.

When she was a child growing up on the farm she was doted on and appeared to be the apple of her father's eye. But once her mother left and moved back to North Carolina, things changed. Yes, she was still given everything she asked for, but she was no longer included in many of the excursions and trips overseas. It was if she was kept around like one of her grandmother, Cassie Lou's, poodles.

Monroe heard "she's just like her mother" so many times she could not count them. Now she was considering the possibility that that was why she was so spurned by the family. Her father was always telling her that she needed to get married and find someone else to furnish her with jewelry and cars. Why didn't he understand those things were not what she really wanted? *But nothing I do, or say means anything, he just buys me stuff to shut me up.*

"I could poop gold eggs and they'd be the wrong size and the wrong shape." She scowled as she unbuttoned the top few buttons of her blouse, fanning herself in the humid night air. "Oh, it's so daggone hot I just can't stand it—no ocean breeze."

Looking at the rings on her fingers and rubbing the handle of the gear shift, she considered what it would feel like, and what the response would be, if she told her father she was going back to Topsail Island. Nodding her head, she knew he would not let her take the car.

She pulled the rearview mirror down to reach her eyes and peered into them by the moonlight. "I do look like Mom." The reflection in the mirror brought a smile to Monroe's face. She loved Ellie, and other than being a little taller and having hazel eyes and auburn hair, she did resemble her quite a bit. More importantly, she felt good when she stayed with her. She wasn't so anxious about things and never felt like she had to kiss up to her.

Of course, all she had ever heard from her father's side of the family was that Ellie was a floozy and cheated on him. Maybe that part was true; her mother did seem to date a lot and had never remarried. But she could understand why perhaps she did those things. Her father was so cold, so accusatory, so belittling. Who wouldn't want to find solace somewhere else?

Scrunching her face into a scowl, Monroe felt the guilt from not having called her mother in over a month. She did miss her and she missed the island. This time of the year was always busy and flooded with people from all over. That was one of the things she really enjoyed about living at Surf City; there was always someone interesting to meet. Such a contrast of lifestyles was exciting; country living and a vacation lifestyle. She rubbed the handle of the gear shift again. "I really need to call Mom," she said aloud. "We haven't talked in so long."

Monroe adjusted her seat farther back and leaned against it, then pulled another cigarette from her purse. She thought again of her father's constant nagging for her to find a husband, marriage. *Do I want to have to wait hand and foot on somebody, like Mona does?* Then she thought of Pearl and her parents and how happy they had always seemed. She simply did not know what to think.

College had been an option at one point. And she sort of regretted not going after graduating high school. Living at the beach offered too many temptations. There, college just did not seem necessary and hardly anyone she knew was going. Maybe some of the boys had enrolled, but most of the girls were getting married; a few went to Miller Motte Business School in Wilmington. Maybe she would do that. Then she'd prove her father wrong about women and business. That was exactly what she wanted to do—*prove that cold -hearted beast wrong.*

Mona moved about the living room turning out lamp lights and gathering glasses and bowls. Monroe watched the house turn dark. Silently she listened to the frogs croaking and calls of whippoorwills. *I'll ask him tomorrow to help me with college expenses.*

****

"The only college I'm paying for is Saint Leo right here in Dade City. You can drive back and forth every day. I'm not paying for anywhere else. You hear me? Nowhere else." Chuck Bridge stared boldly into his daughter's eyes and walked along the sidewalk to his truck. "You'd be a fool to turn me down, but then you always were just like your mother."

In defense of Ellie, Monroe responded, "You know Dad, I don't understand why you even want me around if I'm so much like my mother."

Shrugging, Chuck slid his eyes to the ground; he reached his foot out to squash a cow ant lumbering along the sidewalk. "Think what you want. Do what you want. I don't care. But as long as you're not living with me, you ain't getting a dime of my money and I don't care what it's for."

Balling her fists as she fought back angry tears, Monroe screamed, "You don't care, you don't give a damn about anything except money." She pulled the rings one at a time from her fingers and threw them at her father's feet. "Here, I don't want a damn thing from you—nothing, and nothing is what I've already got." She looked toward the sprawling oak tree in the yard. "That tree has more feeling in it than you do."

Chuck Bridge shook his head and kicked at the rings; his boots crushing the gold and silver baubles. "Just like your mother; give her everything in the world and all she wants is more."

"More? What do you mean—more! Instead of jewelry why don't you pay for my schooling? That would make more sense."

"You need to get married. But more than likely you ain't married because no one would ask you. Once they get to know you and see you're so much like that bitch of a mother, they run like scared rabbits."

She could not stop the tears and they flowed down her cheeks. "I hate you, I hate you," Monroe screamed.

"What's all this now?" Mona questioned as she walked from the back door. Ossie followed behind her and the two stood staring at Monroe.

"Girl? What are you yelling at your father about now?"

The young boy stood next to his mother, scowling he stuck the tip of his tongue out at Monroe.

He's even more spoiled than I was when I lived here, she thought. Shaking her head she glared at Mona. "Nothing. I just want my father to give me as much attention as he does y'all's son, little Ossie, the perfect child."

"Momma, see, she's being mean to me again. I don't like her."

Looking from Mona, to Ossie and then her father, Monroe threw up her hands. "I think the best thing for me is to go back to Topsail. I don't think I'm really wanted here despite your ploys to keep me around."

"It's always been your choice." Chuck half smiled as Monroe bent to pick up the damaged rings near his feet.

"Just tell me one thing, Dad." Her lips tight, Monroe looked at her father defiantly. "Why did you give me all this stuff every time I said I wanted to go back to Mom?"

Without responding Chuck motioned to Ossie. "Come on son, let's go check on those trees out near Bullhead Lake."

The boy quickly ran to his father's side and scrambled into the truck as Chuck opened the door. Kneeling and turning to watch his half-sister from the rear windshield, Ossie grinned and stuck his tongue out once again.

As she suspected, her father forbade her to drive the Corvair to North Carolina. He did let her take whatever clothing she desired, and any jewelry, including the bent and smashed rings she had thrown at him.

"You know, if you go now you'll miss out on the trip to California we've been planning," Mona cooed as she watched her step-daughter pack.

I don't give a fiddle fart about Califoria. Monroe feigned regret. "Well, I haven't seen Mom in so long and I even missed the summer. Last time I spoke with her she said that the Fourth of July was a real big deal this year with more fireworks than ever."

"Does she have a car up there for you to drive?" Mona asked.

"No. I don't think so."

"I'm going to see if your father will change his mind about the Corvair. If not, maybe he will let you have the station wagon."

Monroe was surprised by the offer and lifted her head. "Mona, that is what you drive. What are you going to do without it? You need it for all the toting of animals, buckets and tools that you carry around all the time. What are you going to use?"

"I've been trying to get him to buy me a new car or something besides that old Country Squire. It's older than Methuselah. Around here it's okay, but when I go to church or to town, it's just so big and clumsy," Mona shook her head, "and dirty looking."

They laughed as they sat on the bed together next to Monroe's suitcases. "If you took the station wagon, then he'd have to buy me something else."

"Geez, Mona. What if he got the law after me for taking his car?"

"Oh honey, he ain't going to do that. He ain't going to have his daughter's name in the paper. You oughta know that. He's got two things too much of and that's money and pride. Besides, I bet it's fun driving the Corvair. Ain't it?"

After Mona explained that Chuck wouldn't call the law on her, the thought of simply taking the Corvair entered her mind. But as she studied Mona's face and her beaten down expressions, she decided that the Country Squire station wagon would be just fine. Besides, it had lots more room for her to put a lot more stuff.

CHAPTER TWENTY—FOUR

"I dub thee the 'Big Green Bomb,' Ellie popped the top from a tall Pepsi Cola bottle and poured the contents on the front bumper of the station wagon. Pulling Monroe closely to her she closed her eyes and whispered in her daughter's ear. "You had me so worried dear, I wasn't sure you were ever coming back to your poor ol' Mom."

"Sorry, I guess I should have called more often..."

"At least you're where you belong now."

Monroe was more sure now than she had ever been of where she belonged. She had left her father's home in such an angry state that she thought it may have colored her feelings. But back with the smells and tastes of the ocean and her mother, she knew.

She had been thirteen when she moved permanently to the island, and had gone from getting everything she wanted to being asked, 'do you really need that?'

Soon, with all the new friends and playing on the beach everyday, the *things* lost their luster. She had worked a few summers at the Sea Gull and really had fun doing so. Yes, if any place was where she belonged, it was on Topsail Island.

Kissing her mother hard on the cheek, she returned the warm hug. "I'm so glad I'm home."

"How'd the Bridge family treat you?"

"Like they had to scrape me off their shoes," Monroe turned up her nose, "except for Mona."

Ellie crossed her arms across her chest. "Really?"

"I feel sorry for her Mom; she's just step-and-fetch-it for Dad. And Ossie is a chip off the old block."

"Well, you know what your uncle used to say." Ellie smiled and winked at her daughter. "You can pick your nose, but you can't pick your family."

Both laughed as they opened the doors to the big green station wagon and began pulling boxes and suitcases from it.

"Need any help?" Rawl West's son, David, stood in his swim trunks, sand still clinging to his shins, a beach towel hung loosely from his broad shoulders.

Monroe stepped back and leaned against the car. "Well I'll be, if it isn't David West. I haven't seen you in ages."

"Just got out of the Marine Corps."

"I never knew you enlisted."

"You never did pay me much attention." David grinned wryly.

From the screened-in porch Ellie watched the two young people as they bantered back and forth, obviously flirting with one another. *Well, she's paying attention now,* she thought to herself.

She kept quiet as she moved a few boxes into the small beach cottage, and watched as the two talked and laughed. David sought the heavier items and carried them into the house and before long the entire car was emptied of luggage and boxes.

She heard her daughter tell the young man about living in Florida and how pretty it was and how unbearably hot it could be. And she was surprised when she heard Monroe's response to David's question, 'what are going to do now?'

"I think I'm going to try to go to Miller-Motte."

Ellie's heart swelled with pride when she heard the statement. How wonderful it would be for her daughter to learn how to be a secretary or work in a business office.

Later that evening after David had gone home and most things had been put away, and only a few boxes remained in the living room unopened, Ellie questioned Monroe. "Are you really going to Miller-Motte?"

"I'd like to Mom, but I don't have any money for it."

"I guess your father refused to help you with that."

Nodding her head, Monroe rolled her eyes. "Yep. He said that if I wanted money for school I would have to go to Saint Leo there in Dade City."

Ellie thought for a moment and rubbed her fingers along her jaw line. "Saint Leo is a good school, dear."

"I don't want to be in Florida, Mom. I want to be here with you and my friends."

Ellie stifled the welling of tears she felt behind her eyes. After a deep breath she spoke. "I bet if you asked your Grandma Rosell, she would help you pay for school. Maybe one day this week we'll drive the green bomb up to Raleigh and ask Grandma."

****

Ellie pulled her legs to her chest and scrunched her toes against the seat of the booth where she sat. "Yessirree, my girl is going to go to Miller-Motte."

Pearl leaned across the booth table and grasped Ellie's hand. "I know you're proud, Ellie. Sometimes I wish we would have done that."

"Me? A secretary? Naw, I don't think so. I like things just like they are."

"Well, I can't say I'm too dissatisfied with myself." Pearl fluttered her lashes. "This place has taken off like a rocket—it's doing so much better than I ever thought it would."

"Yeah, it is peachy working here. I usually have a lot of fun on my shift."

A pensive look crossed Ellie's face as she bit her bottom lip; she turned her head to the side and cast a cautious look at her longtime friend. "I used to think that having pretty clothes and being able to have a bunch of nice things, and men fawning all over me were the best things in the world, but I tell you, when

Monroe told me she wanted to be here with me and wanted to go to college, I never felt such a wonderful feeling in my life."

Pearl held her friend's hand tightly. "It's nice. Isn't it?"

Nodding, Ellie plucked a napkin from the napkin holder and dabbed at her massacred eyes. "Still, the second best feeling in the world is having pretty clothes and having men fawn over me," she tittered.

"Could this mean you're going to settle down and get married to one man, now?"

Ellie wiped her nose a bit and balled the napkin in her hand. "All these changes in me, geez...I'm trying to quit smoking and I've had to give up my French fries. Damn, I had to wear a one-piece bathing suit this year, Pearl. What in the world is happening to me?"

"We're getting older, Ellie. In a couple of years we're going to be forty."

"Oh my gosh, forty. That's old." Ellie cupped her breast with her hands. "You know I've even had to start wearing a push-up bra 'cause these babies are hanging down to my elbows."

Laughing, Pearl scooted from the booth table and walked toward the kitchen. "Is this going to be another all-nighter?"

Unwrapping a stick of Dentyne gum from its wrapper, Ellie answered, "It's only ten. We've only been closed an hour, hopefully we won't talk all night long.," She laughed as she popped the gum in her mouth and began chewing. "But I have lots of things to tell you about my little gal and Florida, and I know you have lots of things to tell me about *you know who.*"

"We're drinking Sanka tonight." Pearl settled the two coffee mugs on the table. "I want to get at least a few hour's sleep."

Ellie shrugged and reached for the cream pitcher and sugar bowl on the table. She poured both liberally into her cup of decaffeinated coffee. "You start, I want to know just what is going on with you and Jay. I thought that after that hoo-ha at the Fourth of July shindig you put on here, that things might have cooled down between you two, but a little birdy told me that they saw yours and Jay's cars parked together at the Lumina at Wrightsville Beach last Tuesday. Now, please Pearly White, tell me I'm wrong, because if you want to be talked about remember that lots of folks from around here go to Wrightsville Beach and to the Lumina." Ellie rolled the gum in her mouth; a succession of loud pops followed as she stirred her coffee.

"Are you going to chew gum or drink coffee—you can't do both." Pearl's lips pursed. "Who's the little birdy?"

"Doesn't matter who it is. By now everybody knows."

Pearl took a sip from the coffee then wrapped her hand around the mug. "I suwannee, I don't think I could fart around here without somebody saying they smelled it."

"People are going to talk." Ellie picked the gum from her lips and placed it on her spoon for later use.

294

"They just don't understand, Ellie."

"They understand that he's married and he's slipping around on his wife—slipping around with you."

"Do you know that last Tuesday Jay took Feona back up to Cherry Hospital? She's going to be up there for at least six weeks. He was meeting me there to talk about Fate. He's not sure whether to leave him with Momma or not. You know she watches Emma Jewel and Josie."

"Josie's old enough to watch herself."

"Yes, and she spends most of her days around here—in and out, when she's not working. But E.J. can't do that. I don't feel right with her being so young without some sort of supervision, especially in the late afternoons. Momma usually comes and gets her around four." Pearl straightened the cuff of her shorts and added. "And Jay wanted to talk about having her watch Fate. That's two young'uns playing and getting into all kinds of things, and I don't know if Momma is up to it."

Ellie pondered Pearl's reasoning, there were flaws in it; she took another sip from her mug and studied her friend's face.

"What?" Pearl asked.

"Why did Jay have to ask you? Why didn't he just go ask your momma? And why did y'all have to talk about it at the Lumina?"

"Cause he wanted to dance with me again." Pearl's cheeks flushed red and the corners of her mouth turned upward.

"And you went through all that about your momma and Fate, looking all earnest and sorrowful. Why didn't you just spit it out?"

"Caught me, huh?" Pearl raised an eyebrow and grinned.

"Oh, you've been spending too much time with me old friend. Learning how to lie and cover up. My, my, my—just what is going to happen to my Pearly White, Goody Two Shoes?"

"I hate having to lie. I always wonder if it will be a curse on my kids, if they will be treated differently because people are gossiping about me. But, Ellie, every bone in my body tells me that what I am doing is not wrong. Jay's situation is different. Our situation is different. We were always meant to be together and the war messed everything up for everybody."

"Was Paul a mistake?"

"I wouldn't trade my time with Paul for anything in the world, and if he had not died I would be the happiest woman in the whole world. But he did die and it took me a long time to get past it." Pearl's hand went to her throat as she took a sip of her coffee. "I still love Paul. I carry him with me in a special place. But I can't change a damn thing that has happened. And to be honest with you, I think Paul is in heaven giving me his blessing."

"Really?"

"Yes. Feona is mentally ill. She has no one to go back to in Texas. Her grandmother passed away a while back and she has no other family in Texas that she can rely on. Jay is all she has."

"Really?" Ellie slid the Dentyne gum back into her mouth and popped it loudly.

"Why don't you go back to cigarettes? That gum popping drives me nuts."

"Funny you should say, 'nuts'."

"*You* are judging *me?*"

"The man is married."

"If I recall, when Chuck was away at the war you went out with a few men."

"If *you* recall, I told you that all I did was give them a kiss. I didn't roll around in the hay with them."

Pearl pushed her body back against the seat and licked her lips before speaking. "Just what is he supposed to do? Do you suggest he throw her in the loony bin? Because if he doesn't keep her on medication and tend to her, there is no one else to do it and that is where she will end up."

"Isn't that where she is going for six weeks? That's what you said earlier. You said that Feona was going to Cherry Hospital for six weeks."

Pearl's body relaxed and a slight grin fell upon her lips. "Yes, Jay and I will have six weeks of being together."

"You're glad..."

"I didn't say that. I don't wish anything bad on Feona. I didn't ask for her to go bananas. If she wasn't, I wouldn't be involved with Jay."

"Are you sure?"

"Jay would not need me, Ellie. He would have a wife, a real wife that dotes on him like he says she used to. He's told me that he loves Feona, but he's also told me that he never stopped loving me."

"I wish I had a cigarette." Ellie's fingers drew a make believe cigarette to her mouth and she mimicked a deep draw from it. "I thought my life was a jigsaw puzzle, but I think you have me beat, Pearly." Pausing to stick another piece of gum in her mouth, Ellie's brows drew together. "Did you ever stop loving him?"

"Yes."

"Go on," Ellie's fingers beckoned her to continue.

"I did stop loving him; Paul made me forget about him. Paul was the love of my life, Ellie."

"My scrawny ass cousin?"

"Yes, your scrawny cousin—the most loving, compassionate, understanding man I have ever known."

"And Jay. What about Jay and all that stuff that went between the two of you before the war."

"Love, pure love, Ellie. I loved him beyond belief. But things...happened you know. He wasn't there."

"Through no fault of his own." Ellie raised an eyebrow, "You know, he was going through hell in Germany then."

"I know. He's told me. But he wasn't there for me. Paul was."

"And you say I'm selfish. Shame on you."

"I can't help it. Paul took all my shattered dreams and fashioned them into something new. He made me whole again."

"But Jay can...oh, that's right. There was Roger in there to pick up those pieces."

"Not quite, Smelly." Pearl answered, a harshness coloring not only her words but her demeanor. "Roger picked up no pieces, though in the beginning I thought he could, then he just became nothing. He became a hammer to break even more pieces and I was holding the damn thing."

The intensity of Pearl's words stunned Ellie and she leaned back in the booth. "Gee whiz Pearl, why can't you have a simple affair?"

"I'm not you. I've never been able to have a simple *anything.*"

"You think too much—you care too much."

"Maybe. Maybe you are right, but that is who I am. And I know with all my heart that Jay needs me and that sharing my life with him, whatever part I can—is right—for me."

Nodding, understanding Pearl's dilemma more, Ellie tipped her cup of coffee up and finished the remains. "I think it's time for me to go home and get to bed. Monroe should be home anytime."

"Did she have a date with David?"

"Yes. I like him. He reminds me of my poor old cousin, your husband."

Pearl nodded. "Mmm." She looked out the big plate glass window; a sigh escaped her lips. "It's a lovely night tonight. It will be a nice walk home."

The two women turned off the lights, turned the sign from opened to closed and locked the door.

"I think I'm going to go home and get some sleep," Ellie said.

"Okay, I'll see you tomorrow afternoon. Josie and Nadine have the morning shift and Momma's coming in to start breakfast."

"That woman works like a horse."

"I've tried to get her to quit but she'll have none of it." Pearl shrugged and waved as she made her way down the stairway to the paved road leading to her home. The walk, nearly half a mile, was a lonely walk that she often enjoyed on warm nights.

She could hear the waves crashing and imagined Ellie holding her shoes in her hand as she walked barefoot along the shore. *Pretty Ellie, beautiful Ellie. She would always be beautiful. Her vanity would allow it to be no other way.*

Releasing a giggle, Pearl passed by a clump of hairawn muhly not quite in season, with green and brownish plumes that within a month's time would be a blaze of purple. She thought of Jay. Had she been truthful with Ellie? Had she ever stopped loving him? She thought of the men in her life. Roger briefly swept through her mind and she brushed him away with the flip of her hand.

It was Jay and Paul, Paul and Jay. She pondered their love and suddenly, unexpectedly she realized how fortunate, how blessed she had been. It came upon her like one of those brash, towering waves that crashes ever so loudly upon the beach.

Yes, she had known real love, satisfying, soul-deep love, bone deep love. Pearl threw her head back in laughter and felt giddy, like a seven-year-old on Christmas Day. She closed her eyes and breathed in the salt air and listened to the sounds of the ocean, of the breezes through the trees and faint whistle of the wind. A red-wing blackbird trilled in a nearby scrub oak and Pearl stopped to follow its sound to where it was. He sat low in the branches as she kept herself still and waited for another song from his throat. A moment passed and he trilled again.

CHAPTER TWENTY—FIVE

Lottie stood before the closet, the one in the home she and Jess had shared for so long. Immediately, as she opened the door, her late husband's smell seemed to swallow her entire being.

"Oh Jess, my wonderful Jess, my loving Jess." She wrapped her arms around herself and smiled. "You silly, silly man." Opening her eyes she peered at the accumulation of shirts and trousers hanging closely together. "Now which shirt is it that you want me to wear, sweetie?" She spoke aloud to her husband.

Her fingers traveled across the hangers until she came to the red plaid one Jess had worn a few years back at Jordan's and Tillie's oyster roast—the last oyster roast she and Jess had attended together.

Her fingers rested on the shirt for a moment before she pulled it from the closet. Holding it against her face, she deeply breathed in Jess's scent. Again she smiled. "You beat all, you know that?" She giggled.

"No tears today." Lottie forced any melancholy thoughts from her mind and focused on the task at hand. "Tonight, my dearest, we are going trick-or-treating with the young'uns."

She unbuttoned her polka dot blouse and laid it across the chair in the bedroom, then slipped her late husband's thick red and black plaid shirt onto her body. It fit her well across the chest, but the shoulders were a bit big. The tail of the shirt fit snuggly across her belly and buttocks. "Humph," she tittered. "Yes, I'm a broad."

From outside the house a car horn blared and Lottie heard her granddaughter, Josie, call, "Are you lost in there, Grandma? The party's starting in an hour and I have to go home and get dressed too."

"Me too," joined in Emma Jewel. "I got to get my hair all teased out like a scary person."

Lottie thought for a moment of how impatient her grandchildren were being, but she chose to ignore the thought, feeling that perhaps time had gotten away from her as she reminisced about her late husband. "Okay!" she hollered through the doorway. "I'm on my way." Grabbing her blouse she moved quickly toward the door, then paused for a moment to reach for her late husband's straw hat resting on the nightstand. She continued walking briskly through the rooms she once shared with Jess and Pearl. She could almost hear their voices—their warmness was still there.

Out the front door she flew as if moving from one age into another; the crisp autumn air slapping her in the face, wakening her from the past.

It had felt strange coming to the house again, and she shook the remnants of the visit from her. She had not been there in so long. But she knew Pearl frequented the farmhouse often. A scowl settled on her brow.

"Everything okay Grandma?" Questioned Josie as she noticed Lottie's expression."

Her frown turned promptly to a smile. "Oh yes, yes, dearie. Everything is fine—nothing to worry about." She patted her oldest granddaughter on the arm and turned to blow a kiss to her youngest. "Now, you go slow." She warned Josie. "Be sure to lift your foot from the clutch as you step on the gas."

The car lurched forward as Josie jerked the gearshift into gear and pressed on the gas. Slowly they motored along the worn cart path until stopping just before reaching Highway 50 leading to the beach.

Turning right, Josie pushed in the clutch as she shifted into first gear; the car lurched again.

"You have to feel it with your foot, dearie. Feel just when you have to push on the gas and let the clutch out."

Josie pushed on the gas and slowly let out the clutch; smoothly Josie shifted back into first and then moved into second gear.

"Whoopie! You've done it. That is the way to shift gears. Did you *feel* it, dear?" Lottie asked encouragingly as her granddaughter nodded.

"Yes Grandma, now I know what you mean."

"Good girl. Now drive slowly and keep between the lines, because Stretch Morrison is riding right behind you."

Lottie turned to look the police officer directly in the face. She raised her hand and shook her finger at him. "He ought to know better than riding right behind us when he knows good and well you ain't got no license yet and that you're just learning to drive."

The car lurched again as Josie lifted her foot nervously from the gas.

"No, no, my dear, you go right on. He ain't going to stop you. He's just trying to give you a hard time. Now, if you were drinking he might pull you over and take you home to your momma. But he's just picking on you. He does that with all the new drivers around Topsail. "

Slowly Stretch pulled his car next to Josie. He hollered through the open window as the two cars drove side by side. "You ought to let her learn on an automatic. It's easier."

"Don't have an automatic, Stretch." Lottie called back.

Laughing, the police officer tipped his hat. "Y'all take care, now. Watch out for stray dogs and children." Passing Josie, he honked his horn and waved.

"You just mind that you keep the car on the road and don't run off. If you get in the sand, you'll get stuck and we'll have to call Jay to get the wrecker and pull you out."

"Yes Grandma," Josie spoke shyly as they crossed the swing bridge to Surf City; the grates beneath the car hummed. "I can't wait for the party tonight."

"I want to go to the party," Emma Jewel whined.

"You ain't old enough." Lottie reached her arm into the backseat to touch her youngest grandchild. "It's just for teenagers. You'll be a teenager soon enough." She patted E.J.'s blond head. "Besides, you and me are going trick-or-treating tonight, and I expect we're going to get a lot more candy than your big sister will."

E.J. smiled broadly showing her two missing front teeth. "Grandma, what are you going to dress as for Halloween?"

"I have your grandpa's old plaid shirt and I'm going to roll up a pair of my dungarees, take some eyebrow pencil and give myself a beard, and go as an old hobo. What do you think of that?" Lottie tousled Emma Jewel's already messy hair. "You got hair just like your momma."

"Momma says it's like Daddy's."

"That too. I guess you could say that you got it from both of them. Now tell me, what are you going to be tonight for trick-or-treating?"

"I'm going as the bride of Dracula." E.J. bared her missing front teeth and thrust them forward making a growling sound. "Momma bought me some fangs to wear, then I'll really look scary."

Lottie turned her attention to Josie, still focused intensely on the road before her. "Did you take her to that Dracula movie that was showing at the Starway in Wilmington?"

"She wanted to go."

"She's seven years old. I'm surprised she hasn't been having nightmares about it."

"I did have a nightmare, Grandma. But Josie told me that if I didn't squeal on her for taking me, she'd help me get all dressed up like the lady that married the vampire man."

"Obviously your mother knows about this since she bought the fangs."

Josie rolled her eyes and nodded. "Don't sweat it, Grandma. Momma already gave me the once over for taking her. I don't need to hear it from you too."

"Josephine Loretta Rosell, don't you talk to me like that." Raising her hand to slap Josie, she pulled back. "I ought to, but I won't. I don't know where you get that smart mouth from, but if you want me to help you anymore with driving the car or any other thing, you better start buttoning that sassy lip of yours. Hear me young lady?" Lottie's eyes glared threateningly at the teenager.

"Yes ma'am."

They rode silently the short way from the intersection to the apartments where the family lived. Lottie opened the door to the car and slammed it hard. "Come on, E.J. Let's get you ready for tonight."

****

After Lottie discussed Josie's behavior with Pearl it was decided that she would not be allowed to stay overnight with Gloria Abbott. Instead she would have to ride home with Sarah Butler who, according to Josie, always had to leave the party too early.

Josie stifled her anger, and walked to her bedroom to change clothes. She emerged only a few minutes later dressed in jeans and a sweater, leaving Pearl to wonder why she had not dressed in a costume.

"Costumes are for little kids. This is a real party, Momma. We're going to dance and play records."

Pearl grinned, somewhat confused but satisfied that her daughter was enjoying her youth and going to parties. She herself had never wanted to grow up, and at the age of fifteen, as was Josie, she would still on occasion play with her baby doll.

Pearl had fashioned an old worn out dingy sheet into a makeshift gown for E.J., and had applied the whitest make-up she could find to the child's face making her complexion ashen. She smudged dark circles around E.J.'s eyes and teased her hair to stand directly away from her scalp, and then applied nearly an entire can of hairspray. The child looked adorable.

"Here's your teeth, honey." Pearl handed Emma Jewel the plastic fangs.

"Eek!" Lottie hollered as she feigned fear. "Oh please, please Miss Dracula, don't bite me."

Placing her hand next to her lips Lottie whispered to Pearl, "I still don't like this vampire stuff; the child's too young for this."

"I can't say no now, Momma."

Lottie shook her head at Pearl then shrugged her shoulders.

Baring her teeth, E.J. showed the fangs and brought her hands, with the long plastic fingernails, close to her face. "I vant to suck your blood."

"Ooh, you're so scary," feigned Lottie as she shielded her face. "Don't hurt me Miss Dracula."

"You sit down now E.J., and let me finish fixing up Grandma for Halloween." Taking in her mother's appearance, Pearl laughed. "You look darling, Momma." She tittered as she adjusted her father's hat on her mother's head. "You look just like Daddy."

"Don't say that. Your father was a much better looking man than I am." Lottie giggled. He sure was something. Wasn't he?"

Pearl looked around the room at her costumed family. They were a sight to behold and she held her side as she laughed. "Y'all sure do look good. I sort of wish I was going with you. But someone has to mind the store."

"What are you going to wear, Momma?" Josie asked Pearl as she moved toward the door and peered out.

"I'm dressing as a cat, a black cat." She ran her hand down the length of her torso, displaying the snug black pants and matching turtleneck sweater.

"But...how are you a cat?" questioned Josie.

"Well, I've got a tail." Pearl pulled a length of black cloth from her purse. "I thought I'd make a tail out of this."

"You need to let me make up your face."

As Josie made up her mother's face, Pearl thought of how grownup her daughter was—how so unlike her she had been at that age. Maybe she should not be so hard on her.

Josie finished applying the make-up and stood back to examine her work. "Whatcha think, Momma?"

Pearl stood and looked in Josie's compact mirror. "Wow! I really do look like a kitty."

"Now, let me fix your hair so it looks like you have kitty ears."

Josie pulled her mother's hair tight into two pigtails fashioned high on her head. "There you go, Miss Kitty." Pearl's eyes widened. "That looks outstanding."

Pearl looked at herself in the mirror; she was astonished at how she looked.

"You look like a real cat, Momma," chimed Emma Jewel.

Pearl blushed through the make-up and looked at Josie. "I like this." She kissed her daughter on the cheek. "Guess I better get you to the West's house for that big Halloween shindig their having?"

"Yes ma'am." Josie's face lit up as she moved toward the door.

"If you feel like it, come by and get some popcorn balls."

"Yummy." Emma Jewel licked her lips as she sat cross legged on the sofa. "She won't show up, she's going to a grown-up party," E.J. crinkled her nose. "But I'll be there for sure, Momma."

"I bet you will," she looked down at her daughter and pinched her cheek softly. "Have fun and I'll see you soon at the Gull."

At the West house, cars were parked along the side of the road; no one would have dared park in Miss Francis's yard so neatly manicured and filled with seasonal flowers and plants.

Teenagers stood or sat near the doorway. Pearl recognized the West's youngest children, the twins, Tammy and Terry; they were in the grade above Josie.

Enid and Bella Abbott's daughter, Gloria, was there, Jordan and Tillie Butler's boys, Milo, Junior and Tommy were in a small group to themselves, their cousin Ray Butler was there along with his sister, Dixie, plus several teens whose names she was not sure about, but were more than likely cousins of somebody there.

Nearly everyone around Topsail Island was related in one way or another unless they came from a military family.

Pearl dropped her daughter at the driveway to the West home, held her hand for a moment as she told her to have a good time, and then drove off to work at the restaurant to wait for the younger set of children from the island.

The hum of her tires against the bridge sounded familiar and warming to Pearl, she loved the sound and immediately perked up at the thought of all the little faces that would be opening the door to the restaurant.

311

In past years, when the children came dressed on Halloween night, patrons of the Gull offered nickels and dimes as the children opened their bags before them. Pearl was sure it would hold true this year as well.

Pulling into her parking spot in front of the Sea Gull, Pearl adjusted the tail tied around her waist and smoothed her sweater. She laughed as she thought of how she looked. "Meow, meow," she practiced playfully. Checking her make-up in the rearview mirror she giggled. Her red lips had been drawn on and resembled a cat's tight bee sting shape. "Oh my, I am a sight." Pulling open the door to her car, she sauntered up the steps to the Sea Gull entrance.

"Well I'll be, are you cattin' around tonight, Miss Kitty Cat?" Asked Ellie who stood boldly in the middle of the restaurant in an antebellum dress.

"Well, I know who you are, Scarlet." Pearl stroked the lace and satin of Ellie's broad skirt. "Where did you get that, it is beautiful."

"Last week when I went up to Raleigh to see Mother, she pulled it out of this big cedar box. She said it was her mother's."

"It's got to be nearly a hundred years old."

"Mother said it probably was about eighty or so."

"And she let you have it?"

Ellie nodded shyly. "I know, can you believe it. Mother is being so nice to me lately. She says she wants to visit and she was giving me so many gifts. I could hardly believe that she was the same mother I grew up with."

"Since your father passed on she has changed, it seems."

"Who knows, but she didn't even have any color in her hair. She's let it all go gray."

"Um." Pearl touched the dress again and suddenly realized that Ellie would not be able to go behind the counter because of the width of her gown. "Monroe is here helping, I assume."

"Yes, Miss Pearly. My daughter is here; your precious restaurant has not gone unattended." She leaned in close to Pearl, "If you're going for the cat-lady look, you have it down to a tee. Don't tell me you came up with the idea."

"Josie made me up. She sure is an artist when it comes to applying make-up."

Ellie nodded. "Gets it from her aunt."

Shrugging, Pearl squeezed past her friend and moved behind the counter. "Did y'all finish making all the popcorn balls?"

"Yes ma'am we did." Monroe opened the swinging door from the kitchen. "I think we have over thirty. Do you think that is enough?"

"That's plenty," nodded Pearl. "It's more than enough. It will leave us a few to enjoy after the little darlings are done for the night."

Pearl settled the big glass bowls filled with popcorn balls on the counter then clapped her hands together in an effort to gain the attention of the few customers in the dining area.

"For the next couple of hours children dressed for Halloween will be coming here to get their treats. I hope they will not disturb you too much."

All of the customers were visiting fisherman and had been through Halloween previous years. They reached into their pockets and withdrew the coins.

Turning to Monroe, Pearl thanked her for making the treats, then added, "You're missing a mighty fun party over at the West's. Junior Butler is there, so why don't you go ahead and take off?"

Monroe untied the apron from around her waist. A broad grin settled on her lips. "Yes ma'am. I was hoping you'd let me go early. Momma said you would."

Out the door the teenager scrambled, just in time to hold the door open for the flood of costumed children rushing toward it.

"Here they come," giggled Ellie as she kept her place in the center of the restaurant.

She heard what she was expecting to hear as the children entered. 'Oh Miss Ellie, you look so beautiful.' She heard this numerous times from the young girls. From the young boys she received silence as they walked slowly past her, their mouths gaping as they stared.

"You love all the attention, don't you?" Pearl chided.

"Of course I do. Who doesn't want to be adored?" Ellie rolled a shoulder and flipped her long dark hair to the side. "I *am* a southern belle."

Lottie walked in with Emma Jewel, the Schneider children, Robert and Marla, the Moretti kids, Bart and

Nora, Bobbie Robbins and the Chase children, none of whose names she could recall. There must have been six or seven cousins among the two Chase families that had moved to the island a couple of years ago. To Pearl, they all resembled one another.

Eventually, after all the children were finished oohing and aahing over Ellie's dress and they had picked up their dimes and nickels from the fishermen, Pearl handed out the popcorn balls.

"Here you are, Bobbie, Bart, Nora, Robbie, Marla and you and you and you. My goodness there are so many of you this year." She laughed as she emptied one bowl and reached for another.

"Miss Pearl, hi." Fate Bishop reached out his hand shyly to grasp a cellophane-covered popcorn ball.

She looked into his familiar eyes and then raised her head to look into Jay's. His face flushed lightly; she could feel his eyes running up and down her body. "Nice kitty," he cooed.

Feeling her heart beat faster, Pearl extended a bowl full of popcorn balls toward the children. "Everyone gets only one." She looked once again at Jay's face, "How's Feona doing?"

"Miss Janie is sitting with her tonight while I take Fate out with the other kids."

Among the chatter and push and shove of the children as they reached to grab a treat, Pearl could feel the tension from Jay; her face felt warm as she withdrew the bowl.

Taking his son by the hand, Jay followed the children as they left the restaurant. He turned back at the door and found Pearl's gaze. "Have a nice Halloween."

Emma Jewel, the last of the children to leave the restaurant, ran fast after Fate and called, "Do you want another popcorn ball?"

"You go ahead with the other children, Emma Jewel. I'll be right there with you in a minute." Lottie glared at her daughter. "What was that that passed between you and Jay. Don't tell me I was imagining things—please tell me you're not flirting in front of customers and children."

Pearl blew a sigh, lifting the thin bangs from her brow. "What do you want me to say?"

Lottie shook her head. Muttering to herself, she exited the Gull and caught up with the crowd of children.

Within a few minutes the remaining patrons of the Sea Gull Restaurant paid their bills. Most commented on the costumed children and how they remembered going out on Halloween when they were young.

Ellie and Pearl watched as the last one exited the building. They waved and smiled back.

"Whoa Nellie, you could have cut the tension with a knife. The *black* pearl is on the prowl tonight, dressed like the cat she is." Ellie blurted out as she shut the door and turned the sign to Closed. She slid her eyes smugly toward Pearl and shook her head.

"What in the world are you talking about?" Pearl turned and sat on a stool at the counter.

316

"Uh huh, don't give me that baloney; Jay couldn't keep his eyes off you."

"Maybe."

"Mirror, mirror on the wall who's the prettiest girl of all." Ellie twirled in her wide, fluffy, dress. "Sure as heck wasn't me tonight. Jay's eyes were all over you. You could dress in a croaker sack and he'd still think you lit up the world."

She watched as Pearl lowered her head and spun around on the stool. "You are one lucky girl, to have someone love you like that."

Raising her eyes to meet Ellie's, Pearl grinned. "I guess it's time we cleaned up and went on home. The kids will be finished trick-or-treating soon. I want to be there when they get to the house."

Sashaying across the floor of the restaurant, Ellie turned off the porch lights. "What is to become of you two?" Ellie asked.

"I really don't know." Pearl paused. "I love Jay, I can't wait to see him. I feel so complete when I am with him."

Ellie turned her back to Pearl. "Would you please unfasten this daggone thing. I can hardly breathe. No wonder those southern belles died so young, they couldn't get enough air.

Unbuttoning the many tiny buttons, Pearl leaned her head against the small of Ellie's dress. "This is a pain in the butt, my fingers are tired already."

"Just finish it; I don't think I could stand another minute in this dress much less this darn girdle I got on."

As she felt the last button pop, Ellie pushed the dress to the floor and stepped out of the hoops and crinolines. She stood before Pearl in her push-up bra and thigh length girdle.

"Somebody's going to see you, Ellie," Pearl admonished.

Ellie posed a hand on one hip and the other behind her head; she wiggled from side to side. "La tee dah,"

Pearl laughed, "Well, I guess you got on more than you do when you wear your bathing suit to the beach in the summer."

"She sure does." Jay's voice came from the beach entrance where he stood beyond the screen door. He walked into the room and leaned against a booth, his eyes steadily on Pearl.

Unabashedly walking past Jay, Ellie tossed the gown in an empty booth and made her way to the kitchen. "My clothes are in here, so I'll just get dressed in here, if you two don't mind." Sarcastically Ellie added, "When are you going to get some *indoor* bathrooms? Surf City and Barnacle Bill's piers have them. So does Thompson's Restaurant and even The Mermaid Bar."

Jay held his hand out to Pearl as she rose from the stool. Silently they walked back to the beach entrance.

"Be sure to lock up *all* the doors before you go home Ellie." Pearl called loudly.

"Okay. See you tomorrow." Ellie called from the kitchen. Hearing the door shut she walked back into the dining area; she heard Jay's and Pearl's footsteps fade away as they walked further along the patio.

318

Pressing her face to the window, Ellie peered out into the night and watched as the two lovers, wrapped tightly in an embrace, kissed. She watched as they stepped, arm in arm, down the stairway to the beach.

Engrossed in the scene, she watched them disappear into the night. "I always knew they would be together," she smiled and whispered to herself.

Turning to finish closing up the restaurant, Ellie was startled by a rattling of the locked front door and the sound of fists banging against the window panes.

"Where's he at? Where's he at? I know he's over here." Feona's wrenched features glared through the glass.

Ellie walked to the door. "Jay's not here, Feona."

Fate sat on the top step, he turned as Ellie spoke; his face told a story of confusion and fear.

Made in the USA
Charleston, SC
19 May 2015